SNOW HILL

Mark Sanderson is a journalist. Since 1999 he has written the L[illegible] *[illegible]raph* and he revie[illegible]me fiction for the *Evening Standard*. His memoir, *W[illegible]g Rooms*, a moving account of his relationship with hi[illegible] partner who died from skin cancer, was published in 2002 to widespread critical acclaim. Melvyn Bragg described it as 'one of the most moving I have ever read'.

By the same author

Wrong Rooms: A Memoir

MARK SANDERSON

Snow Hill

HarperCollins*Publishers*

This novel is entirely a work of fiction. The names, characters and incidents portrayed in it while in some instances based on real historical figures, are the work of the author's imagination. Any resemblance to actual persons, living or dead, events or localities is entirely coincidental.

HarperCollins*Publishers*
77–85 Fulham Palace Road,
London W6 8JB

www.harpercollins.co.uk

Published by HarperCollins*Publishers* 2010

1

A catalogue record for this book is available from the British Library

ISBN: 978-0-00-729679-8

Set in Sabon by
Palimpsest Book Production Limited, Grangemouth, Stirlingshire

Printed in Great Britain by
Clays Ltd, St Ives plc

In memory of Drew Morgan
(1964–1994)

Now from all parts the swelling kennels flow,
And bear their trophies with them as they go:
Filths of all hues and odour, seem to tell
What street they sail'd from, by their sight and smell.
They, as each torrent drives, with rapid force,
From Smithfield to St 'Pulchre's shape their course;
And in huge confluence join'd at Snow Hill ridge,
Fall from the conduit prone to Holborn Bridge,
Sweepings from butchers' stalls, dung, guts and blood,
Drown'd puppies, stinking sprats, all drenched in mud,
Dead cats and turnip-tops come tumbling down the flood . . .

From *A Description of a City Shower*
Jonathan Swift, October 1710

FOREWORD

I went to my funeral this morning. I expected more people to be there – if only, like Simkins, to make sure the coffin lid was nailed down properly. The turnout was so disappointing I felt like joining the mourners as they huddled round the gaping grave – but, of course, I couldn't. It was short notice, and it is the week before Christmas, so I suppose it's a miracle that anyone, apart from Matt and Lizzie, bothered to traipse from Fleet Street to Finchley. Mr Stone told me that more came to the service in St Bride's. Then my colleagues only had to walk about a hundred yards to the church. At least they made the effort. My killer didn't.

I've been through a lot in the past few days. I nearly froze to death. I nearly burned to death. Daisy's walked out. I've been blackmailed and nearly framed for murder. And I know there's worse to come. The bastard thinks he's got away with it. He won't stop now. I can't wait to see his face.

It began to snow as Lizzie threw her handful of earth into the grave. Not the usual thin, grey flakes that look like dandruff: thick, white, fluffy ones, the sort you see in children's picture books. The gardens of stone soon disappeared under a shroud: God was organising his own cover-up. A real snow-job.

It is weird watching yourself being buried. I was a wraith at my own wake – which is somehow rather apt. This whole affair is about ghosts, bringing the dead back to life, giving a shape to the past. The world is not the sort of place I thought it was.

I'm still not sure what went on in the small hours of 5th December, but I do know it should never have happened. I know it was evil.

I will uncover the truth even if I have to kill to get it. A dead man can't be tried for murder.

From the diary of John Steadman
Friday, 18th December, 1936

PART ONE

Smithfield

ONE

Monday, 7th December 1936, 12.35 p.m.

About bloody time. Johnny Steadman stood up and yawned. No matter how much he kicked and cursed, Quicky Quirk, a lantern-jawed youth from Seven Sisters, was off to Pentonville for a five-year stretch. Judge Henshall, hungry for his club's steak-and-kidney pie and claret, had decided to overlook the house-breaker's deplorable lack of respect in favour of a quick exit. Johnny was starving too. He would grab a sandwich on the way back to the office.

As he emerged from Court Number Three and slipped into the stream of gowned functionaries, witnesses and spectators, a large hand gripped his shoulder. It belonged to a policeman.

"Ah, Inspector Rotherforth. Congratulations. Another thief off your patch."

"Unfortunately there are plenty more where that

blighter came from. Poverty breeds prisoners." The cop smiled but did not relinquish his grip. He was known for always getting his man. At six foot two he towered over Johnny, but his height was not exceptional; some members of the City of London Police were seven feet tall. "I trust you'll give me a mention in dispatches."

"But of course." Johnny relaxed as the long arm of the law finally released him.

Rotherforth was one of the first people he had interviewed for the *Daily News*. The senior officer had rescued a young girl from drowning. One moment she'd been playing happily on the beach beside Tower Bridge, the next she was being swept away by the current and dragged under the surface of the crowded waterway. With no thought for his own safety, Rotherforth, alerted by the screaming mother, had dived off the bridge into the Thames. To the applause of a crowd of red-faced Cockneys – who would be feeling cold, sick and dizzy by the end of the day, despite the knotted handkerchiefs on their heads – the policeman had dragged the unconscious child from the filthy water and administered mouth-to-mouth, undoubtedly saving her life.

To begin with, Johnny had been slightly intimidated by Rotherforth. He was strong as well as long, a well-trimmed moustache accentuating the whiteness of his even teeth, with handsome features that were remarkable for their perfect symmetry. There was a glint in his black eyes that, depending on the occasion, could promise mischief or menace. Johnny had gradually warmed to the man as he described his distinguished war record and showed off his "pip squeak", the set of medals awarded to those servicemen who – unlike Johnny's father – had somehow survived the Great War. Rotherforth had the full set: the 1914–15 Star, the General Service Medal and the Victory Medal, affectionately named by their proud bearers after the characters in a *Daily Mirror* strip cartoon called *Pip, Squeak and Wilfred*.

Anxious to be portrayed as a devoted family man as well as a career cop, Rotherforth had talked about his three daughters – Edith, Elaine and Elsie – before going on to describe how he had come to join the "gentlemen cops", as the City of London Police were known. Like many officers, when the war ended he'd found that he missed the discipline and camaraderie. Pressed for anecdotes, Rotherforth's face lit up as he began to recount various exploits involving an old comrade-in-arms by the name of Archie, only for his voice to catch with the recollection that his friend had not returned from France. Johnny had caught a glimpse of the titan's vulnerable side as he refused to elaborate any further on Archie's fate.

Rallying swiftly, Rotherforth stated that the only lie he'd ever told was giving his age as eighteen when he enlisted in the Black Watch. Johnny did not believe him; he knew that Rotherforth had knocked two years off his real age. Now in his thirty-ninth year, the inspector was popular with his men but no push-over. Any constable who went off his beat even for a minute, no matter what the reason, would be immediately recommended for dismissal.

"I'm glad I bumped into you," said Johnny. "Did you lose a man over the weekend?"

"No. Who suggested we had?"

"I received an anonymous tip-off this morning."

"Someone must have it in for you," said Rotherforth, flashing his teeth. "It's pure balderdash." His sharp eyes lit up. "Ah, here comes my favourite PC."

Another helmet with its distinctive crest and Roman-style comb – a tribute to the City of London Police's civic-minded predecessors – was bobbing towards them through the mob.

"Matt!" said Johnny. "I didn't know you were here."

"PC Turner to you, sunshine."

Johnny laughed. At six foot one, his closest friend was a lot taller than he was: then, since he was only five foot six, most people were. He was about to come back with some cheeky retort when he remembered Rotherforth, but on turning he realised that the inspector was no longer behind him.

"I've just been speaking to your boss." Johnny stepped out of the path of a clerk laden with a perilous pile of folders. "He called you his favourite PC."

"That's because I won the match on Saturday. Rotherforth made a packet betting on me. He's a good trainer, considering he's never boxed himself."

"Afraid of damaging his pretty face." Noticing that Matt's face was marred by dark smudges, the colour of raw liver, under his deep-blue eyes, Johnny asked: "Everything okay? Is Lizzie all right?"

"She's fine," said Matt. "And so am I."

His tone of defiance could not disguise the fact that he was lying. Matt did not lie very often, especially to him. In their own way, both men had an ingrained respect for the truth. Johnny wondered how he could help.

"Got time for lunch?"

"No," said Matt. "They've done cross-examining me so I'll have to go back on duty till two."

"That's a shame," said Johnny. "I wanted to ask if you'd heard anything about a cop dying over the weekend."

"Which station was he based at?"

"Snow Hill," said Johnny.

"That can't be right," said Matt. "We'd know if one of ours had bought it. Besides, if a cop from any station had been killed, there'd have been a huge to-do by now."

"I didn't say the cop had been killed," said Johnny. "He could've been run over by a bus."

"Still, if he worked at Snow Hill, we'd have been told," said Matt. "Bad news travels fast, and losing one of our own – whatever the cause – always affects morale. I'll ask around, but don't hold your breath. I reckon someone's having you on."

"Rotherforth said much the same thing." Johnny half turned, then swore under his breath. "Don't look now."

It was too late.

"What's this? Hobnobbing with the boys in blue, Steadman? You know full well officers of the law are forbidden to talk shop with gentlemen of the press."

"You're no gentleman," said Johnny.

"Oh, but I am – and that's what really gets your goat, isn't it?" Henry Simkins smirked as Johnny, despite his best efforts, flushed. It was not just the fop's sandal-wood scent that got up his nose.

For some reason, instead of squandering the Simkins family fortune in the time-honoured fashion – drink, drugs and debutantes – Henry preferred to use his wealth, public-school education and social connections to further a career which his father, a Member of Parliament, considered no better than venereal medicine. Then again, perhaps Simkins senior wasn't so far off the mark. Like doctors, journalists got to see mankind at its most naked.

As always, Johnny felt scruffy standing beside Simkins in his Savile Row suit and a shirt from Jermyn Street. What rankled even more was the fact that the slim and slimy Henry was a blood with brains – and an excellent crime reporter.

Grudgingly, Johnny introduced his arch rival to Matt. As Simkins launched into his usual self-congratulatory spiel, Johnny let his eyes and attention wander around the foyer. Multicoloured marble seemed an odd choice of building material for an arena in which everything was cast in black and white. Barristers might argue for hours about the minute variegations of the law, but when it came down to it the defendant was either guilty or not guilty, freed or for the drop. The smooth stone and polished wood of the Sessions House appeared impervious to the torrent of human misery that swept through its portals.

His thoughts were interrupted by Simkins braying:

"You may congratulate me, Steadman." Grinning at the scowl which had instinctively appeared on Johnny's face, Simkins turned to Matt. "Look at that! He's piqued by my latest exclusive. Did you see it in the *Daily Chronicle*?"

"I read the *News* myself," said Matt. Johnny was touched by his loyalty. He knew his friend usually just made do with whatever was lying around the canteen.

"Never mind. Two million other people saw it." Simkins gave a sigh of satisfaction.

Johnny's reply was lost as around them the crowd swelled as yet another court emptied of spectators; the prospect of some hapless fool losing their liberty or life was always enough to add an edge to even the most jaded of appetites.

"Well, gentlemen, must dash," said Simkins. "I've got a table at Rules. Coming, Steadman? Fancy a nosh-up on my expenses? Success should always be celebrated." He looked Johnny up and down slowly, then tossed his flowing, chestnut locks. "Perhaps another time then. I think you'd like the restaurant."

Johnny resented the assumption that he had yet to darken the doors of the fashionable restaurant. What made it worse, Simkins was right. Johnny was more of a greasy-spoon gourmet.

He wondered what lay behind the invitation. Had Simkins received the same tip-off? Was it a fishing expedition, hoping for corroboration, or was he just seizing an opportunity to rub Johnny's nose in his expense account?

With a final nod in Matt's direction and a smarmy, "PC Turner, it's been a pleasure," the tiresome toff shot off, oozing self-assurance, seemingly oblivious to the female heads turning in his wake.

"The world is his lobster," murmured Johnny.

"You've used that one before," said Matt, watching Simkins sweep through the doors, arm already raised to hail a taxi. "Are you free tomorrow night?"

"I can be," said Johnny without hesitation, hoping that Daisy, his latest cutie, would understand. A chorus girl who, of course, harboured acting ambitions, she had asked him to get tickets for Mazo de la Roche's *Whiteoaks*, which had been running at the Little Theatre in John Adam Street since April. Daisy, who had a fiery temper and big breasts, would inevitably make a fuss at missing out on a promised treat, but he would enjoy making it up to her later.

"How about the Viaduct at seven?"

"Great. I'll see you there." Matt gave him the ghost of a smile and hurried towards the daylight.

Intrigued, Johnny watched his friend's broad back negotiate the milling crowd.

Clearly Matt had heard something after all.

TWO

Johnny crossed Old Bailey and hurried down Fleet Lane. Weaving through the crowds of office workers on Ludgate Hill would take too long, and he was spurred on by the thought that, even now, Simkins was probably trying to find out what he had been talking to Matt about. Wondering how much his rival had heard of the conversation, he took a short cut through Seacoal Lane – a dark, narrow passage which burrowed under the railway from Holborn Viaduct Station – and emerged into Farringdon Street just before it gave way to Ludgate Circus. He was in the foyer of the *Daily News* before it occurred to him that he hadn't eaten, so, spinning on his heel, he went straight back out again to the café next door. Three minutes later he was dropping crumbs over the piece of paper that had been preoccupying him all morning.

The newsroom was unusually quiet. Most of the

reporters were out chasing stories or sinking a lunchtime pint in one of the dozen or so pubs that fuelled Fleet Street. A faint cloud of cigarette smoke lingered. Telephones went unanswered. Typewriters remained silent. Johnny preferred the place when, deadlines looming, it buzzed with barely controlled panic. He enjoyed the banter, the friendly rivalry which ensured he always tried his best. Moreover, since he'd found himself all alone in the world, his colleagues had become a sort of surrogate family, keeping the emptiness at bay.

He breathed in the sweet, acrid smell of ink from the presses on the ground floor. For once, it wasn't mingled with the scent of a hundred sweaty armpits. Even in December, it was always hot in the newsroom. All around him, whirring fans fluttered papers on empty desks. Despite frequent requests from upstairs, no one ever bothered to turn off their fan or angle-poise lamp. The air of ceaseless activity had to be maintained at all times.

No matter how often he entered the newsroom, Johnny just couldn't get over that sense of stepping out on to a stage. His heart rate would pick up each time he came through the door, and he still experienced the same adrenalin rush he'd felt on his first day in the job.

Four years on, he could not quite believe he had made it to a desk in the newsroom of a national daily. In the scheme of things, his was still a lowly position. In the newsroom, your place in the pecking order was reflected by your location in the vast maze of desks: the closer you were to the centre – where the news editor held court – the more senior you were. Johnny was only a couple of yards from the door.

Getting a foot in the door had been a struggle. With no connections in the industry, Johnny had had to do it the hard way. On leaving school a week before his fourteenth birthday – the same day Johnny Weissmuller broke his own hundred metres freestyle world record at the Amsterdam Olympics – the young would-be journalist had landed himself a job running editorial and advertising copy down to the typesetters. From Sunday to Friday, he would put in long hours at the day-job, then three nights a week he'd head off to evening classes at the Technical College to get his diploma in Journalism.

With working days that sometimes didn't finish till after midnight, it had been difficult for Johnny to keep up with the rest of the group even though he was a quick learner. But he'd persevered, and armed with his shiny new diploma he'd secured a job on one of the local rags in Islington. Not that there seemed much call for a diploma; his tasks ranged from listing jumble sales, weddings and funerals; reporting committee meetings and company outings; casting horoscopes; concocting letters to the editor; compiling easy-peasy crosswords; and, most important of all, making tea. In the end it paid off though: his efforts got him the coveted position of junior reporter on the *Daily News*.

Much to his dismay, it turned out that his new role entailed doing exactly the same things.

Fortunately for Johnny, he'd been taken in hand by Bill Fox. An old hack with nicotine-stained fingers to match his yellowing short-back-and-sides, Bill had been in the business for more than forty years, working his beat even through the war years, asthma having kept him out of the army.

Perhaps Bill recognised something of himself in the eighteen-year-old human dynamo, or perhaps he was impressed by Johnny's sharp mind and fierce ambition, then again, maybe he was just won over by the cheeky grin. Whatever the reason, Bill had begun teaching the newcomer everything he knew, ranging from the intricacies of the *News*' house style to the tricks of the trade: how to grab a reader by the lapels and not let him go, how to cut and cut until every word was made to work.

Each time Johnny delivered a piece of copy, Bill would lean precariously back in his chair and deliver words of wisdom, punctuating his speech by stabbing the air with the 2B pencil he kept behind his ear: "Remember, Coppernob, with the honourable exceptions of wine and women, less is more."

But Bill's advice went beyond the craft of writing and fine-tuning copy. He had covered subjects that Johnny's Technical College diploma hadn't touched upon. For him, journalism meant pounding the streets, ferreting out facts and stirring things up. While others his age had opted for a managerial role, sitting behind a desk telling others what to do, Bill preferred a more hands-on approach. He'd been delighted to have Johnny tag along as he demonstrated how to make the most of a lead, and to watch Bill in action was to enjoy a master-class in the art of interviewing reluctant witnesses and worming the truth out of those who were determined to bury it. Persistence, patience and curiosity were his watchwords.

As a result of this apprenticeship, Johnny learned how to turn to advantage the very things that might have worked against him: his deceptively young looks and short stature. He no longer minded being underestimated – if anything, he encouraged it. His job became so much easier when others lowered their guard.

Fox himself was prone to be underestimated by colleagues who judged him on his lack of promotion or love of booze, but to Johnny, he was a hero. Bill was the only person Johnny would tolerate calling him Coppernob – even though his hair was quite obviously strawberry blond.

The crime desk was, in reality, made up of six desks pushed together in a cramped corner of the third floor. These were occupied by a junior, four reporters – two for the day shift and two for the night – and the crime correspondent. Having made his way up from junior, Johnny was determined to gain his next promotion as soon as possible – preferably before his twenty-third birthday. Under a different boss, he would have been moving up the ladder much faster, but Gustav Patsel was a little bully in an age of bullies. While Hitler in Germany, Franco in Spain and Mussolini in Italy ranted and threw their weight about, Patsel swaggered and held sway in the newsroom. Everything about this cantankerous, capricious bore was round: his piggy-eyes peered out from behind round, wire-rimmed glasses.

His white bald head was reminiscent of a ping-pong ball. His belly seemed to bulge more by the week: probably a result of too much bratwurst. Proud of his German heritage, Patsel was not shy of vaunting the führer's galvanising effect on his homeland: the Volkswagen "people's car", designed by Ferdinand Porsche and launched in February, was the best car in the world; the Berlin Olympics in August had been the best games ever *und so weiter* – though he'd been strangely silent back in March when the Nazis invaded the Rhineland.

His colleagues had unaffectionately dubbed him Pencil and ridiculed him behind his back, but Patsel survived by virtue of a Machiavellian grasp of office politics. Even so, it was an open secret that the humourless Hun was looking to jump ship – he had been at loggerheads with either the night editor or the editor-in-chief ever since Johnny had joined the paper.

As much as he longed for Patsel's departure, Johnny was terrified by rumours that Simkins might be poached to replace him.

The sooner Johnny got promotion, the more secure he'd be. However, to achieve that he needed to make a splash – and that meant a spectacular exclusive. The one that had made his name was a piece exposing a drugs racket at St Bartholomew's Hospital. A senior pharmacist had masterminded a scheme whereby he and his cohorts were making a fortune on the black market, selling drugs from the hospital's pharmacy. At a time when patients were struggling to pay for every pill, his cut-price rates had, he claimed, been an act of charity

– a noble motive undermined by the fact that not many people needed addictive painkillers in wholesale quantities.

The whole thing had been going on under Johnny's nose for a while before he smelled a story; back then, his mind had been on other things. It was during a visit to his dying mother that he had been surreptitiously offered cheap morphine by a member of the medical staff. He would have accepted, except that the drug was useless when, as in this case, the patient had bone cancer.

Johnny used his rage at his mother's imminent death to work tirelessly – with Bill's help – to expose the racket. The finished piece had raised questions in Parliament and renewed demands for the establishment of a National Health Service. However, apart from a few more prison cells being filled, nothing came of it all.

Johnny's reward had been promotion from office junior to fully-fledged reporter. Unfortunately, thanks to Patsel, that had translated into the dubious distinction of reporting from the Old Bailey.

Court reporters – not to be confused with those that dealt with the affairs of the once German residents of Buckingham Palace – were afforded little respect because their authors were spoon-fed the copy. They did not have to sniff out stories, follow up leads or track down witnesses. They only had to get off their backsides when the judge stood up. Trials dealt with the aftermath of crime in a calm and clinical fashion. There was none of the excitement of the hunt, no vying to get ahead of the pack in pursuit of your quarry.

To make matters worse, Simkins – who was not confined to the courtrooms of the Old Bailey – had just landed a scoop that had eclipsed Johnny's drug-ring effort, being simpler and juicier.

On the very morning that the police released details of the murder of Margaret Murray, a nineteen-year-old girl who worked for a firm of solicitors, the *Chronicle* had run an interview with the killer's wife. It was an excellent piece of reporting – except, in Johnny's indignant opinion, it should never have been written at all. Simkins had come by his exclusive using dubious means.

The moment the tip-off came in from his source inside the Metropolitan Police, Simkins had got on the phone to Scotland Yard. Realising that no information would be forthcoming if he identified himself as a reporter, he'd passed himself off as the concerned spouse of the man in custody. Though his normal speaking voice was tainted with the trademark drawl of an Old Harrovian, Simkins was a master of verbal disguise. Shortly after their first meeting, he had taken to calling Johnny at the crime desk with bogus complaints about his latest report or cock-and-bull tip-offs delivered in a variety of accents ranging from a thick Irish brogue, Welsh lilt or stage Cockney. His ability to mimic women's voices as well as men's was uncanny. Nevertheless, Johnny, who was not that wet behind the ears, soon caught on. The pranks had, however, taught him a valuable lesson: it was always advisable to meet informants face-to-face. In the flesh it was easier to be certain that someone was who they said they were, and he could watch for the tell-tale clues that revealed when they were lying.

Unfortunately the dozy detective Simkins spoke to at the Yard had fallen for the ruse and told him everything he needed to corroborate the story. Having winkled out the address of the arrested man – "He's told you where we live, has he, officer?" – Simkins had gone straight round there.

Turning up on the poor woman's doorstep ahead of the local constabulary, he'd given her the impression that he was a plain-clothes detective, and then delivered the news of her dear husband's arrest.

Until that moment, Mrs Shaw had believed her Arthur, a travelling salesman for a toy company, was away on business in Newcastle. Within minutes she had learned that he'd been unfaithful to her, that he'd got a young secretary not even half his age in the family way and, in the heat of a furious post-coital row about a back-street abortion, had strangled the poor girl to death. Mrs Shaw had thought the worst she had to fear was a visit from the tallyman. That was before Simkins came along and revealed that her husband of seventeen years was destined for the scaffold.

Simkins' exclusive had not stinted on the woman's shock, anger and grief. He had captured in minute detail every aspect, right down to the dreary landscape reproductions on the wall of the spick-and-span parlour where she sat sobbing uncontrollably; the ember-burns on the hearth rug; and the half-excited, half-fearful reactions of the neighbours who, alerted by her cries, had gathered in glee by the railings, peering through the open door for a glimpse of whatever misfortune had befallen the Shaws.

Part of Johnny admired Simkins' skill and brass neck, but he'd vowed he would never stoop to such underhand methods. It wasn't that he was a prig: he simply refused to inflict such pain on another human being – especially when it was for no better cause than the amusement of others. Bill's motto when it came to composing a report was "titillation with tact". Well, Simkins had no tact. If he had stopped for one moment to imagine how his mother might have felt if she'd found herself in Mrs Shaw's position, then Johnny was sure his conscience, however atrophied, would have silenced him.

Johnny had lost his own mother two years ago. Watching her die a long and painful death had knocked the stuffing out of him. An only child with no near relatives, he'd had no one to turn to but a few close friends, like Bill and Matt and Lizzie. It was only afterwards that he'd learned how much they'd been worried about him. Somehow, he'd bounced back. Instead of letting the bitterness overwhelm him, he'd managed to maintain his cheery outlook – in public, at any rate. He had learned how to conceal his emotions. Professional callousness, a prerequisite of the job, often clashed with personal compassion, but the two were not mutually exclusive. The best journalists were those who managed to bring both detachment and compassion into play when writing their copy.

Wiping away the last crumbs of his lunch, Johnny shook off all thought of Simkins and returned to studying the typewritten note that had been delivered by the District Messenger Company soon after eight thirty that morning. He had no idea who had sent it. The thin white envelope was sealed and stamped with thick black letters: PRIVATE & CONFIDENTIAL. The tip-off inside could not have been more succinct:

A SNOW HILL COP HAS SNUFFED IT.

Johnny had checked all the news agencies for bulletins on a dead or missing policeman and drawn a blank. He'd tried calling the press bureau at Scotland Yard and the desk at Snow Hill but in both cases the response was the same: they had no idea what he was talking about. The messenger company claimed they had no record of who had paid for the message to be delivered. Now he pulled out his notepad and drew a line through Rotherforth and put a question mark next to Matt.

He stared at the piece of paper. Those seven words hinted at so much and revealed so little. Mishap or murder? True or false? Could it be one of Simkins' tricks? Johnny dismissed the idea; it wasn't Simkins' style. Besides, even though he had so little to go on, there was something about this tip-off that made his nerves tingle. Something told him this was genuine.

"What you got there, Coppernob?"

Startled, Johnny looked up. Bill was swaying down the aisle towards him.

"Something or nothing. I can't decide," he said,

handing over the flimsy slip of pink paper. "For your eyes only."

"Say no more," said Bill. A blast of beery breath hit the back of Johnny's neck. "Very interesting."

"I've just asked Inspector Rotherforth if he's lost a man, but he said the suggestion was – and I quote – 'balderdash'."

"Well, he would, wouldn't he?" said Bill.

Johnny could almost hear the liquid lunch sloshing around in his stomach.

Bill handed back the message. "I'll make a couple of calls."

"Thank you." Johnny checked his watch and began gathering up his things. "It's time I got back to court." His voice was heavy with resignation: the mere thought of sitting in those punishing pews made his backside ache.

"Very well." Bill dropped into his battered chair. As always, it rocked alarmingly, on the verge of tipping over backwards, then somehow defying gravity to remain upright. "Off you go then." He sighed heavily. "You know where I am if you need me."

Putting his feet up on the desk, Bill watched as his protégé scurried out of the office. A frown spread across his crinkled face. As soon as Johnny was out of sight, he picked up the telephone receiver.

THREE

Monday, 7th December, 8.30 p.m.

Lizzie was waiting on his doorstep. This was a pleasant surprise. His thoughts had been taken up with Daisy, wondering whether he should nip round to explain face to face that he'd arranged to spend tomorrow evening with Matt instead of taking her to the show, debating whether she could be persuaded to let him make it up to her tonight. Seeing Lizzie, he felt a stab of guilt and then mentally scolded himself: you could not be unfaithful to a fantasy. Mrs Matt Turner was, and always had been, strictly out of bounds.

"Come on! Open the door," she said, brushing off his attempt to kiss her. "I'm half-dead with cold, standing out here. Been at that flea-pit again?"

She meant the Blue Hall Annexe on the corner of Packington Street. The cinema had started life as a district post office before being converted into the Coronet.

Twenty-five years on, its four onion-domes remained but the blue-and-gold tiled façade had worn as thin as the velveteen covering the oversprung seats inside. The only thing the new owners had changed was the name.

The little cinema was a favourite haunt of Johnny's, his mother having introduced him to the delights of the silver screen back in the days when talkies were still a novelty. As a boy, he'd been fascinated by the actors who'd sometimes appear during screenings, striking up conversations with members of the audience. He remembered one paid stooge who always seemed to mangle his lines and would invariably end up being pelted with peanuts. It wasn't until years later that Johnny learned the man had a habit of preparing for his appearances by nipping into the Queen's Head next door for a quick one, or two, to steady his nerves.

Lizzie made her way straight through to the kitchen and Johnny followed, turning on lights and through force of habit switching the wireless on. "The Way You Look Tonight" came warbling out. He filled the battered kettle, lit the gas and set it on the stove.

"What did you see?" she asked, sitting down at the table with her coat still wrapped around her for warmth.

"*Bullets or Ballots*. A gangster pic. Edward G. Robinson, Joan Blondell and Humphrey Bogart."

"Any good?" She was toying with her gloves. Johnny could see she was nervous. Why? Was it because she was uncomfortable being alone with him nowadays? She knew his feelings for her had not changed when she'd married Matt.

"The action sequences were great: tommy-guns spitting fire everywhere. Robinson plays a detective called Johnny Blake who feigns dismissal from the force so that he can go undercover to smash a major crime ring."

Johnny had been a fan of Robinson's ever since he'd seen him in *Five Star Final,* playing a ruthless editor whose investigation of a murder case drives two of those involved to suicide. Earlier that year he'd gone along to see the remake, *Two Against the World*, with Bogart in the starring role, but it wasn't a patch on the original. The focus had been shifted to the goody-goodies who thought the story should not be published, and the worthy result had only provoked yawns.

Hollywood had nurtured Johnny's ambition to be a journalist. It set him dreaming of a global exclusive where he'd interview Al Capone through the bars of his tiny cell in Alcatraz. He did not care if cinema was "neither art nor smart": it offered a picture window into other people's lives. Movies could provide an escape from reality or turn powerful searchlights on it. The same could be said of the press – and Johnny's sense of fair play made him determined to use that power to right wrongs. Social inequality made his blood boil. What was so bad about making breakfast stick in the throats of the bourgeoisie when many children did not have their first meal till midday?

"You might as well tell me the ending," said Lizzie. "It'll save me going to see it."

"Robinson gets a bullet in his belly."

"Now there's a thing – especially since I've got something in mine. Well, more or less. I'm pregnant."

Johnny, who was spooning tea into the pot, froze. He turned slowly. Lizzie was regarding him quizzically, trying to gauge his reaction.

"Lizzie, that's wonderful news!" He bent down and kissed her on the cheek. This time she did not shy away.

"Is it?" Her brown eyes blazed.

What was she so angry about? Even as he registered her mood he couldn't help thinking how beautiful she was. No one else made his heart leap the way she did.

"Of course it is. Unless . . . you don't you want it?"

Lizzie, much to the annoyance of her long-suffering parents, was an independent woman who knew her own mind. They thought their one and only daughter had married beneath her – Matt was a good chap, salt of the earth, but indisputably working class. What's more, they seemed to think she'd done it just to spite them. Johnny knew better.

She had once told him that it had been love at first sight: *He seemed so comfortable in his own skin.* She knew instinctively that Matt was a man who could look after her and who would be a wonderful father to the children he gave her. His good looks were almost an irrelevance – but not quite. She still got a thrill each time she set eyes on him. As for Matt, it had never occurred to him that she might be out of his league. He had the confidence of a natural athlete, one who was used to setting goals and achieving them.

Johnny recalled only too well the moment he had

grasped how true and deep their love was. The realisation had crushed him.

It had taken Lizzie ages to persuade her father, a surgeon, to give his consent to the morganatic marriage – let alone allow her to get a job. Her mother, a raging snob, still disapproved of both. They were the sort of people who took a hotel room to afford themselves an excellent view of the Jarrow marchers as the "agitators" had reached the end of their 291-mile journey. Lizzie was outraged that the public had only donated £680 to the demonstrators and thought it obscene that people should sip champagne while unemployed men fought for an opportunity to put food on their families' tables.

Lizzie's mother had relaxed a bit when her daughter's employer – Gamages, the "People's Popular Emporium" – had promoted her from kitting out middle-class brats in Boy Scout uniforms to the more genteel cosmetics department, where her high cheekbones, straight nose and fashionably short, black hair could be shown off to commercial advantage. Although secretly impressed, she could still not understand why her daughter had decided against becoming a secretary to a chief executive and opted to stoop to common shopwork. She was blind to the fact that the lowliness of the position was precisely the point. Lizzie, indignant that British women had only won the right to vote eight years previously, was showing solidarity with her sisters. She wanted to prove herself, succeed according to her abilities rather than her social connections, though she would have been the first to acknowledge that she was fortunate enough to have the luxury of choice. Matt had been only too glad to take advantage of the fact that his father had been a policeman.

"I do want it, I think." She sighed. "It's just happened sooner than expected – and, well, look what happened last time."

The Turners had lost their first child the year before in a miscarriage that the doctor had put down, in part at least, to stress. Lizzie was highly strung by nature, but Matt, bitterly disappointed, had blamed the loss on her refusal to give up her job immediately the good tidings were announced. Neither her family nor his had said anything to contradict this opinion. She was bound to be fearful of a second tragedy.

"Promise me you won't tell Matt. He's got enough on his plate at the moment."

"What d'you mean?"

"He's been sleeping awfully badly of late. He has the most terrible nightmares. Wakes up shouting and crying. The sheets are positively sopping with sweat. He won't tell me what's the matter and gets cross when I try and find out. I want to help the silly billy, but he won't let me."

Johnny couldn't imagine Matt crying. In all the years they'd known each other he had never seen him shed a tear. Matt had been the calm, even-tempered one – unlike Johnny, whose quick tongue often landed him in trouble with bigger lads who didn't like being made fools of by a short-arse. Back in their schooldays, Johnny had shed many a tear, but invariably they were tears of fury and frustration at his opponents' refusal to stay down when he finally succeeded in landing a punch. All too often they'd just pick themselves up and knock him down. It was only when Matt intervened that they'd give up the fight. He was a year older than Johnny and had three elder brothers who'd taught him how to look after himself. A talented southpaw, he'd amassed quite a collection of silverware over the years, first at schoolboy level and then representing his station in the amateur league. He seemed to soak up the punishment, showing no sign of emotion even when a vicious warhorse, anxious to prove he was not quite past it, almost beat his brains out; somehow Matt just hung in there, patiently waiting for the opening that would allow him to land the knockout blow.

To Matt, Johnny was the kid brother he'd always longed for – he hated being the baby of the family. He'd been only too happy to pass on the lessons he'd learned from his brothers: teaching Johnny how to turn and throw his weight from the hip, not the shoulder. As his confidence grew, Johnny learned an even more effective form of defence: making people laugh. Where once his big mouth had landed him in trouble, he began to rely on his wits, an engaging smile and a clever way with words to get him out of sticky situations. And when Matt began turning to him for advice he realised that he was no longer the junior partner in their friendship but an equal, their different talents complementing each other and making them a winning combination.

It had been a highlight of both their careers when Matt arrested the crooked pharmacist exposed by Johnny's investigation.

"Is everything else all right?" said Johnny. He was flattered that Lizzie had chosen to confide in him, but uneasy about being asked to keep a secret from Matt. They told each other everything. Lizzie looked up sharply.

"Perfectly, thank you."

"I was only asking. Look, I'm seeing Matt tomorrow night so I'll try and find out then what's troubling him. Don't worry, I won't say anything about the baby – but you should tell him soon. He'll be over the moon."

He wished it were his.

The kettle started to rattle on the stove and he busied himself pouring water into the teapot, conscious of Lizzie watching his back. It was so hard to keep up the pretence, constantly trying to hide the way he felt towards her. In those dark days following his mother's death, she more than anyone had pulled him through. She was the one who'd got him out of the house, made him forget his troubles, taught him to laugh again. It was ironic that one of the things that united them was their love for Matt. He was the one who needed help now.

"Don't bother." The bentwood chair scraped on the bare floor as she got to her feet. "I'd better be heading off – Matt finishes at ten."

"I thought he was on six till two."

"He's doing a double shift. They're short-handed

because of the 'flu. Everyone seems to have it. Mrs Kennedy popped her clogs this morning."

"The old dear who lived at the end of Rheidol Terrace? Always sucking a humbug? She looked after me a few times when I was a kid. Here, it won't be too long before you'll be needing a babysitter."

"I'm sure Bexley's full of them."

Johnny's heart sank. It was as if she couldn't wait to increase the distance between them.

"So you're definitely moving then?"

"The house is supposed to be ready by March. It's a lovely semi – exactly what we were after."

"Just like the ones in the posters on the Tube." He could see them now: chessboards with model homes instead of pieces. "How does their slogan go? 'Your next Move and your best is on to the Underground. Houses to suit all classes.'"

"There's no call to be sarcastic. Islington's no place to bring up children. The air's much better in Bexley."

"It didn't do me and Matt any harm."

"That's what you think!" She put her gloves on. "I'll see myself out. Do let me know how you get on tomorrow night." She was already halfway down the hall.

"Hey! Don't I get a goodbye kiss?"

Of course not. He never got what he wanted.

The door slammed shut. And it was then the full force of her two bombshells finally hit him.

FOUR

Tuesday, 8th December, 6.45 p.m.
The last edition had gone to press. The familiar scramble was over – until tomorrow. Johnny grabbed his coat. Those starting on the night shift chatted to their daytime counterparts. The cracked leather of the seats they traded did not even have a chance to cool down. The search for stories, the proprietor's pursuit of sales and money, never stopped.

"Coming for a livener?" said Bill, licking his lips. "I'm spitting feathers."

"I'd like to . . . Thing is, I've got a date," said Johnny. It was not a lie . . . exactly. He did have a date with Daisy for tonight – until he broke it off. He just needed some pretext to ensure that his mentor would not want to tag along.

"Just one, old boy, I promise." Bill's bloodshot eyes took on a pleading expression.

Johnny felt guilty. Bill had gone to the trouble of calling round his contacts, all of whom assured him everyone was present and accounted for at Snow Hill. He owed the guy a drink, at the very least. But he knew from experience that there was no such thing as "just one" drink where Bill was concerned; invariably their sessions would expand into full-blown binges and another evening would be lost before he knew it.

"Let's make it Thursday instead, eh?"

"Right you are." Bill rubbed his hands together. "Happy spooning."

Wasting no time, Johnny legged it along Fleet Street before any other colleagues tried to waylay him. He headed up Shoe Lane, past the cacophonous printing works, and under Holborn Viaduct. As he ran across Farringdon Road, skirting the western end of Smithfield Market, he glanced up Snow Hill, wondering whether he'd see Matt leaving the police station. The steep, winding road was deserted. Back before the Viaduct was built, all traffic from the City to the West End had been forced to negotiate Snow Hill. Nowadays it was something of a backwater. The police station was one of the few places showing any sign of life: its reassuring blue light was a beacon in the dark.

Built just over a decade ago, the station was an odd, bow-fronted building in the middle of a curving terrace. Five-storeys tall, narrow and gabled, it was reminiscent of a uniformed constable standing to attention. The compact façade was deceptive: Snow Hill station-house extended all the way back to Cock Lane at the rear, so there was plenty of room inside for the whole of B Division. A blue plaque informed passers-by that it stood on the site of the Saracen's Head Inn. Matt, who often had to endure the protracted company of Philip Dwyer, a desk sergeant who fancied himself something of a local historian, would occasionally regurgitate the fascinating facts – especially concerning murders and executions – with which he had been forcibly fed. Johnny knew a few additional facts of his own: it was in the Saracen's Head that Nicholas Nickleby had met the one-eyed Wackford Squeers.

Dickens, who'd started out as a newspaperman, was Johnny's idol. He had been introduced to him at school by Mr Stanley, otherwise known as Moggy. The English teacher had returned from the Great War with an artificial leg which his pupils took to be mahogany. As Silas Wegg in *Our Mutual Friend* would have said, he was "a literary man – *with* a wooden leg." Moggy's lessons became the highlight of the week. Dickens' stories were funny and scary and he was writing about the place where they lived. He had walked the same streets, passed the same buildings, seen the same things. He made Johnny want to be a journalist. Even today, a part of him still could not believe he was writing for the newspaper that Dickens had once edited.

His most treasured possession was a mildewed set of Dickens' novels that he'd found one Saturday afternoon on a second-hand bookstall in Farringdon Road. He'd paid for it with the money he had made hanging around Collins' Music Hall on Islington Green with Matt, collecting discarded programmes and selling them on at bargain prices to the punters going in for the next show: the better the clothes, the lower the discount. He'd continued faithfully working his way through the set all the way through school and college.

Dickens' work provided a living map of the capital. He did not care if it was out of date; the characters lived on in his mind and the echoes reverberated each time he visited a location which had featured in one of the novels. The Old Bailey, for example, had been built on the site of Newgate prison; in the confines of its stuffy courtrooms, whiling away the hours as lawyers argued and judges jawed, Johnny could not help but recall Dickens' "horrible fascination" with the gaol which featured in *Barnaby Rudge*; in whose condemned hold Fagin awaited his end; and where, in *Great Expectations,* Pip viewed the Debtors' Door through which doomed culprits were led to be hanged.

It was inconceivable to Johnny that anyone could be bored by Dickens; but Matt – lulled by Moggy's droning and the hissing of the gas-lamps – would invariably drift off to sleep. The English master took a sadistic pleasure in twisting Matt's ear as slowly as he could, seeing how far he could go without waking him, and then, having fully regained his attention, dragging him to his feet and rapping him on the knuckles with the edge of the ruler, all the while continuing to read. Moggy never lost his place; Matt never made a sound.

By now, Johnny was drawing near to the Rolling

Barrel – a favourite watering hole for many of Matt's colleagues. The pub was said to have derived its name from a local legend: the site was apparently notorious for a gang of tearaways who used to snatch unsuspecting little old ladies off the street, stuff them in a barrel and roll them down the hill.

Finally he reached St Sepulchre's churchyard and the Viaduct Tavern came into view, just across the road on the corner of Giltspur Street and Newgate Street.

A Victorian gin palace glittering with cut glass, painted mirrors and plush seats, its regulars were mostly off-duty postmen from the General Post Office in King Edward Street. The ornate clock behind the bar told Johnny he was five minutes early.

It was only when he had been served and wriggled his way through the crowd – without spilling more than a few drops of Ind Coope Burton – that he saw Matt sitting alone at one of the small, round tables at the back. His friend was staring morosely into the empty glass in front of him.

"Penny for them."

Matt looked up. His handsome face, white with exhaustion, did not bother to smile. The liver-coloured welts under his eyes seemed to have deepened.

"Evening. One of those for me?"

"Who else?"

Johnny handed him a pint. He downed half of it in three gulps.

"That's better."

"Bitter, actually."

"Jack the Quipper strikes again." Matt drained his glass. "Refill?"

"Hold your horses – what's the rush?"

"D'you want another or not?"

"Go on then."

Johnny watched, concerned, as his friend lurched off towards the bar, the mass of bodies miraculously parting before him like the Red Sea. Matt was too big to argue with. It looked as though he'd downed a few while he was waiting.

With Lizzie's words of the previous evening running through his mind, Johnny lit a cigarette and leaned back on the banquette, watching the smoke spiral towards the high, intricately patterned ceiling. Its once white mouldings were now stained the yellow of bad teeth.

"Here we are." Matt suddenly reappeared with two glasses, took a slurp from one and smacked his lips. "I needed that." He flashed a grin that was half-grimace. "It's good to see you."

"Likewise." Impatient as ever, Johnny cut to the chase: "So, what have you got to tell me?"

"Nothing about a cop dying, if that's what you mean. I checked the Occurrence Book."

"Oh." Johnny could not keep the disappointment out of his voice.

"I told you yesterday, I haven't heard anything."

It wasn't like Matt to clam up this way. One of the things he loved about police work was the range of characters it brought him into contact with – the suspected burglar who turned out to be a doctor on his way to deliver a child at three in the morning; the incontinent woman who wandered the streets in a coat made from the pelts of her pet cats; the boy who thought he was a Number 15 bus. Usually he couldn't wait to describe his latest odd encounter to Johnny – but not tonight. Clearly there was something else that he needed to say, something he could not say to anyone else.

Whenever Matt needed advice, Johnny was invariably his first port of call. He'd always been clever, and since he'd gone into journalism he'd begun to build up an impressive network of informants and experts and people who owed him favours. His contacts book, scrupulously maintained and augmented throughout his career, was one of his most prized possessions.

Resisting the urge to fire questions at his friend, Johnny took a pull on his drink and waited. But it seemed Matt still wasn't ready to get to the point:

"On the other hand, there's been quite a bit of talk about your friend Mr Simkins," he stalled.

"Go on," coaxed Johnny.

"Mrs Shaw – the murderer's wife – killed herself last night. They found her this morning. It looks as though she drank a bottle of bleach."

Johnny put down his glass. He couldn't imagine a more agonising death; her vital organs dissolving bit by bit in the chlorine. As if she had not been in enough pain already, what with her husband confessing to the murder of Margaret Murray. Murder rarely involved just one victim.

"I feel sick," he said.

"Me too," said Matt. "Back in a tick."

He certainly looked queasy as he picked his way through the crowd, making a beeline for the gents. Matt was not squeamish – in his job he could not afford to be – and could hold his liquor better than most.

A few moments later, Matt returned, negotiating the packed bar with uncharacteristic caution. His slightly exaggerated air of being in control could not disguise the fact that he was well on the way to being blotto.

"Come on, Matt – tell me what's up."

Turner shook his head in confusion. Advice was one thing, but he'd never found it easy to ask for help: to him, it was an admission of weakness. Johnny was the one person he trusted enough to turn to. When they lost the baby, Matt had been desperate not to add to Lizzie's pain by burdening her with his grief; he'd tried drowning his sorrows and venting his fury on a punch-bag or some over-confident sucker at the gym. It was only when all else had failed that he turned to Johnny. It helped that his friend had experienced loss himself and knew that words, however well meant, changed nothing.

"I'm having these nightmares . . ." He lifted his gaze as if challenging Johnny to laugh, then continued: "I've tried to ignore them but, rather than going away, they're just getting worse. It's got to the stage where I'm almost afraid to go to sleep."

"Can you remember much about them?"

"They're always the same. It's pitch black . . . very hot. I can't move. I can't breathe. Just when I think I'm going to suffocate, there's this incredible pain – pain like nothing I've ever felt before. Then there's this blinding white light and I wake up." Matt wiped away the perspiration on his upper lip. He was so blond he only needed to shave every other day.

"Have you been to see the doctor?"

"Of course not! There's nothing wrong with me physically. And can you imagine what they'd say at the station if I went to see a head-doctor? I'd never hear the end of it. I'd lose my job."

"What about Lizzie's father? He could give you something to help you sleep."

"And have him think his son-in-law is a lunatic as well as a prole?"

"You're not mad. Besides, you needn't tell him *why* you can't sleep."

"True." He did not seem convinced.

"When did the nightmares start?"

"About three weeks ago. It wasn't too bad at first. They weren't that frequent. Now, though, I'm having the same dream every night. It's like I'm dying."

"Well, you're not." Johnny patted his forearm. "You're only supposed to worry when you dream that you don't wake up."

"That's a big help. Thanks a bunch!" Matt slid a finger round the inside of his collar and glowered. His rage had come from nowhere. Johnny, for the first time, felt afraid in his friend's company.

"Matt . . . what is it you want me to do? I could speak to a psychiatrist . . . I can get you some pills. Just let me know what it is you want. No one will ever know."

"Just forget it. Sorry to bother you." Matt drained his glass and made as if preparing to leave.

"Don't be like that," said Johnny, suddenly feeling out of his depth. "Give me a chance. There's got to be a reason why you're having these nightmares. Did anything significant happen three weeks ago?"

"No. I've thought and thought about it. There's nothing. It was the usual routine: work, bed, work, bed."

"Anything out of the ordinary at work?"

"Nothing. I was on point duty, freezing my balls off on Blackfriars Bridge. The sooner I stop being a straight bogey and pass my sergeant's exams the better. We were short-staffed that week so I had to go out on the beat for a couple of nights as well. The extra money will come in handy – you know we want to start a family – but I didn't make it home for three days."

"Well, houses in Bexley don't come cheap."

Matt's eyes bored in to him. Their blueness deepened. "So she's told you, has she?"

Johnny cursed himself. He would have to lie. In his current state of mind, Matt would kill him if he thought he had been seeing Lizzie behind his back. Besides, he would want to know why – and, at this stage, the knowledge that he was about to become a father would only increase the pressure on him.

"Nobody's told me anything – I'm just teasing. I know you prefer Stanmore. Why Lizzie wants to live south of the river is a mystery to me."

"Well, as it happens, you're spot on. She's got her own way – again. We signed up for a house in Bexley a couple of weeks ago."

"Congratulations." Johnny raised his glass even though his heart was sinking.

"My dad's pleased, at any rate."

Turner's father had been a detective inspector when he had retired five years ago. His son was very conscious of following in his footsteps. Although he made an exemplary constable – a friendly face to those in need and a daunting prospect to villains – Matt was determined to reach a higher rank than DI, and passing his sergeant's exams would see him progress to the next step on the ladder. His athletic prowess had stood him in good stead so far, but he wasn't a natural when it came to matters academic; knowing he daren't leave anything to chance, he'd been spending all his spare time cramming for the upcoming exams. He'd need to attain first-class certificates in English Composition, Arithmetic, General Knowledge and Intelligence, Geography and Preparation of Police Returns to get through. But even if he passed with flying colours, any whisper of mental instability would undo all his good work and instantly scupper his chances.

"So Bexley it is. Lizzie must be delighted."

"Yeah, she is. Course, once we move, I'll have to sleep most nights at Snow Hill until I get promoted, just like I do when I've got a double shift. Lizzie's never liked the idea of Ferndale Court."

Constables were not permitted to live more than thirty

minutes from their station-house, and with affordable housing hard to come by in central London, the force provided its own accommodation. Ferndale Road, Stockwell, was the nearest base for married officers.

"At least we'll still see as much of each other as before." Matt stared into the bottom of his pint glass.

"I hope so," said Johnny, and meant it.

The level of conversation around them had risen to a roar. The drinkers had become more raucous as the alcohol transformed cold, dog-eat-dog reality into a warm fug of camaraderie and security.

"Look, I've got to go." Matt suddenly got to his feet. He seemed unsteady, holding on to the table for support. "If you can have a word with someone for me, I'd be grateful. And if I hear anything about a dead cop I'll let you know. Bye."

He laid his hand on Johnny's shoulder as he passed; Johnny covered it with his own.

When Matt had moved away, Johnny turned, craning his neck to scan the crowded bar. Something had happened to make Matt leave so abruptly. He'd looked as if he had seen a ghost. All Johnny could see was a wall of backs.

He fought his way to the bar. It was not yet seven thirty; he needn't have cancelled his date with Daisy after all. True to form, when he broke the news last night she had wildly over-reacted then pretended not to give tuppence. This time she might not even let him make it up to her. Well, it wouldn't be the end of the world if it was all over between them.

Why did he keep chasing after these good-time girls? He was the ultimate stage-door Johnny. He'd asked Daisy out because she reminded him of Carole Lombard in *My Man Godfrey*, but for all that her glossy, black hair, curly lashes and pouting lips made him hot under the collar, there was a hardness about her that repelled him. Like the other actresses and dancers he'd dated, the only thing she cared about was getting some publicity for her stuttering career. If he hadn't been a reporter on a national daily, she wouldn't have given him a second glance. And he had no real interest in her – so why did he persist?

Because he was lonely.

It was odd how, after their encounters, he felt even lonelier.

Rather than head straight home, he decided to order one for the road.

The man who would kill him watched him in a mirror.

What the devil were those two talking about? That Steadman's getting to be a real nuisance, always sticking his nose where it's not wanted. Persistent little bugger. So determined to get a big scoop, make his name as a reporter – that ambition's going to land him in trouble if he's not careful.

Still, there's no way he knows what happened Saturday night. It's impossible. I made damn sure there was no one else around. Christ, it felt good.

Pity I needed help with the clearing up, but I picked the right lads for the job. They won't breathe a word – they've got too much to lose. Not as much as me, mind. Won't hurt to remind them that I'll do whatever it takes to avoid discovery. Even if it means killing them too.

FIVE

The cold air slapped his face. It was like walking into a washing line on Monday morning. He was half-sober already.

"Had a good time?" A policeman blocked his path, towering over him. Was he a marked man? He could not seem to turn round this week without bumping into a cop.

"Yes, thank you, officer."

"Johnny Steadman, isn't it?" His interrogator smiled pleasantly. All City cops were neat but this one somehow seemed neater. He had an open face and kind, slate-grey eyes.

"I'm Tom Vinson. I believe we have a mutual friend. Matt Turner?"

"You've just missed him."

"Actually, I haven't. I saw him just now, heading back to collect something from the station-house. That's how

I knew it must be you." He took off a black glove and held out his hand. Johnny shook it.

"How d'you do." Vinson's grip was warm and firm.

"It's a pleasure to meet you after all this time," said Vinson. "Matt often talks about you. He looks up to you." Johnny was surprised – and embarrassed.

"We've known each other since we were four years old."

"That's some friendship. Matt's a good man to have on your side."

"Indeed." There didn't seem much else to say, but Vinson was still blocking his way. "Well, it's been a pleasure to meet you." Johnny moved to the right. Vinson followed suit. He moved to the left. So did the policeman. "Was there something else?"

Vinson hesitated and looked round to check no one was within earshot. "This did not come from me, right? I believe you want to know if a cop has gone missing from Snow Hill. There's only one person who was at the station last week who isn't there now – a wolly who's transferred to the Met."

"That's a bit odd. It's usually the other way round."

The City of London Police – stationed at the hub of the British Empire and accustomed to rubbing shoulders with the bankers and brokers of the financial capital of the world – considered themselves a cut above the Metropolitan Police who patrolled the rest of London. Rozzers were not being complimentary when they referred to their City counterparts as "the posh lot".

"And how come a new recruit was given an instant

transfer?" Johnny was fully alert now. "These things normally take weeks to arrange."

"I don't know when he applied to be moved," stated Vinson. "The notice doesn't say. What it does say is that it was for personal reasons. Something to do with a family tragedy."

"What was his name?"

"Ah, I can't help you there. It's forbidden to divulge operational information."

"Then can you at least tell me where he was transferred to?"

"Sorry. Still, there's no need to go wasting your time investigating that dodgy tip-off now."

"Thanks very much. It was good of you to tell me. I owe you."

"Don't mention it – really!" With a cheery nod, Vinson continued on his beat.

As Johnny continued down Giltspur Street his mind was so full of questions he barely registered his surroundings. Why was Vinson being so helpful? Had Matt told him about the tip-off? Was he trying to put him off the scent? It would be easy enough to find out the recruit's name – Matt would tell him tomorrow – so why had Vinson withheld it? Was he afraid that Johnny would want to interview the lad? That didn't make sense; policemen were forbidden to talk to the press – officially, anyway.

If Vinson was being straight with him, it would explain the absence of an outcry: nobody had died and there was nothing to hide. But if that were all there was to it, why bother to tell a journalist anything at all? And why had Bill not come up with anything about the transfer?

Johnny smelled a cover-up.

Johnny closed the front door and did not bother to lock it behind him. He stood in the narrow hallway shivering as the cooling sweat trickled down his back. It had unnerved him to see Matt so disturbed; he resolved to do everything he could to help without betraying Matt's confidence. He felt he owed it to his friend, who had never ceased to trust him – even though he was in love with his wife.

One moment he had never been in love, the next he was head-over-heels. Lizzie was unlike any other woman he knew. She was witty, not flighty; independent, not clingy. She wore Chanel No. 5, not Coty Naturelle. Although middle class, she never betrayed the slightest hint of condescension. She infuriated her father by voting for the Labour Party. She liked Molière as much as musicals; read Compton Mackenzie, Elizabeth Bowen and Pearl S. Buck as well as movie and fashion magazines. And she loved Dickens.

Occasionally, when Matt was boxing in a tournament or wanted to meet up with his brothers to go to a match, he was only too happy for Johnny to take Lizzie to a matinee; earlier in the year the two of them had sat enthralled in a Shaftesbury Avenue theatre while Matt watched Arsenal beat Sheffield United in the FA Cup final at Wembley.

Back in the days when they were courting, Matt and Lizzie had often gone dancing with Johnny and whichever chorus-girl he was seeing at the time. It was only when they swapped partners, and Johnny slipped his arm round Lizzie's slender waist, holding her tightly, sweeping her across the polished floor, her breath tickling the hairs on the back of his neck, that he felt truly alive. She had known how he had felt before he did. Nothing was said; nobody was to blame. It was not Johnny's fault he loved her; it was not Lizzie's fault that she merely liked him.

He could see why she'd fallen for Matt – he was good-looking, fearless and kind, someone who never hesitated to go to the aid of those in distress whether he was in uniform or not – but he could not help being disappointed. However, he put on a brave face – thus gaining stature in Lizzie's eyes – and tried to concentrate on Matt's blind happiness rather than his own overwhelming misery.

There was no doubt they made a beautiful couple. His speech had made every one laugh: "The trouble with being best man is that you don't often get a chance to prove it."

Standing in the darkness and silence of his empty house he wondered what the hell he had hurried home for. There was only his journal and a few family photographs to keep him company. Johnny's father, Edward, had been killed at Passchendaele when he was three. He knew all too little about the short, stocky infantryman grinning proudly at the camera with a baby in his arms.

At school he had pored for hours over history textbooks, hoping to find out what men like his father had been forced to endure, but mostly the authors skated over the realities of warfare and instead focused on the causes and consequences of the conflict, with a paragraph or two of waffle about the honour and heroic sacrifice of the troops. He had tried to imagine the blood and the mud; the stench of the trench; the crawling lice and gnawing rats; the random, wholesale carnage and the mind-splitting shriek of the shells. However, reading was no substitute for the real thing. He had tried to talk to those who had returned from France, men who had seen the atrocity of war at first hand, but most of them, like Inspector Rotherforth, had clammed up or changed the subject, clearly reluctant to release the painful memories. The wounded look in their eyes was similar to the one now staring back at him in the mirror.

Johnny was haunted by his mother's death. Having to stand by while she had screamed and screamed in agony – not for a few seconds, not for a few minutes, but until she was too exhausted to scream any more – had taught him all there was to know about powerlessness. He had been totally unprepared for the messiness of death.

He tramped up the wooden stairs to the bathroom that had once been his bedroom. The cold always made his bladder shrink. After the funeral he had made a conscious effort to jettison the past. Most of his wages as a reporter – which, although pretty low, were far more than he had ever earned before – had gone on converting the terraced two-up, two-down in Cruden Street into a modern bachelor pad. When the landlords learned about his new bathroom they had increased the rent and said they would do so again if he made any further alterations. He was on the mains now, what more did he want?

Why was it that any attempt to better yourself or your situation always proved, one way or another, so costly?

SIX

Wednesday, 9th December, 4.05 p.m.

Johnny breathed a sigh of relief when the trial of Rex v. Yelloff, a fruit importer accused of torching his own warehouse in Australian Avenue, was adjourned until the following morning. He'd have to be back at the office to file his daily round-up of court news by the 5.30 p.m. deadline, but in the meantime there was someone he wanted to see.

Imprisoned in the Old Bailey for most of the day, Johnny had been unable to contact Matt to find out the name of the rookie cop. That would have to wait now. It was more important to establish whether a body had turned up over the weekend. The dead cop – if there was one – might not have been a new recruit. Whoever the supposed victim might be, their body would have to have been taken somewhere.

The City of London Police comprised four divisions:

A Division, based in Moor Lane; B Division, in Snow Hill – where the tip-off said the victim was stationed; C Division, in Bishopsgate; and D Division, in Cloak Lane. Although the headquarters of the "gentlemen cops" was in Old Jewry, the mortuary for the force was in Moor Lane. Johnny's contact there had assured him that no officer or unidentified person had been brought in over the weekend. His opposite number at the Metropolitan Police mortuary in Horseferry Road, a truculent tyke, swore that "no dead pigs of any sort" had been delivered there. That left only one other place a corpse could feasibly be taken: Bart's.

Johnny crossed the courtyard, its fountain chuckling to itself in the gloom, and went round to the pathology block at the back where, via Little Britain, black vans could come and go day and night without attracting too much attention.

It felt warm in the morgue. The sudden contrast to the Arctic air outside made his nose run. He let his eyes adjust to the dim lighting. He was looking for Percy Hughes, the mortuary assistant. Ever on the lookout for money-making opportunities, Percy had been a part of the Bart's drugs ring. He was only a lowly delivery boy to the pharmacist, but it would have been enough to get him sent down had it not been for Johnny agreeing to keep his name out of the investigation in exchange for his services as an informant.

Today he was sluicing the black-and-white tiled floor with some sort of brown disinfectant.

"Mind where yer standin'!"

"Sorry, sorry." Johnny stepped back in the nick of time, the puddle advancing within inches of his toes. It looked like diarrhoea. "Have you got a minute?" He glanced round. The basement was empty. He jingled the change in his pocket.

Hughes' hand shot out and grabbed the two half-crowns from Johnny's palm.

Johnny laughed and said: "I'm looking for a policeman."

Percy carried on mopping. He had none of that cheerful callousness which those who work with the dead sometimes adopt to disguise their true feelings. Johnny could not imagine how he got through the endless night shifts with only corpses for company. No wonder he was always miserable; his normal expression was that of a moose not getting enough moss.

"Yer won't find one 'ere – dead nor alive."

"What d'you know about a dead cop?"

"Nuffink." Percy kept his eyes on the floor. He was clearly uncomfortable. As he spent most of his time with folk who would never talk again, he was usually glad of the chance to chat. Not today though.

"Cat got your tongue?"

"Nope."

"Well, what's up then? Your price gone up?"

"Nope." He squeezed his mop out and began to push the last of the foul liquid down the drain. There was something in it that made the eyes sting. It did not smell too good either. Johnny took a deep breath and, looking around, waited for Hughes to break the silence.

There were three slabs in the mortuary. The green curtains used to screen cadavers from view were at present pushed back against the tiled wall. On the opposite wall were six refrigerators, each with three drawers: filing cabinets for stiffs. Johnny's eyes took in the glass-fronted cupboards with their intimidating array of glistening surgical instruments: saws and scalpels, trepans and trocars, forceps, xysters and specula. He tried not to linger too long on the specimen jars, labelled in copperplate, which held various body parts pickled in formaldehyde, like denizens of an obscene aquarium.

Johnny tried again:

"Forget about the patients. Were any corpses brought in over the weekend?"

Hughes concentrated on making figure-of-eight swirls with the mop.

Johnny snatched it off him. "Have you been told to keep your trap shut?"

"What d'yer mean?"

"Percy, I won't ask again. It's not too late for me to turn you in – one phone call, that's all it would take."

"Okay, okay. Keep yer 'air on. A dead 'un did come in, early Sunday mornin'."

"Thank you. Was it a cop?"

"'Ow the 'ell should I know? 'E was in 'is birthday suit."

"Now we're getting somewhere. Name?"

"Dunno. They didn't tell me 'is name. Said they didn't know it either."

"Who's 'they'?"

"The two geezers what brung 'im in. And before you ask, I'd never seen 'em before in my life."

He was lying.

"How old was he?"

"Early twenties, I reckon."

"Was there a post mortem?"

"Nope."

"Cause of death?"

"Dunno. Register says hypothermia."

"Is there going to be a funeral?"

"'Ardly. The body's bin donated to medical science. Stuck-up students'll be chopping 'im into cat-meat as we speak."

"On whose authority?"

"None needed. No next of kin. Barnardo's Boy, so they said."

"Very convenient . . . Go on."

For a moment, Hughes had been about to say something. He was not usually so reluctant to spill the beans. Seeing how afraid Percy was, Johnny was certain that he must be on the right track. He took out another half-crown. To a lad who earned less than £3 a week, this was significant encouragement. It was a pretty significant amount to Johnny, too; well beyond his usual budget for informants. He prayed that Patsel would sign off his expenses.

"I 'aven't spoken to yer, awright?"

"Yes, yes. Get on with it."

"Mr Steadman, I'm serious. Sumfink's up, but I don't want to lose my job."

Johnny suddenly wondered if Percy had a wife and family to support. Probably not. Few women, knowing what Percy did for a living, would want those hands touching their flesh.

Realising that he was still holding the mop, Johnny handed it back.

"Here you are. Don't worry, I won't say a word. And don't you go talking to anyone else either. We've got an exclusive arrangement, remember."

"No danger of me blabbing." Percy dropped his voice. "As it 'appens, I did know one of the geezers. Don't get me wrong, 'Arry's a good lad. Wouldn't 'urt a fly."

"Who is this Harry? What does he do?"

"'Arry Gogg's 'is name. 'E's a porter at Smithfield. Drinks in the Cock most days."

"Thank you."

Johnny glanced at his watch. He had under an hour to get his copy to the subs. As usual, most of it was already written in his head.

Someone was coming down the corridor with a trolley. Its wheels needed oiling.

"What made you decide to tell me?"

"I 'aven't said nuffink, remember." Percy was whispering now. "But it's the only case of hypothermia I've seen wiv broken bones sticking out the skin."

SEVEN

Thursday, 10th December, 5.50 a.m.

Johnny got off the tram in St John Street. It had been clear at the Angel but down here the capital was gripped by a choking, freezing smog. Smithfield appeared as a yellow shimmer straight ahead of him.

Even though daybreak was a couple of hours away, it was busier than Piccadilly Circus. Trucks, wagons, vans and carts jostled for position like pigs round a trough. As soon as one lorry had loaded its cargo of meat, the next was sounding its horn, determined to take its place. Others, on an equally tight schedule, were just as desperate to load up and deliver their new stock to butchers' shops across London. As he approached, he heard raised voices then shouts and the sound of pallets being overturned as a scuffle between drivers broke into a fist-fight. Most of the market workers barely gave the combatants a glance; flare-ups like this were an everyday occurrence at Smithfield.

Still excited by the lead Hughes had given him the night before, Johnny made his way through the mêlée like a man on a mission. The vast iron-and-glass building was a cathedral of corpses, complete with nave, transepts, and aisles. The interior had been decorated with an almost fetishistic attention to detail: every arch, spandrel and lunette was filled with a swirling mass of ferric foliage painted not green but blue. The nave was lined with stalls that stretched as far as the eye could see. Hundreds of skinned and gutted animals, their carcasses shining dully in the electric glare, swung on rails bristling with giant steel hooks. It was a forest of flesh through which strolled potential buyers, some from the kitchens of the very best hotels, inspecting meat and comparing prices.

There was, however, nothing spiritual about Smithfield; under its roof the "inner man" meant the stomach, not the soul. It was devoted to carnality, its services designed to assuage man's hunger for beef, pork, lamb and poultry. Money was the religion here.

The Central Markets even had their own men of the cloth: porters, known as bummarees, who acted as intermediaries between buyers and sellers. Their white coats and strange hats – a cross between a havelock and a wimple – made them stand out from the mass of black and grey. They were freelances who got paid for what they did, which was why most of them worked on the run, lugging carcasses on their shoulders or dragging wooden carts behind them. As time was money, they brooked no interruption.

Trying not to get in their way, Johnny hurried to keep up as he asked one after another where he might find Harry Gogg. Those that did not ignore him simply professed ignorance. The market workers were a bolshy lot, only too happy to go on strike. The last one, in February, had cut off the meat supply to the whole capital.

Finally Johnny gave up and wandered through the halls. Although the floor was scattered with sawdust, the dripping blood, melting ice and trudging feet had turned it into a gruel-like sludge. If Smithfield was no longer the filthy abattoir described by Bill Sykes in *Oliver Twist*, it remained a steaming, swarming hive that reeked of death.

As a reporter, Johnny was used to being unwelcome. Most people looked down on journalists. He'd hear them on trams and in cafés and pubs, tut-tutting whenever the tricks of the inky trade got so bad they ended up making the headlines. But it didn't stop them devouring their newspaper each morning. Looking around him, it occurred to Johnny that it was much the same with the contents of their breakfast: if people were to see the process that led to the bacon and sausages ending up on their plate, many of them would lose their appetite. The consumer was not interested in the means of production, what counted was the finished product.

Anyone of the cowled creatures roaming the aisles of Smithfield could have been Harry Gogg. Cursing himself for not getting a description from Percy, Johnny decided there was nothing more to be gained from hanging around the market. Besides, he needed to take refuge from the cold.

A board outside the Cock Tavern announced that it was permitted to open at 4 a.m. "for the accommodation of persons following their lawful trade and calling as salesmen, buyers, butchers, assistants, carmen and porters and attending a public market at Smithfield". Taking a seat at the bar, Johnny ordered a "wazzer", the speciality of the house. It tasted like a cup of tea laced with whisky. Whatever it was, it did the trick. Soon even his toes were warm.

Those around him were tucking into plates piled high with bacon, eggs, fried bread, sausages, liver, kidneys and black pudding. With the salty, prickly smell of raw meat still in his nostrils, Johnny made do with a cigarette.

By half past seven most of the day's business had been concluded so far as the market workers were concerned. A group of bummarees came in and sat in a corner.

The landlady went over to take their orders. She was a dumpy, middle-aged woman with a mop of long, lank curls that looked as though someone had tipped a bowl of cold spaghetti over her. She did not seem to mind that their white coats were smeared with gore and had no problem countering their ribald banter with some of her own. Johnny watched in the mirror behind the bar as she served the five men their wazzers then went off to the kitchen.

Fortified by the alcohol, he slipped off his stool and made his way to their table.

"Sorry, mate. Never 'eard of 'im," said the oldest, a grizzled bear of a man. His colleagues looked at each other.

"He's one of your lot. Look, he's not in any trouble – I was told he may be able to help me, that's all."

One of the younger ones muttered something. They all laughed.

"There'd be a few bob in it for him," said Johnny.

"As I told yer, never 'eard of 'im." The bummaree raised his voice so the whole pub could hear. "Anyone 'ere know of an 'Arry Gogg?"

Silence fell. Everyone in the room was staring at Johnny. He returned their stares until they turned away. Slowly the conversation resumed.

"Well, that is odd," said Johnny sarcastically. He was riled. He hated being treated like an idiot. "Harry Gogg works in Smithfield. There can't be that many of you – someone must know him."

The brute who'd spoken before lumbered to his feet. He could easily have carried half an ox on each shoulder.

"You calling me a liar, son?"

There was nothing Johnny could do. If he didn't back down he'd be going head-first through the swing-doors before he knew what hit him.

"No, no, not at all. Sorry to have disturbed you." He retreated to the bar.

"You're pushing your luck," said the landlady, introducing herself as Dolly. A pink wart nestled in the cleft between her nose and right cheek. "They're a close-knit bunch and don't like strangers. They've probably got you down as working for the taxman." She set another wazzer in front of him and, when he insisted on paying, promised to tip him the wink if Gogg came in.

He did not have long to wait. Harry was a winsome lad, fair-haired and fresh-faced. He scanned the room as if looking for someone then came and stood by Johnny at the bar. Although roughly the same height, he was twice as broad. He also seemed nervous. Instead of joining the other bummarees, he went and sat by himself. The only thing he ate was his thumbnail. It would be pointless talking to him now.

Ten minutes later, Gogg drained his mug and left. Johnny, making sure he avoided eye contact with the porters, followed. His senses quickened: he was on the trail again.

Legwork was an essential part of the job. The best stories usually involved pounding the streets: chasing leads, witnesses and suspects – sometimes literally. Johnny knew what Matt was talking about when he complained of being footsore.

The smog was beginning to thin now. Dawn was glimmering in the east. Johnny finally caught up with Gogg as he crossed the recreation ground. The statue of *Peace*, erected to allay the spirits of William Wallace and others who'd been executed on this very spot, ignored them.

"Harry Gogg?"

The bummaree looked over his shoulder and regarded him with suspicion. He kept on walking.

Johnny followed.

Without looking back, Gogg asked, "Who wants to know?"

"My name's Johnny Steadman. I'm a reporter on the *News*. I was told you might have some information for me. I'm willing to pay."

The boy stopped to use the drinking fountain. It was frozen.

As Johnny caught up with him, he hissed, "Don't look at me."

Leaning against the fountain, Johnny stared off into the distance, trying to look casual, as if it were normal to be loitering in the freezing cold.

A moment later he heard the boy whisper: "Information about what?"

"The death of a young man on Saturday night."

"Jesus Christ!" The lad looked round the park in panic. Shapes seemed to shift at its edges. "We can't talk here. Follow me . . . Wait! Don't make it obvious. Keep your distance."

They left West Smithfield and entered Cloth Fair. Johnny hoped they were not going far: he was supposed to be at the office by now. Well, if questioned, he could honestly say he had started work hours ago.

Around him the medieval houses leaned out over the street as though whispering gossip to each other. Through the gloom he could just make out Gogg's chunky frame on the left. He assumed the boy was heading for the pub on the corner of Rising Sun Court. However, when he reached it he suddenly veered across the lane and disappeared into an alley which ran alongside

St Bartholomew-the-Great. Hesitating to check that he had been seen, he then went into the church.

A few moments later, as the bells in the brick tower chimed eight o'clock, Johnny raised the latch and pushed open the heavy oak door.

Although he had often heard the evening peal of London's oldest parish church on his way to meet Matt, he had never been inside its flint-flecked walls before. He walked down the long nave. The black tiled floor was dangerously uneven. Gogg was waiting for him beside the choir screen, which showed monks going about their daily business. It looked brand new.

"We should be safe here. Let's see the colour of your money."

The ten-shilling note brought the pink back to Gogg's cheeks. It was the equivalent of a day's earnings. His melting brown eyes darted here and there, seeking eavesdroppers. His cowlick flickered in a draught. Satisfied that the church was empty, he nodded in the direction of the choir-stalls and they took a seat.

"Why did your colleagues say they didn't know you in the pub?"

"Sheer bloody-mindedness. I'm not exactly popular round here."

"Why not?"

"It's a long story – and it's not why you're here."

"True." Johnny would have liked to hear the story nonetheless. Nosiness was another prerequisite of the job. "Okay, first I'd like to assure you that whatever you tell me will be in the strictest confidence."

"I've heard that before. Who put you on to me?"

"A friend. No names – I don't betray confidences, remember? What can you tell me about a dead cop?"

The porter froze.

"He was a cop? A bloody cop? That fucking bastard – he didn't tell me that. I knew something was off – he was too generous."

He put his head in his hands. Was he crying? Johnny was filled with concern. There was something innately attractive about the boy.

"Harry, what's going on? Don't be afraid. I'll protect you." He put his hand on the boy's shoulder.

Suddenly Gogg leapt to his feet. Someone had lifted the giant latch.

"Green Hill's Rents," he whispered. "Three thirty tomorrow morning. I start work at four, so don't be late. I'll tell you everything then, I promise. The bastard's gone too far this time. He's got it coming."

Johnny realised the boy had been thinking, not crying. His frustration must have shown in his face, for Gogg flashed a grin and said, "Trust me." Then he scurried off.

For a while, Johnny remained seated, listening intently. He could not hear a thing: no receding footsteps, Harry leaving, the hum of traffic, birdsong . . . The silence was unnerving.

Knowing that if he sat any longer he would fall asleep – or freeze to death – Johnny got to his feet. To kill time while he waited for whoever had disturbed their encounter to show themselves, he decided he might as well take a look round the church.

He wandered through the ambulatory, investigating the numerous nooks and crannies, trying – and failing – to identify the period and style of the various additions and renovations. The piecemeal quality of the church's construction actually served to enhance its austere charm. Of all the memorials that embossed the walls, that to Margaret and John Whiting, who both died in 1681, made the greatest impression:

Shee first deceased, Hee for a little Tryd
To live without her, likd it not and dyd.

Johnny knelt down in a pew and said a prayer for his parents. He no longer believed in an all-merciful God. He was not sure what he believed in any more. Truth? Justice? Love? Did any of them endure?

As he got to his feet he noticed an oriel window above him, beautiful if incongruous. The central panel of its stone base was decorated with a cloverleaf. It contained a rebus, a visual puzzle, in which a crossbow arrow pierced a cask. A bolt and a tun.

Something moved: there was a figure in the window, dressed in black. Johnny tried not to appear startled. He pulled himself together and exited the pew. In the distance a door slammed.

"Have you worked it out yet?" A young man, his palms pressed together, approached.

"Who was Bolton?" Johnny, having compiled crosswords, considered the rebus insultingly simple.

"Ah, very good, very good. The Prior was a fascinating

man but completely loopy. He built the window so he could observe Mass without having to enter the church."

"Rather voyeuristic of him, wasn't it? Religion as a spectator sport."

"Well, in a manner of speaking, it's all theatre, isn't it? But, like most pursuits, it's more fun taking part." He smiled conspiratorially. There was a blob of food on his dog collar. "Prior Bolton also built Canonbury Tower in Islington. Have you seen it?" Johnny nodded. "He was convinced that an apocalyptic tidal wave was going to wash away the City in 1524. Something to do with a conjunction of water signs, apparently. That's why he built the tower – and he didn't stop there. He went on to have a house built on the highest spot in Harrow-on-the-Hill. It seems he thought the flood wouldn't reach him there."

"*Après lui, le deluge*."

"Fortunately not. The end of the world still awaits us. Came pretty close though in the Great War. The church was hit during a Zeppelin raid in 1916, but the bomb only damaged the west gateway. The Lord looks after his own."

"And the people blown to bits? Who was looking after them?"

They had learned all about the Zeppelin raids at school. It was impossible to imagine how the victims must have felt. Death from the air: another great technological advance.

The verger cleared his throat. "You're a non-believer then? Never mind. You may not love Jesus, but He still loves you."

Well, at least that made one person. Johnny did not think it appropriate to share the thought. He said goodbye to the silky cleric and headed back to the real world.

The market had gone to bed. It was so cold he could feel the shape of his lungs. The smog had all but vanished. The sun, a wan disc, was having as much difficulty rising as Johnny had experienced several hours earlier. Justice, the golden lady who presided over the Central Criminal Courts, her arms akimbo like a traffic cop, was already on duty. Now all he had to do was put in a full day's work. Even so, his spirits lifted. At last he had a definite lead.

EIGHT

Friday, 11th December, 3.05 a.m.

An impromptu chain of Christmas lights gave Upper Street the faltering jauntiness of a seaside resort after the tide has gone out. He was the only visitor. Islington had become a ghost town: its bus, tram and Tube drivers still lay farting in their beds. A faint, freezing mist cast a grey pall over the slumbering terraces, tenements, shops and factories. Each lamp-post was graced with a halo: gold in the centre, surrounded by rings of cream, orange, violet and purple, then brown at the edges. Nothing, not even a yowling dog, broke the uncanny silence.

Johnny strode out, trying to strike sparks on the Tri-pedal road surface with his segs. The iron was supposed to give tyres and rubber-soled shoes a better grip but in such icy conditions it just made it easier to skid. He returned to the pavement.

The crossroads where Pentonville Road turned into

City Road was clear of traffic in every direction. A lone policeman stood in the doorway of the Angel cinema. He nodded but did not bother to extinguish his cigarette. Johnny's head ached. Lack of sleep or excess alcohol? Both, probably.

He knew it was a bad idea to go for a drink with Bill, but he hadn't had the heart to put him off two evenings in one week. Even so, as they had sat in the Tipperary, which Bill still insisted on calling the Boar's Head – printers returning from the Great War had given the pub its new name – it was all Johnny could do to stay awake. He could not tell him that he had been up since five, and that he would have to be up again in a few hours time, because that would only invite questions.

He did, however, have one question of his own.

"How come you didn't tell me that a wolly had transferred from Snow Hill to the Met?"

"Sheer ignorance, dear boy." Bill's bloodshot eyes – like road maps of Great Britain – regarded him quizzically. "What's the matter? You think I'm holding back on you?"

"Your calls turned nothing up?"

"Nothing relevant." Bill leaned forward. "I promised not to run the story."

"What story?" Johnny was struggling to mask his trepidation. Even if Bill had given his word that he would not write about the death of a cop, that didn't mean he too was sworn to maintain his silence.

"Nobody's been transferred. A constable has been

sacked – and you know how the powers-that-be like to keep such matters hush-hush."

"What did he do?" asked Johnny.

Bill chuckled. "It sounds like this feller was a chap after my own heart. You know how they're introducing bicycles so that the boys in blue can patrol longer beats?"

"Yes." Matt had told him: he preferred being footsore to being saddle-sore.

"Well, the blighter was winding a piece of string round the odometer and pulling it back and forth so that, when his sergeant checked, it looked as if he was covering the requisite distance instead of just sitting on his arse and smoking."

"I have to admit, it demonstrates a certain ingenuity. What was the cop's name?"

"Don't know. Rotherforth wouldn't tell me."

"Rotherforth? *He*'s your source? When I spoke to him he rubbished the tip-off."

"Keep your hair on. He and I go way back. I got you the dope, didn't I?"

"Yes, thanks a lot, Bill."

There was no way he was going to mention the dead cop after that. He tried changing the subject, but Bill had known him long enough to sense when his protégé was withholding something. Again and again, he kept asking if Johnny had anything else to tell him. Johnny kept mum: he knew that the tighter Bill got, the looser his tongue became.

It went against the grain to deceive Bill. In addition to being his mentor, the older man had helped Johnny pay his mother's medical expenses. Without his generosity, she would not have been able to stay in hospital until the end. Bill knew what it was to lose someone to cancer: his wife had died of it. He did not talk about her much, brushing off Johnny's questions with: "It was a long time ago, dear boy, when you were still sucking your mother's tits." Even with those closest to him, Bill preferred office gossip or conversation about books to personal disclosure. He rated Thackeray, Gissing and Jerrold above Dickens – which often led to heated arguments. Spouseless and childless, Bill did not seem to have a life outside work. His colleagues appeared to be his only friends. Drinking and smoking were his major hobbies. He said the tobacco was good for his asthma. Johnny wondered what Bill would do with himself when he retired the following year.

He felt especially guilty because only that morning, Bill – as helpful as ever – had given him the telephone number of an alienist after he'd made up a story about Daisy having nightmares and wanting to find someone who could treat her.

During his lunch break, Johnny had sounded out Dr Meikle. After listening to Matt's symptoms the doctor said it sounded as though his friend was refusing to face up to a traumatic event in his past. If he continued to do so he could well suffer a breakdown. Meikle had warned Johnny: "He should come to see me at once."

When he relayed the suggestion, Matt had been swift to reject it. "There's nothing in my past that would explain the nightmares. I haven't got the time to lie around on a couch all day. Besides, it would no doubt cost a pretty penny. I've got this far without a man in a white coat. The bad dreams'll probably stop as suddenly as they started."

Johnny hoped so. Before Matt hung up, he'd filled him in on the previous night's brief encounter with PC Vinson, and secured a promise to find out the name of the apparently non-existent transferred recruit.

There was no moon and the absence of street-lights made progress tricky as he made his way downhill along St John Street. Smithfield was still asleep. Drivers who had arrived overnight snored on in their cabs. The clock in Grand Avenue said 3.27.

Johnny turned into Cowcross Street. Green Hill's Rents was just past the Hope on the left. It was a dead-end, only about three hundred yards long. Why had Gogg suggested meeting here?

There was only one building of consequence in the cul-de-sac: a cold store. Its huge double doors were unlocked. Johnny pushed them open and slipped through the gap. He found himself in a wide hallway plastered with posters of prize bulls advertising the Smithfield Club Cattle Show at the Royal Agricultural Hall, Islington, from 7th December through to the 11th.

Deep humming filled his ears and tickled his feet. A corridor lined with poky offices ran off to the left. The plywood and glass partitions were unlit and unoccupied. The narrow stairs on the right presumably led to the cellar. Perhaps Gogg was down there.

The humming got louder. The foundations of the building seemed to pulsate with barely suppressed energy. It was suffocatingly warm.

A gigantic refrigerator filled the gloomy basement. A vertical strip of light told him that the door was ajar. Wisps of steam streamed out.

"Hello? Harry?"

There was no reply. Where the hell was the boy?

He pulled open the steel door. Winter blasted out. He blinked and felt the skin on his face shrink.

Wooden duckboards ran down the middle of the fridge. On either side frozen carcasses hung from hooks attached to two circular rails. Ball-bearings ensured every cadaver could be reached without stepping on to the stainless steel floor.

"Harry?"

He hunkered down and looked underneath the hanging meat. Nothing.

Johnny was about to close the foot-thick door when he realised that the freezer was much larger than he had originally thought. There was a panel of light switches by the door. Only one of them had been turned on. He flicked on all the others and gasped.

The cold-store was vast. Its duckboards stretched on and on. In the distance he could make out another door, which presumably led to the underground rail depot that allowed dead livestock to be unloaded directly off the train. The ice-chamber was filled to capacity. Although the lights were bright, the mass of meat reduced their glare to a reddish glow. Gogg must have had second thoughts.

The threshold of the fridge was a foot off the floor. Johnny tripped over it and fell head-first against the nearest side of beef. It was like hitting a brick wall. He swore and lay sprawled on the duckboards rubbing his brow.

What sounded like an angry rattlesnake could now be heard above the hum. He had set the carousel of corpses in motion.

The well-oiled ball-bearings spun round and round. The slaughtered animals slid past him one by one. Frosted sheep, headless pigs, hollow cows . . . and Harry.

He was hanging from a hook which protruded from his neck. His head lolled to one side. The eyes stared at him glassily.

There was something stuffed in his mouth. It looked like a fat, tropical slug: purple, red and yellow.

Johnny was transfixed. Harry continued rolling towards him. He was naked. There was a black gash in his groin. Blood trickled down his thighs, streaked his calves and dripped off his hairy big toes. Nearer. Nearer. Johnny gazed into the bloated face.

The boy had been made to eat his own genitals.

Gagging, Johnny scrambled to his feet. He was now shaking with fear as well as cold. Whoever had butchered Harry might still be in the freezer. He had to get out.

Too late. The door slammed in his face.

He jumped back and yelled as Gogg brushed past him. He looked round wildly. There was no handle on this side of the door. Nor was there an alarm.

One by one, the lights went out.

NINE

Johnny hammered and hollered for all he was worth, but the door remained shut and the lights remained off. Slowly the swinging stiffs clicked to a stop. The vast chamber fell deafeningly quiet.

Although he could no longer hear the massive generator, Johnny could still feel a muffled vibration. In such utter darkness it made no difference whether his eyes were open or closed. It was like drowning in ink.

Panic began to writhe in the pit of his stomach. He sat on the floor and strained his ears for the slightest noise. All he could hear was Gogg's life-blood slowly ebbing away: tick, tick, tick. He was alone – that was something. The killer was not trapped in there with him.

The temperature continued to fall.

It would not be long before the staff turned up for work. However, if he could not hear them, they would not be able to hear his cries for help.

His teeth sounded as though they were sending a mayday message in Morse code. It was too cold to sit around on the off-chance of being rescued. Besides, how long would the air last? Which would kill him first: suffocation or hypothermia? He wasn't going to wait to find out. He had to keep moving.

Perhaps the door at the other end of the freezer had a handle on the inside. Johnny began to crawl along the duckboards. He had no wish to bump into any more nasty surprises.

His overcoat cushioned his knees a little, but his hands were unprotected. He rarely wore gloves: they were too restrictive. Each time he missed the edge of the board he left behind a layer of skin on the metal floor. A splinter sank under the nail of a forefinger, piercing the quick. He was almost relieved when his head finally butted the door.

It was exactly the same as the one at the other end.

Johnny crawled back the way he had come, this time using a none-too-clean handkerchief and his hat to protect his sore hands.

Rime was forming on his hair, eyebrows and eyelashes. It was exhausting and progress was excruciatingly slow. Iron bands seemed to be tightening round his head. He forced himself to carry on.

Surely he should have reached the door by now? He could feel claustrophobia creeping up on him. The darkness took on a glutinous quality, glugging into his mouth, trickling into his nostrils, filling his lungs. He squeezed his eyes shut. Purple and orange burst out of the black.

It was becoming increasingly difficult to think. Johnny knew he must not panic. He yelled again, his lips splitting open, the blood shockingly hot.

The effort sapped what strength he had left. It was no good: he would have to rest for a moment.

The vibrating hum sent ripples through his bone marrow. It was strangely soothing.

He was asleep in seconds.

After her husband's death, Johnny's mother, like many other grieving widows of the Great War, had ordered a "spirit photograph". The simple but expensive process involved super-imposing an image of the dead person on to one of the living. The magic of double exposure thus bridged the gap between this world and the next. A separated couple could be reunited by a mere trick of the light.

His mother was delighted with the result. A studio portrait of her sitting solemnly on a straight-backed dining chair beside the obligatory aspidistra on a stand had been merged with her favourite from the half-dozen that the same photographer had taken of her husband shortly before he had been shipped to France. The good-looking soldier standing confidently in front of the camera had been transformed into a shadowy figure whose right hand seemed to rest on her left shoulder.

It was a touching memento from which she derived great comfort and reassurance. Her Edward was still with her. He was looking after her now and always would be.

The picture was on her bedside table when she died. Johnny brought it home from the hospital and put it back on the mantelpiece where, throughout his childhood, it had given him the creeps. He had not liked the idea that a man he did not know could be watching him every minute of every day. However, the fact that his mother had since joined his father, that the longed-for reunion had finally been achieved, made it impossible for him to put away, let alone throw away, the sinister souvenir.

Johnny did not believe in ghosts: they were just external manifestations of internal disorder, grief, fear – or, in the case of Ebenezer Scrooge, a guilty conscience. Marley and Christmasses Past, Present and Future were harmless messengers from his own troubled mind.

And now here he was, suspended between life and death, feeling the big chill, sinking deeper and deeper towards oblivion.

Johnny knew he ought to fight, to go against the flow, but he did not have the energy to resist. He really could feel himself swaying. It was as if someone had picked him up. Was he back in his father's arms?

Someone slapped him across the face, hard. They did it again, harder. He registered the impact but not the pain.

"Johnny! Snap out of it. Wake up!"

Whoever it was hit him again.

"All right, all right." He opened his eyes. His lashes

were frozen together. Warm thumbs melted the ice. Johnny blinked. It was Matt. "I'm not crying," said Johnny.

Matt hauled him to his feet and gave him a bear-hug. "Are you okay?" His strength was astonishing.

"I am now," said Johnny. However, as soon as Matt let go, his knees buckled.

Matt, expecting this, was ready to catch him. He lay him down on the floor and roughly rubbed his limbs to increase the circulation.

"My head hurts," groaned Johnny. It was as if someone were twisting a knife in his eye. "How did you find me?"

"There was a tip-off about a burglary planned for tonight. This place is on my beat," said Matt. "I found the doors open and decided to wait and see what came out. I stood in a doorway, had a spit and draw, then you came along. Didn't know it was you, of course. Thought you were a sneak thief. After a bit, when you didn't come out, I thought I'd better investigate."

"Didn't you see anyone else leave?"

"No."

"Then where's the person who shut me in?"

They looked round anxiously. Johnny's teeth would not stop chattering.

"Here." Matt produced a hip-flask. "It used to be my father's. Only thing that gets me through nights like this."

"Don't get caught."

Commissioner Turnbull of the Metropolitan Police had recently sacked two frost-bitten constables for having a cup of tea in the street. Turnbull thought he was God and acted accordingly. While his men could be fired for "idling and gossiping", rumour had it that Turnbull himself got away scot-free after he threw scalding water over his long-suffering wife to "teach her a lesson".

"Don't you worry about me. Stay here. I'll go and have a butcher's."

"Ha, bloody, ha." The whisky burned its way to his stomach. "Matt, don't go. There's something you should see here first. A porter called Harry Gogg's been murdered. He's in there."

Matt turned on all the lights in the freezer and, glancing back to check that he was not being had, crossed its threshold. He did not trip as Johnny had.

Johnny remained shivering on the stone floor and took another sip. He heard Matt take three tentative steps on the duckboards then stop. He did not say a word.

Johnny pictured the scene back in St Bartholomew-the-Great just twenty-four hours earlier, saw Harry grinning at his frustration, his brown eyes sparkling with life; his brawny body radiating health. Now he was just so much dead meat: his own balls stuffed in his mouth.

Anger surged through him. Johnny clambered to his feet, wincing at his stiffness, and hobbled over to the door.

Matt was staring at the corpse. He was no stranger to death: year in, year out children were crushed by cartwheels, workers were mangled by machinery, floaters were fished out of the Thames and tramps found frozen to the ground. Murder, though, was different. It had its own gruesome glamour.

"Matt?"

He turned round. Instead of being pale and calm as expected, he was flushed and excited.

"Did you touch him?" His voice was shaking.

"Not bloody likely."

"Good. You better get out of here now that you can stand on your own two feet. I must report this right away. Should be worth a few brownie points. I can't believe my luck. My first murder case!"

"Matt, the boy's dead. It's hardly a cause for celebration."

"I know that. You don't have a monopoly on compassion. I'd given up nicking the poor sod. He spent more time in the toilets under the market than he did in it. Being sorry won't help him now. I want to find out who killed him – and who tried to kill you." Johnny was shocked. The rent-boy had been nothing like the nancies he usually saw snivelling in the dock.

"He and an accomplice were paid to take a body to Bart's early on Sunday morning," said Johnny, realising for the first time that he had lost his only lead. "He was going to tell me everything. It must have been the dead cop."

"Well, you're wrong there," said Matt with barely suppressed irritation. "The wolly who got transferred to the Met is called George Aitken. He's a fine chap – from

Aberdeen, I think." Men were often recruited from outside the capital: farm-hands and soldiers had better lungs than those who had grown up in the Smoke. "We were in the same tug-of-war team. He called me yesterday afternoon to say goodbye. I did warn you that the tip-off sounded dodgy. Just drop it: someone's pulling your leg."

Johnny was surprised – and disappointed. He had been so sure he was on to something.

"Whose body was it then? Why has someone choked Harry with his own cock?" The very idea made his gorge rise. "And why did someone try to kill me? I nearly died, for Christ's sake." His rage returned. The blood surging through his veins felt good.

"Calm down. You were only in there for ten minutes or so. You'll be okay. We'll get the killer, just you see if we don't. You wanted an exclusive and now you've got one."

He was right: Gogg's murder would still make a good story.

"Sorry. You saved my life and I haven't even thanked you."

They shook hands. The shadows under Matt's eyes were darker than ever. Johnny felt a pang of sympathy for his friend. However, this was not the time to try and persuade him to see Dr Meikle.

"Go on. Get out of here. I won't mention your involvement unless I have to. I take it you're unwilling to make a statement at this stage?"

Johnny nodded. "Let's meet up over the weekend."

"It'll be difficult. All leave'll be cancelled. The detective squad will need help with their enquiries."

"You'll let me know what happens, won't you?" Johnny did not want Simkins queering his pitch.

"If I can."

They went upstairs to the ground floor. A startled man in a white coat came beetling towards them.

Matt blocked his path. "Morning, sir. May I use your telephone? There's no call to be alarmed."

Johnny left him to it and emerged into a world he had not been meant to see.

In the event, he could not see much. The mist had thickened so much it was like swimming through porridge. His clothes, already damp with melted frost, seemed to soak up the moisture. The cold seeped back into his bones.

Blast! He had left his hat in the freezer. It was too risky to go back to retrieve it now. He quickened his pace, hoping to stave off the cold that way, and hurried towards home and a hot cup of tea.

As he approached the mouth of the cul-de-sac he heard a low muttering. He slowed down, stepping softly. Poking his head round the corner he could make out two men, standing at the far corner. Johnny crept closer, trying not to give himself away.

"Do it, damn you!" said the taller of the two.

The other man took something from him and headed off towards Farringdon. The one who had spoken pulled up his collar and took off in the direction of Smithfield, which, judging by the noise, had already come to life.

There was a little more light in Cowcross Street. Johnny realised the shorter man was wearing police uniform. He had no choice: he had to follow him.

Making no allowance for the fog, the cop charged on up St John's Lane, leaving murky swirls in his wake.

As Johnny followed, a pile of paraffin rags in the doorway of an ironmonger's assumed the bleary form of a tramp. The man grunted and tried to sit up. A battle-scarred moggie escaped from his arms with a yowl.

The rapid footsteps ahead of him suddenly became muffled. The cop had turned into Passing Alley. Within seconds of entering the dark passageway, Johnny was reminded of its former name – Pissing Alley – which had been amended to something more respectable by the prudish Victorians. Human nature was harder to change: men still used the snicket as a urinal. In summer the stench was overpowering, but even in winter a persistent tang hung in the air.

Johnny would have held his nose except that he needed both hands to guide himself. It was an unusually long passage, so narrow that it was impossible to pass someone coming in the opposite direction without rubbing up against them. Women tended to avoid the place.

Although the fog could not penetrate the gap between the five-storey buildings, it was pitch black in the cut-through. Slimy brick walls closed in on him. His head began to throb. The claustrophobia, which had threatened to overwhelm him in the cold-store, returned. Should he go back?

Johnny stared ahead, straining his eyes to make out any sort of shape in the dancing darkness. Nothing. There was no light at the end of the ginnel.

The footsteps stopped. Johnny froze. For a moment there was silence then the footsteps started again.

This time they were coming towards him.

Johnny turned and began to retrace his steps. A bad move: he was making too much noise and, if the cop had suspected he was being followed, this would only have served to confirm his suspicions.

Heart thumping, Johnny halted and prepared to confront his quarry.

He counted the slow, deliberate steps.

One. Two. Three. Four. Five. Six. They stopped.

The cop was listening. If Johnny could not see anything, neither could he.

Johnny held his breath and prayed that the cop would not come any closer. He should have known better.

Seven. Eight. Nine. Ten. He could not be more than six feet away now.

He would have to punch him in the balls and run like hell.

Eleven. Twelve. He could hear him breathing. His own lungs, meanwhile, were about to burst. Sweat prickled his upper lip and armpits.

Thirteen. Fourteen. The cop sniffed. Paper rustled.

The point of the knife pricked his skin just above the Adam's apple.

"Keep your eyes shut."

Hot breath brushed his left ear. He concentrated on

trying not to swallow. Seconds passed. Was this how he was going to die? Stabbed in a back alley reeking of piss? This was not how it was supposed to be: he had not got where he was going, still had many things to achieve. Promotion, a novel, a wife and lots of kids. Well, what was the bastard waiting for?

The knife moved. Johnny, full of fury, braced himself.

However, the cop did not kill him.

He kissed him.

I had to do it – he left me no choice. He started babbling as soon as he saw the hat-pin. He was on his knees straight away – invert that he was, he'd already spent half his miserable life on them, begging for it – but I wasn't in the mood for forgiveness or anything else.

He swore he hadn't tipped off Steadman, promised he'd given nothing away. I almost believed him.

When I produced the knife, he stopped squealing. He was crying as I made him strip, snivelling like some little kid. His cock shrivelled to almost nothing. Fear or the cold? Both most likely. It actually grew afterwards – which made it easier to slice off. The blood was so hot.

I can still hear him screaming.

Steadman's a lucky blighter. I thought he'd cop it for sure. Didn't expect anyone to be on the scene that time in the morning. He must have a guardian angel. We'll see.

The murder might *stop him sniffing around. I doubt it, though. Most likely there'll have to be another mishap . . . and I won't leave anything to chance next time.*

TEN

The man's tongue was in his mouth before he knew it. An image of Gogg's severed penis slid into his mind. He jerked his head away and retched. Why the hell would a cop do that? His terror turned to rage. He spat savagely at his assailant but the pervert was already making his getaway, whistling a familiar tune which, for the moment, Johnny could not name.

A clink and a clatter echoed down the alley. The knife had been dropped – or discarded. Johnny wiped his cracked lips with the back of his hand. He supposed he ought to go and check.

The alley became even narrower as it neared its end. He found the knife by kicking it. He hated to think what his peeled fingers were touching as he groped about on the filthy ground. He took off his muffler – a present from Lizzie last Christmas – and picked up the knife with it.

Back in St John Street he stood beneath a lone gas-light and examined the blood-stained blade. He shuddered. It was a butcher's knife, about ten inches long, and very sharp. The blood was no doubt that of Harry Gogg.

Why had the cop thrown the murder weapon away? If the men he had seen were responsible for Harry's death, why on earth had such incriminating evidence been left for him to find? Did they *want* to be caught?

His mind was racing but he could not think about it now. He was shaking with exhaustion. Shock and the cold, plus his hangover and lack of sleep, were taking their toll. He did not have the energy to trail all the way home then back to the office.

The Cock would be opening soon. There he'd find warmth and safety in numbers. Wrapping the knife in the muffler, he carefully placed it in an inside pocket of his overcoat. It was an awkward fit. The blade had to point upwards otherwise it moved around too much. He would just have to make sure he did not fall on it.

He could not face going through Passing Alley again so he trudged down to Peter's Lane. Already he could hear the shriek of the first freight trains of the day pulling into Farringdon. The fumes from the gin distillery in Turnmill Street hung heavily in the damp air.

By the time he re-emerged into Cowcross Street, the tramp had disappeared. A single policeman was on guard duty at the entrance to Green Hill's Rents. A group of his colleagues were standing outside the cold-store, which was now ablaze with light.

Pulling up his collar to hide his face, Johnny walked

by on the other side. When a black van pulled up at the entrance to the cul-de-sac, the constable waved it on.

The meat market was in full swing. The big hand of the clock in Grand Avenue now pointed north-east. A lot had happened in forty minutes. The recreation ground where he had first spoken to Harry was deserted.

Perhaps it had been a mistake to tell Harry that the body he had helped to move was that of a cop. The knowledge that he was involved in serious skulduggery must have spooked the boy. Harry could have told someone that a newshound was sniffing around – and if it was the person who had paid him to dispose of the corpse, they might have decided to shut his pretty mouth for ever.

"Look what the cat's dragged in!" Dolly regarded him with a mixture of amusement and concern. The few early customers smiled into their beer. Johnny sat on the same stool that he had occupied almost twenty-four hours before. "What on earth have you been up to?" She nodded at his coat, which he could now see was smeared with streaks of green and brown filth.

"Don't ask. I'll have a wazzer please."

"First things first. Come on, take it off."

"It's all right, thanks. I'll drop it off at the cleaners on my way to work."

"Oh no you won't. What'll you wear in the meantime? You'll catch your death in this weather."

She was right. He was such an idiot. He should have hidden the knife or, better still, handed it to the cop on sentry duty. It was too late now.

There was nothing else for it. Dolly looked honest enough – not the type to go through a bloke's pockets. He undid the buttons.

"What's that on your neck? Looks like blood to me. Cut yourself shaving?"

He handed the coat to her over the bar. "I'll go and clean myself up."

"I should think so too. Those hands are a disgrace."

The wazzer was waiting for him when he returned from the Gents. He concentrated on not spilling it. The hot tea tasted like nectar. His shakes slowly subsided.

"There you are!" The landlady slammed a full English breakfast down in front of him. "Get that inside you."

Food, especially meat, was the last thing on his mind, but he was too tired to argue. He started slowly but soon picked up speed as the salt and spices aroused his appetite. It felt obscene to be stuffing his face after what he had just seen, yet the hot meal reminded him that he was still alive.

He so easily might not have been.

Dolly looked on with approval. He washed the last of the grease down with the dregs of the wazzer.

"Another one?"

"Please."

She picked up the plate and went off to the kitchen. "Stella? You done with that coat yet? Stella! Where are you?"

"Here you are."

Johnny spun round. His eyes met those of a girl. They were dazzlingly green and fringed with long, dark lashes.

The day had hardly begun, yet she seemed all set for a night on the town.

"What's up? Never seen a beautiful woman before?"

"One or two," said Johnny with as much nonchalance as he could muster – which was not much. He stood up and put his coat back on. "Thank you, it's as good as new." He patted his pockets.

"Don't worry, the knife's still there."

A smile played on her full red lips. He wanted to kiss them. Before he could think of what to say, they were interrupted.

"I see you've met my Stella," said Dolly. "She's not a bad girl. Considers herself too good for this place though." The landlady winked.

"She is," said Johnny.

"Don't say it." The green eyes bored into him.

"What?"

"Let me take you away from all this – or words to that effect."

"I wouldn't dream of it. You must've heard every chat-up line going." He cleared his throat. His life had suddenly become a surreal series of misadventures. What else could possibly happen to him? He had nothing to lose. "So how about letting me take you to dinner to say thank you? Anywhere you like. I wouldn't mind being taken to the cleaners by you."

"Okay."

He tried to mask his astonishment by fishing a business card out of his wallet but only succeeded in dropping it at her feet. They both knelt down to retrieve it.

Out of sight of her mother, she blew him a kiss. "Monday night. Six o'clock. Pick me up here. If you're a second late you'll be sorry." Then she swanned out of the bar.

"So tell me, Mr Journalist," said Dolly. "Did you get what you wanted from Harry Gogg?"

The question brought him down to the ground with a bump.

"'Fraid not. Nice lad, though."

Dolly nodded sagely. The spaghetti hair swayed.

"He is. Harry's a lovely boy, no harm to anyone. It's a shame the police won't leave him alone."

The lift-boy raised his eyebrows when he asked for the seventh floor. Galley-slaves like Johnny did not visit the bridge very often.

The first time he'd entered the editor's suite had been the day he joined the *News*; like all new employees he'd been summoned up to receive a welcoming handshake.

The second time he'd got a pat on the back to congratulate him on becoming a junior reporter, a reward for a series of articles on childhood poverty which Captain Vic had found "both passionate and pioneering". The series had generated a lot of comment and not a jot of change.

The last time he crossed the carpeted expanse he'd been given a bottle of champagne – the paper had an excellent, extensive wine cellar – and promoted to the post of fully-fledged crime reporter. His exclusive about the drugs ring at Bart's had caused a sensation and had been much appreciated by the high-ups. He was told he had a great career ahead of him – and then he went back downstairs where Patsel promptly sent him into exile at the Old Bailey.

Johnny was determined that his current investigation would prove to be his means of escape.

The well-appointed calm of the top deck was in stark contrast to the raucous chaos of the engine rooms below. It housed, in addition to the editor's suite, the proprietor's apartment, six offices for senior management and their secretaries, and a boardroom with a table the length of a cricket pitch.

At 6.30 a.m. there was no sign of the snooty brunette who controlled access to the editor. Johnny thought he could hear grunting coming from the other side of the door. He knocked anyway.

"Enter!"

As the door swung open, Johnny was confronted by the sight of the editor, wearing nothing but a pair of soiled combinations, hanging upside down from a set of wall-bars. Sweat dripped on to the carpet.

"Ah, Steadman. What can I do for you?" he panted, immediately resuming his workout.

Victor Stone was a dedicated newsman who burned off excess nervous energy with callisthenics. "Beauty hurts" was one of his favourite catchphrases. Rumour had it that he and his wife were committed members of the Open-Air Tourist Society – which meant they spent their holidays running around with no clothes on. Bill reckoned it was how they got their OATS. Whether this was true or not, worshipping the sun had certainly given Stone a Mediterranean complexion – and his darker skin made his teeth appear even whiter. He claimed to be forty-five but looked much younger, especially when he was surrounded by his grey-haired superiors.

Johnny told him about the tip-off, his meeting with Harry Gogg, his murder and mutilation, the attempt on his own life and the knife.

He did not tell him about his encounter with the policeman in the alley. He could not get it out of his mind. The one consolation was that nobody need ever know. Why had the cop kissed him? Had he known whom he was kissing? Did he think he was a shirt-lifter? Thinking about it, Johnny found it hard to resist the urge to spit.

"Almost done."

Stone embarked on a final set of chin-ups. Johnny, unsure what his story amounted to, or what his editor would make of it, took the opportunity to inspect the room more closely.

There was little to show that this office housed a member of the fourth estate. Rather, it resembled the library of a stately home. Two of its walls were lined with leather-bound books. Busts of famous authors surmounted the shelves: he was gratified to spot Dickens standing shoulder to shoulder with Tennyson and Thackeray. The huge double-pedestal desk was lit by a brass lamp with a green, opalescent glass shade. Its surface, inlaid with tooled green leather, boasted an eau-de-nil leather blotter, olivine pen-stand and no less than four Bakelite telephones, all of which were black. A chesterfield, set against the front, prevented anyone getting too close. The three square windows, their baize blinds still drawn against the December darkness, looked down on a table and eight chairs. Next to them stood a pair of drawing-boards, still spread with pages from the previous day's final edition.

Stone, his exercise routine completed, dropped to the floor. The telephones tinkled faintly. He grabbed a towel from the back of a chair and rubbed himself down.

"So there are two dead men, one of whom was definitely murdered, and you've only a hunch that their deaths are connected. Since you were the man on the spot I'm going to let you write up Gogg's killing – but leave out any mention of your own involvement and the other death. The murder of a male tart is a great story, but it won't cause much of an outcry."

"The murder of a cop would, sir."

"Indeed. Unfortunately, apart from the anonymous tip-off, you don't have any evidence that the body delivered to Bart's by Harry Gogg and his mystery accomplice was a cop's – or that he was actually murdered. You'll have to dig around some more before we can run anything on that."

"Yes, sir."

"Let's suppose, just for a moment, that your hunch is correct. What d'you think this cop was up to that landed him in the morgue?"

"I've no idea, sir. Maybe nothing at all."

"No one, especially a cop, is totally innocent. I know

you, Steadman. You can't read someone's copy month after month and not get an insight into their character. You instinctively saw the dead man as a victim, didn't you? This is another opportunity for you to champion the underdog, to rage against the cruel workings of faceless authority. But there are other possibilities. The bluebottle may have been a bad 'un who ended up being squashed when one of his scams went wrong."

"He was naked, sir."

"Was he now? Perhaps he was stripped afterwards to hide his identity. Perhaps he was attacked at home in bed. Perhaps he was blackmailing someone who couldn't pay any more. Perhaps he fell out with an accomplice who came after him seeking revenge. Find the motive and you'll find the killer. The connection with Gogg may be pure coincidence."

"I don't think so, sir," said Johnny. "Surely the fact that the death has not been reported is suspicious? If it was a cop, bent or otherwise, Scotland Yard could have issued a press release full of the usual lies and that would have probably been the end of the matter. They'd have been quick enough to put out a statement if he'd died in the line of duty. Everyone loves a dead hero." He shook his head. "No. Something, somewhere's not right. I can feel it in my bones. Bill Fox was told that a cop had been sacked, but I've now heard from two sources at Snow Hill that the only officer unaccounted for was a rookie cop who transferred to the Met. Which is it? Someone certainly doesn't want the truth to come out: why try and kill me otherwise?"

"They might have just been trying to scare you off. After all, you're here now."

Johnny nodded. That would explain why the cop had not killed him in the alley – after all, there would have been no witnesses, and had he used the knife instead of just holding it to Johnny's throat it would all have been over in a matter of seconds. Of course, it still didn't explain why the cop had kissed him.

Stone began undoing the buttons on his vest. He strode over to the bookshelves and pressed a copy of Ruskin's *Sesame and Lilies*. A hidden door sprang open to reveal a small, black-and-white tiled bathroom. It was not unknown for him to conduct editorial meetings from his bathtub.

"Sit down before you fall down," he ordered.

Johnny plonked himself on the sofa and listened to the soothing sounds of running water. A long soak was just what he needed to thaw him out; he felt as though the cold hadn't left his bones since he'd been locked in the freezer. His eyelids drooped . . .

Two minutes was all he got.

"Steadman! Come and make yourself useful!"

He staggered into the bathroom. Stone handed him a loofah. "Don't be afraid of rubbing too hard."

Johnny, wondering how much more bizarre his life could get, perched on the edge of the bath in a daze and started to scrub his editor's back. Stone had a decent body for an old man. Then, if you liked to flaunt yourself in public, it made sense to ensure you had something worth flaunting: hence the morning manoeuvres.

"So, sir, you'll place me on special assignment?"

"I'll give you one week – but the sooner you get to the bottom of this the better. You might not be the only reporter to have received the tip-off."

Johnny would have turned cartwheels had his hands not been so sore.

"Have you spoken to anyone else about it?"

"Just Fox, sir."

"Very well. Don't be shy of asking him for help. If you don't make much headway I'll have to bring in others with more experience."

"Thank you, sir, that won't be necessary. All expenses paid?"

"Within reason. You'll need a cover story."

"How about a series on the daily life of a City policeman? We could call it 'Life on the Beat'. It'd give me an excuse to talk to the cops."

"Okay. And if you don't find anything juicy you can write the series anyway. I do hope your hunch is right, though. Exposing a police conspiracy would give us back some credibility. God knows, after Beaverbrook's brown-nosing, we need it."

The British press had been virtually the last to report Edward VIII's relationship with Mrs Simpson making it a laughing stock around the world. Beaverbrook, owner of the *Daily Express*, in response to the King's plea to spare his lover embarrassment, had not only sat on the story of a lifetime but also persuaded Esmond Harmsworth, owner of the *Daily Mail* and chairman of the Newspaper Proprietors Association, to follow suit.

The whole country, thanks to foreign newspapers, had been rife with rumour and speculation before the *Yorkshire Post* finally reported the affair on 3rd December – at least a month after Fleet Street had first got wind of the scandal.

"I'd be grateful, sir, if you didn't tell anyone else about this," said Johnny. "I don't want gossip to complicate matters."

"Of course, of course," said Stone. "Any problems, call my office. Now, go and file your report. It should be an exclusive, in the first edition at least. Well done, Steadman. And try not to snore at the judge."

"I thought I was on special assignment!"

"You are – from Monday. Mr Patsel will need time to arrange the necessary cover. Besides, you've got the weekend to get going. Good luck." He stood up, aglow with health and vigour. "Towel please!"

Somehow Johnny resisted the urge to throw it at him.

Four cups of tea later, Johnny had written his account of Gogg's murder. He thought it prudent to omit Matt's name as well as his own. He hung around to check the subs did not mangle his pristine prose and, in the meantime, received a slap on the back from Patsel, who appeared to be in an unusually good mood. Perhaps he had found another job.

"Good stuff, Steadman. It reads as if you were actually there. Were you?"

"A friend in the force tipped me off, sir."

"*Sehr gut.* That's what it's all about: information, information, information."

When he got back to his desk he found Bill standing beside it reading the carbon copy.

"Morning, Coppernob. Rough night, was it? Worth it, though, for this. Should be one in the eye for Simkins."

"Hope so."

"Is this what you've been up to then? Consorting with lunch-mashers?"

"Only the one," said Johnny, trying not to think of the cop's tongue in his mouth.

"Enjoy yourself?"

"Not much."

"By the way, this came for you." He held out a thin white envelope.

It was stamped PRIVATE & CONFIDENTIAL. Johnny tore it open. This time there were just three words:

DON'T STOP NOW.

PART TWO

Honey Lane

ELEVEN

Saturday, 12th December, 12.50 p.m.

Johnny decided to call into Gamage's on his way to meet Matt. The Holborn department store, decked with fairy lights and paper chains, was packed with Christmas shoppers. Lizzie, fetching as ever in her uniform, was standing by one of the cosmetics counters, dabbing perfume on any passing woman who wished to sample the latest fragrance from Paris.

As usual, his heart leapt. Even though she was constantly in his mind's eye, it still sent a jolt through him whenever she was actually present in the flesh. He wondered if he should buy some scent for Daisy, but was unsure whether he was ever going to see her again.

Their last encounter had not gone well. Accusing her of playing hard to get had, as it turned out, not been the best of tactics: it had only increased her indignation. He felt he'd had a good excuse for postponing their date. Matt would always come first, and on this occasion he had been in real need of help. But Daisy had been in no mood to listen to explanations. He suspected she rather enjoyed a blazing row: as if there were not enough drama in her working, workaday, life.

Even so, a gentleman should make it up to her. Besides, selecting a gift for her would provide him with an excuse to talk to Lizzie.

Lizzie's supervisor seemed unconvinced by the charade. Under her disapproving gaze, Lizzie took various samples down from the display so he could sniff each one in turn. As soon as the woman's back was turned, she told him that Matt was still unaware that he was a father-to-be and that he was still having nightmares. When he departed empty-handed a few moments later, the supervisor gave a loud snort of disdain.

It was obvious that Matt had not caught up on his sleep. The face that looked up as Johnny entered Gianelli's was haggard. Edvard Munch's *The Scream* sprang to mind. Usually Matt radiated an air of well-being and vitality: whenever the station-house was struck by flu, he'd be the last man standing, more than happy to do a double shift to cover for a colleague and pick up some overtime to boost Lizzie's "get-out-of-N1" fund.

Johnny felt sure that the news about the baby would buck him up. However, it was not down to him to break it. Besides, he had promised Lizzie.

The caff in Limeburne Lane, round the corner from

the Old Bailey, was crowded. A miasma of cigarette smoke and cooking fumes hung above the tables. The musty smell of damp wool mingled with the aromas of fried bacon and minestrone soup. The conversational hubbub was intermittently drowned out by the violent hiss of the hot-water machine.

Matt was sitting at a table for two at the back. It was hardly private, but it would have to do.

"Have you ordered yet?" asked Johnny, taking off his gabardine. He draped it over the other coats that hung from hooks in the corridor leading to the toilets. An image of Harry Gogg, naked and bleeding, came into his head. As of last night, Matt was not the only one having bad dreams.

"I'm not hungry."

"Come on! You know I hate eating by myself," said Johnny.

"You should be used to it by now." Matt glanced up to ensure that the barb had hit its mark. He winked. For a moment he was his old, teasing self.

"Thank you, *Cunt*stable."

"Don't mention it."

Johnny had already decided not to mention the kiss in Passing Alley. He was ashamed. Besides, it would only complicate matters.

Making sure no one was watching, he handed Matt a parcel – the knife carefully wrapped in newspaper – and gave him an edited version of the previous day's events.

Matt listened without comment then slid a Manila

envelope across the ring-stained wood. Before he could open it, Arturo, the barrel of a proprietor, loomed over them.

"Aha! Bigger plates! City cop!"

This was an oblique, ironic reference to police corruption. It was endemic in every force but – in a perfect example of double-think – it was deemed not to interfere with their capacity to uphold the law. Not seriously, anyway. The Home Secretary or the Big Five, as the top brass at Scotland Yard were known, would occasionally make noises about stamping it out, but nothing much was ever done.

The corruption was casual rather than corporate: taking back-handers from street bookies for turning a blind eye; zealously enforcing traffic regulations, then dropping any charges in return for a generous gratuity; selling tickets for non-existent lotteries to local shopkeepers who knew they could not win. The bobby remained a pillar of the community – someone who could be relied on in a crisis; a source of reassurance in everyday life – even though it was known that such protection money was a perk of the job. A little graft was a small price to pay: the rozzers worked hard, they deserved it.

If a copper chose to be honest – and Johnny assumed Matt did – then that was fine too, as long as he did not peach on his colleagues. However, in the Robbery Squad, things had started to get out of hand: detectives were more interested in arranging break-ins than arresting thieves. The keepers of the peace invariably kept a piece for themselves.

Arturo suggested the dish of the day: fresh mutton pies with mushy peas. Johnny tucked in straight away.

"What?"

Matt glowered at him. "Open the envelope!" He lowered his voice. "And don't let anyone else see."

"Sorry," said Johnny. He reluctantly laid down his knife and fork. It was just as well: what he was about to set eyes on would have made him choke.

The envelope contained a picture of Matt and another man whose head was out of shot. Both of them were naked. Matt was sitting in front of the other man with his back towards him: a pair of rowers, perhaps, except that they were on a bed not a boat and the man behind was not holding an oar but the shaft of Matt's cock.

Johnny did not realise he was staring at the photograph until Matt, with a muttered curse, snatched it off him, turned it face down on the table and slid it back. Johnny blushed. He had not seen his friend in the nude since they had gone skinny-dipping in the canal as kids. The water by the power station in Poole Street was always warm.

They'd swim every chance they could get when they were kids. Wednesday's swimming lesson had been one of the highlights of their school week. Johnny could still smell the chlorine of Hornsey Road Baths. It was so strong it stung your eyes and tickled your nostrils. The water, which was never warm enough, appeared green rather than blue. The walls, lined with wooden cubicles, were decorated with horizontal stripes of black and white tiles; the roof bare corrugated iron. Together they created an echo chamber in which the teacher's whistle and the cries of the excited boys (for many of whom this was their only bath of the week) bounced off each other. The noise was deafening. It was much quieter under the water. Johnny, letting himself sink to the bottom of the pool, would see how long the air in his lungs would last. The pale, kicking legs above him looked like the tentacles of an enormous sea anemone. As the oxygen slowly dispersed, the heaviness in his chest gradually increased. How could the absence of something weigh so much? It was his first glimpse of the paradox.

"Now I see why Lizzie chose you and not me," said Johnny, resorting, as he usually did in difficult situations, to flippancy.

No wonder Matt looked tormented. His heart went out to him.

"Is that all you can say? My marriage and career are on the line."

"Sorry." Johnny picked up the photograph again, and studied it, searching for tell-tale signs such as blurred edges, weird variations in contrast or odd angles. The focus and lighting were so good you could see the tuft of black hair between Matt's pecs. There was no doubt the picture was genuine. It was not a trick shot, a composite of two or three others: it was a print from an original negative. "Have you any idea when it was taken?"

"Of course not! D'you think I'd have let them take it if I'd been conscious?" Matt hissed. "I don't make a habit of rubbing willies with other men. I am not a pervert!" Anger exacerbated Matt's anguish.

"Calm down," said Johnny. "I didn't say you were."

It was true Matt's eyes were closed, but it was impossible to tell whether he was in a state of ecstasy or out for the count. He could have been lying back in abandon or being propped up by his molester.

Johnny, however, knew that there was no way Matt would have been photographed willingly in such a compromising position.

"I don't suppose you recognise the other chap?"

Matt examined the shot as if for the first time.

"No. There's not much to go on is there? Funny that." He put the photograph back in the envelope and pushed it across the table. "Here, you keep it. I can't have Lizzie finding the bloody thing."

Johnny tried to hide his surprise. If it had been him he would have destroyed the incriminating evidence. Then he realised Matt was not embarrassed by it but enraged. As a boxer he was used to appearing virtually unclothed in public; he was, quite rightly, proud of his body. Besides, no newspaper would ever be able to publish it.

"When could it have been taken?"

Surely Matt must have some idea, thought Johnny. How on earth could you be in such a situation and not know about it?

"I've been racking my brains and I just don't know," said Matt. Then, as if sensing Johnny's scepticism, he added: "I've woken up in my own bed at home – or at the station-house – every single day."

Four workmen were sitting at a nearby table. One of

them made a remark, provoking a burst of laughter. Matt shot to his feet and went over to them.

"Care to share the joke, gentlemen?"

Silence. The whole café was listening. The quartet stared at him insolently. Their regulation brown coats suggested they were porters at Bart's. The one with a hook-nose and sunken eyes took exception to Matt sticking his nose in.

"Fuck off!" It was said with real venom. The man's thin, grey lips hardly moved.

"I'd make that *Fuck off, Constable*, if I were you," said Arturo. "And if you want to use the foul language, do it somewhere else. Say sorry to my friend."

The vicious porter mumbled an apology and stormed out with his cronies, one of them smashing a cup on the floor.

Matt was about to set off after them, but the proprietor told him to sit down while he brought some more tea.

"When did you receive this?" asked Johnny, for once knowing better than to offer a wisecrack.

"Yesterday afternoon," said Matt. "The desk sergeant handed it to me before I went on duty."

"I got this yesterday." Johnny produced the second telegram.

"*Don't stop now*," said Matt. "I presume you think it's from the same person who said a Snow Hill cop was dead?"

"Who else?" said Johnny. "You think there's a connection?"

"Hardly," said Matt. "You're being told to carry on whereas I'm being warned off."

"I suppose you're right," said Johnny. "But what does the photograph mean? It's an exposure in both senses of the word."

"It's certainly a threat," said Matt. "What I don't understand is what I'm being warned off from. I'm not doing anything I shouldn't."

Arturo placed two cups of tea – and two thick slices of chocolate cake – in front of them. "There you go." He removed Matt's untouched plate without comment.

"The pies were delicious, thank you," said Johnny.

Arturo sniffed and went back behind the counter.

"Well, you're talking to me," said Johnny. "Not that you've told me anything. If we can find out who sent it, we'll soon know why. What about fingerprints? You'd only need to submit the envelope."

"True," said Matt. "It's been through too many hands though. Including yours. Besides, I don't have the authority to send it to Dabs and I don't want anyone in the force involved unless it's absolutely necessary. I'd be a laughing stock if this got out. Can you imagine what the lads in the locker-room would say? My father might even get to hear about it." He shook his head. "We've got to try and keep this between ourselves. You're the only person I can trust."

"It's a strange coincidence, though, isn't it?" said Johnny. "I discover Harry's corpse. You rescue me. Then you receive this and I get the telegram. You said Harry was off-normal – and the other chap in the photo definitely must be – so could he be Harry?"

"No," said Matt. "The thought had occurred to me. Check out the biceps. Harry's were much beefier."

Johnny glanced at the picture. It was not difficult to compare the arms with Harry's. The image of the dead bummaree was burned into his brain.

"The photo has nothing to do with Harry's death – it can hardly have been taken in the time since we found his body yesterday. Just forget about this dead cop nonsense, Johnny."

"Then who was taken to Bart's on Sunday night?" demanded Johnny.

"I haven't the foggiest," said Matt. "Look, never mind your so-called tip-off. Try and find out what you can about the photo – discreetly. Look, I've got to blow. There's a tug-of-war tournament this afternoon in Bunhill Fields. It's for charity, but Rotherforth has promised us free beer if we beat the Bishopsgate mob. Let me know how you get on."

It was only when Matt had gone that Johnny remembered he had not asked him about his lost hat. It was probably in an evidence box by now.

Matt had not eaten his slice of cake. It would be a shame to waste it. As Johnny savoured its rich, sweet moistness he chewed over what he had just learned: and what he had not told Matt.

He knew exactly where the photo came from.

Underneath the caption on the reverse – *PC Matt*

Turner and friend – it was embossed with the symbol of a snake swallowing its own tail.

Johnny had recognised it immediately but deemed it prudent to say nothing. He did not want Matt, overwrought as he was, going round there and causing a scene. He would go himself right now.

Reaching for his wallet, he waved to catch Arturo's attention. But the proprietor looked at him incredulously when he asked for the bill.

"But you are the guest of the constable – it's on the house, Signor."

TWELVE

Situated in Amen Court opposite Stationers' Hall, the Urania Bookshop was within shouting distance of the Old Bailey. This was convenient for the proprietor, who regularly found himself called to appear, facing charges under Lord Campbell's Obscene Publications Act.

Johnny had recognised the logo of the self-swallowing snake from court sessions where he'd watched prosecuting counsel brandishing items seized from the shop. Their hypocritical show of recoiling in horror invariably had the jury craning their necks for a closer look.

Today there were no bystanders ogling the dingy array of plaster-of-Paris statuettes in various athletic poses – window undressing rather than window dressing. Johnny pushed open the door, hoping that the shop would be quiet on a Saturday afternoon, its regular clientele poring over their pornography in the privacy of their own homes.

The jingle of the bell over the door summoned a personable young man in a burlap apron from the back room. He closed the door behind him. He seemed more nervous than Johnny.

Having checked that he was the only customer, Johnny retrieved the envelope from his inside pocket and placed the photograph of Matt on the counter.

"Seen this before?"

"What," said the assistant. "A bit of the hard stuff?"

"Don't try and be funny," sighed Johnny. "I know you've got all kinds of filth under the counter. I've seen your boss fined several times for peddling smut. Do you recognise the men in the picture?"

"Why you asking?" The boy, blond and blue-eyed, was barely out of his teens but must have been over twenty-one else the proprietor would have faced yet another court visit. Chosen for his looks, no doubt. He licked his lips. His air of bravado wasn't convincing.

"Stop wasting my time," said Johnny, keen to be out of the place as quickly as possible.

He had never realised so many picture books on Ancient Greece and Rome had been published. Then there were the usual suspects: Edward Carpenter, Richard von Kraft-Ebbing, Baudelaire, Verlaine and, of course, Oscar Wilde. The novels in the fiction section looked particularly well-thumbed.

There was a rack of postcards by the door. It creaked as it turned. Cecil Beaton's swooning portraits of Johnny Weissmuller; Leni Riefenstahl's Olympic heroes clad only in loincloths; raunchier pictures featuring the Ritter

Brothers, gym-toned and brilliantined, black dots obscuring their genitalia. They may have had perfect bodies but the Americans still looked ridiculous playing tennis in the nude.

"See anything you like? I'd never have guessed you were into Greek love – but that's half the fun, isn't it? You never can tell." The boy had regained what was clearly his usual cockiness. "D'you want to see what I've got underneath?"

Johnny tried not to laugh. "Fuck off! Have you seen this picture before or not?"

"It was developed, along with several others, for a gentleman who came in last week. The photographer made a good job of it, don't you think?"

"Name?"

"I maybe a sissy, but I'm not stupid." He rubbed his fingers together. "My memory's ever so rusty. It could do with a bit of lubrication . . ."

"You should be on the stage." Johnny produced a half-crown.

The boy's eyes lit up. "Boris Ignatovich."

"Nice try." Johnny put the money away. He pulled a postcard from the rack. A naked man sat looking at half a dozen others with their backs to him. It was titled "The Bath". According to the credit on the back, it had been taken by Ignatovich.

"It was worth a go." The boy shrugged. "I could give you a gam instead . . ." He licked his lips lasciviously.

Before Johnny could reach over to punch him, the bell rang and someone entered the shop. Keeping his back to the newcomer, Johnny moved over to the book-shelves. He stood there fuming at the titles: *Man and Boy*, *Henry's Heroes, Arthur and George* . . . Footsteps crossed the ceiling. What – and who – was up there?

The customer had his collar up and his hat pulled well down.

"Good afternoon, sir. The usual?"

The man murmured his assent, palmed something off the counter and slipped it into his pocket. The cash draw slid open and closed. The whole transaction was over in less than a minute. The doorbell tinkled again.

"Come on then, if you're going to give me one."

Suddenly Johnny just wanted to be out of the place. Its sordid silence, the flaunting of flesh for money not love depressed him. He held up the half-crown again. "Have you developed other photographs for this chap?"

"Yes."

"Who keeps the negatives?"

"He does, of course."

"D'you know someone called Harry Gogg?"

He wasn't sure what had made him ask the question. Perhaps it was the fact that the shop-boy, though slimmer, bore a passing resemblance to the dead bummaree with his fair hair and blue eyes.

It was as if Johnny had lunged across the counter and landed a punch in the boy's solar plexus. He uttered a low moan and burst into tears.

As the boy stood there, wailing, Johnny looked on in amazement. Men did not cry. Well, not often. He had cried at his mother's funeral, but not during the endless weeks leading up to her death. It was the final act of throwing earth on to her coffin that had set off the waterworks – and once they had started it felt as if they would never stop. He could still smell Lizzie's perfume as he had sobbed into her shoulder.

He stood there awkwardly, not knowing what to do. He could hardly put his arms round the nancy to comfort him as he would have done with anyone else. The gesture might be misinterpreted.

"I loved him so much," said the boy. "He meant the world to me. I don't know what I'm going to do now. I feel so alone."

The doorbell rang again. Johnny – thinking that only he could get himself into such a compromising position – wished the ground would swallow him up.

Fortunately the prospective customer, seeing the state of the boy and sensing trouble, turned on his heels and fled.

As the boy's convulsions finally began to subside, Johnny patted his arm and did his best to express his sympathy.

"I'm sorry about Harry. I only met him the once, but I liked him."

"He was a lovely boy, wouldn't hurt a fly," sniffed the assistant. "No one deserves to die like he did – butchered like one of the beefs he carried." He wiped his nose on the back of his hand.

Johnny gave him the half-crown and picked up the photo of Matt, grateful that the first customer had not swiped it. Matt would have killed him.

"Are you sure there's nothing you can tell me? I'm a reporter investigating Harry's death."

There had to be a connection between the business with the dead cop and the photograph. It was too much of a coincidence that Harry's lover knew who had developed it. Anyway he did not believe in coincidence: it was simply the moment when preparation met opportunity.

"Sure as hell. Anyway, what's his death got to do with that photo?"

"Nothing, as far as I know. That's why I'm asking around."

"Well, do us both a favour and do it somewhere else. Mind you," he said, adopting a more conciliatory tone, "tip us the wink if you do find out anything."

"You have my word."

"Rather have your arse. You're not bad-looking, for a ginger."

Johnny, who had heard all the jokes before – in Cockney rhyming slang *ginger beer* meant *queer* – did not bother to answer.

It was a relief to step back out into the cold.

For a few moments the boy stood at the counter. He watched in silence until Johnny had disappeared from sight.

The door behind him opened.

"Well done, Joseph."

I can't believe he's given the photograph to Steadman. It was meant to be a warning, to put an end to him consorting with the press. Instead, he hands the bloody thing over. Who in their right mind would want their mates to see them looking like that? The big bastard clearly has no shame.

Well, it looks as though I'll have to find another way to shut him up.

I'm going to have to fix that ginger bastard too. The last thing I wanted was to hand him a new lead. I should have been more careful, made sure there was nothing on the photo that would connect it to the shop.

Still, Joseph did well. He's a good lad – for a turd-burglar. Good for business, too. He makes a splendid usherette.

Of course, if he ever finds out who killed his bum-chum, that would be the end of the affair – and the end of him.

THIRTEEN

Saturday, 12th December, 8 p.m.

Daisy had finally said yes. It had taken all his powers of persuasion during another pleading telephone call to her digs in Camden – and the promise of a pair of art-silk stockings – before she accepted his invitation to dinner and a film. Halfway through the call he wondered why he was going to so much trouble – he would much rather have been with Lizzie – but, and he would not have admitted this to anyone, the photo of Matt had made him randy, frustrated and hungry for sex. Daisy was a cert.

From the minute he picked her up he was regretting it. She kept reminding him how lucky he was to have her company – she was not short of offers for a Saturday night out. However, Johnny suspected she *was* short of cash: her latest show, *Revudeville*, had closed the week before so she was kicking her heels until another chorus line required her dubious talents.

To prove how sorry he was for standing her up earlier in the week, he whisked her off to the luxurious Carlton Cinema. Its Egyptian façade dominated the crossroads of Essex and Canonbury Roads. The sumptuous interior – a riot of marble, mirrors, silver and gold – boasted 2,500 seats. Johnny splashed out on a couple that cost two shillings each, the most expensive, which positioned them right underneath the chandelier that hung from the centre of the vast domed ceiling. They had eaten in the lounge – every single wicker armchair and glass-topped table occupied – before entering the auditorium to hear the orchestra perform before the main feature: *Sabotage*.

Johnny was amused to see that Verloc's dirty bookshop had been turned into a small independent cinema in Hitchcock's version of Joseph Conrad's novel, *The Secret Agent*. And the film being screened was *Who Killed Cock Robin?* The director had a warped sense of humour.

Daisy screamed when the bomb went off on the bus. "Who would ever do such a thing?" she said. She did not shrug him off when he put a comforting arm round her shoulders.

The other fine feature of the super-cinema was that it was less than five minutes away from Cruden Street. Daisy, not even bothering to ask for a cup of tea, went straight upstairs, stripped off her second-best dress – the sight of her breasts making him instantly hard – and slipped into bed. She lay there shivering, her shiny black hair caressing her bare shoulders.

"Come on! What are you waiting for?"

He did not need asking twice. She watched him as he threw his clothes off, eyeing his erection with hunger, and giggled as it bounced when he leapt beneath the blankets. He put his arms round her and sighed: she was so warm and curvy and smelled so sweet. However, when their lips touched he involuntarily recoiled. The kiss in the alley flooded his brain. It had felt just the same: just as soft yet strong and tender, filled with the promise of pleasure to come.

"What's the matter?" Daisy stared into his eyes. "You seeing someone else? You couldn't look more guilty if you tried." She grabbed his balls and squeezed. Hard. "Tell me the truth."

"Ow! Let go. Of course not. Why would I be treating you like royalty if I were?"

"Guilt. Tell me again why you couldn't see me on Thursday." She gave his balls an extra squeeze.

"For fuck's sake, Daisy. I told you: I had to meet an informant. Now let go or I'll be sick all over you."

"Charming." She relinquished her grip and turned her back on him. He lay there limply, staring at the ceiling.

"How many more times do I have to say I'm sorry?"

"Something's going on. I can tell. You've changed."

"How?"

"Don't know. Can't put my finger on it."

"You can put all five on it if you like . . ." He was not going to tell her about the murder or the kiss. He had to pretend that the latter had never happened.

Afterwards he went downstairs to make some tea. Daisy, satisfied for the moment – although she always demanded an encore – had fallen asleep. She was prettier when she stopped pouting and relaxed her face. The bloom on her cheeks, the redness of her swollen lips, were beautiful.

He was on his way back when a shriek almost made him drop the tray. Now what?

When he got back upstairs Daisy was scrambling into her clothes, her face white with rage. Brandishing the photograph of Matt with one hand, she took a last drag on her cigarette and flung the dog-end at him.

"Pervert! You haven't heard the last of this."

"I'm not queer. Let me explain –"

"So what was this doing in your bedside drawer?"

"I might ask what you were doing looking in there in the first place."

"I was looking to see if you had any more French letters, okay? Instead I find this filth."

"Don't pretend to be shocked, Daisy. The theatre is packed with poofters."

"Yeah, but I don't sleep with them."

She slipped on her high heels, shoved past him and clomped down the stairs. The front door slammed shut.

Johnny sat on the edge of the bed and helped himself to one of Daisy's fags that she had forgotten in her fury. He would not miss Daisy – she was not interested in his explanation or, when it came down to it, him; she had got what she had come for, a free night out and an uncomplicated fuck – but he would miss the company. He slept better with a woman beside him.

He wished Lizzie was with him – then, with a stab of guilt, immediately reproached himself for the thought. Why was it so difficult to find intimacy rather than sex? He was alone again.

Lost in thought – angry, disappointed and upset – the tea grew cold beside him. Eventually he picked up the tray to take it back to the kitchen and gazed at the rumpled sheets where, only half an hour before, he had lost himself in the mindless pleasures of sexual abandon.

His eyes drifted to the bedside table, its drawer wide open. He had thought it was the safest place to keep the incriminating evidence. Where was the photograph now? He checked the bed, the floor, emptied out the drawer of the bedside table. No sign of it. Had Daisy thrown it down on her way out? He ran through the house, searching everywhere he could think of.

The photograph had vanished.

The ungrateful bitch had taken it.

The hall in King Street, round the corner from Snow Hill, was heaving. The roar of conversation, competing with the band, threatened to lift the roof. Paper chains swung gaily in the hot air. Matt watched his colleagues, all in casual clothes, knocking back the beer and Scotch that had kindly been "donated" by various local publicans.

The tug-of-war team had won the tournament. Unlike the rest of them he had been in no mood for a celebratory Christmas party, but despite that he was now well on the way to being drunk.

For some reason, Lizzie had said she could not face the annual event but insisted he go ahead and enjoy himself. He was usually never happier than when he was in the centre of a crowd, joking with friends, flirting with their wives. His sporting prowess earned him plenty of admiration in and out of the ring. However, the fact that both men and women sought out his company had not made him arrogant. Modest to a fault, he could not understand what they saw in him – apart from his biceps. Johnny said he made people feel good about themselves.

He was no longer feeling good though. His initial elation, as the alcohol took effect, had turned to exhaustion. It was time to go home. He had to be at work tomorrow. Most of his superiors, including Rotherforth, had already left.

A loud crash, followed by the sound of smashing plates, came from the other end of the room. Several women screamed. The band, out of curiosity rather than necessity, stopped playing. Matt pushed his way through the throng.

Herbert Watkiss, his sloe-black eyes wide open in surprise, lay sprawled amid the debris of a broken trestle table. Meat pies, sausage rolls and shards of crockery littered the floor. Tom Vinson stood over him, his fists still clenched.

"What happened?" asked Matt. Watkiss took the

proffered hand and allowed himself to be pulled to his feet. They had been in training together at Bishopsgate. The constable rubbed his chin. He glared at Vinson. "Tom?"

"It was nothing, Matt. I overreacted, that's all."

"You can say that again, Vinson." Watkiss tried to brush off the food that smeared his Sunday best.

"Everything all right?" Sergeant Dwyer surveyed the damage. "Get this lot cleared up."

The band started playing "I've Got You Under My Skin".

"You haven't heard the last of this," said Watkiss.

Vinson smiled. "I can't wait."

"I suggest you go and clean yourself up, Watkiss," barked Dwyer.

"Yes, Sarge." He shoved past Vinson, muttering something that was drowned out by the music.

"I'd make myself scarce, Tom, if I were you," said Matt, steering Vinson away before Dwyer started asking questions.

"He doesn't scare me." Vinson yawned. "But you're right. It's time for bed. You kipping at the station or going home?"

"Home."

"In that case, I'll see you tomorrow."

Any other time, Matt would have tried to find out what Watkiss had said to make Vinson fly off the hook like that. He must have really struck a nerve to provoke such a reaction. But Matt had enough problems of his own, without sticking his nose in anyone else's. He decided to make a speedy exit before Watkiss reappeared, looking for someone to tell his side of the tale to.

Grabbing his coat, he stepped out into the cold night air, hoping the effects of the drink and tiredness would last long enough to keep the nightmares at bay.

FOURTEEN

Sunday, 13th December, 4 p.m.

Johnny hated Sundays. The shops were shut, the pubs were closed most of the time and, once he had worked his way through the newspapers, he was at a loose end.

He could have gone to visit his mother's grave, but Finchley cemetery was such a trek. Anyway, she was no more there than she was here. A schoolboy memory of a saying by the Venerable Bede flitted through his brain: life is as brief as the time taken for a single sparrow to fly into and out of a lighted hall in winter wherein the feasting goes on regardless.

He could have gone round to Daisy's lodging house, but there seemed little point: she would only slam the door in his face. Best give her time to cool down. He would only have one chance to get the photograph back; he didn't want to waste it by picking the wrong moment.

Besides, the photo aside, he had no desire whatsoever to see her. Stella was a much more attractive proposition. He was already looking forward to their date.

He could have gone to a matinee to idle away a few hours, but there was too much on his mind. His special assignment would start tomorrow. The five days Stone had given him would soon fly by, so he needed to come up with a plan of attack to make every second count.

Who had sent him the notes? Apart from being more certain than ever that it was not one of Simkins' tricks – there was no way he could have foreseen the murder of Harry – Johnny was no nearer to finding out who had tipped him off.

There was really only one thing he was certain of: somehow Smithfield was at the heart of the mystery. It was where Harry had worked. It was a mere stone's throw from Snow Hill police station. The dead cop – if the naked, unidentified corpse Harry delivered was indeed a cop – had been taken to Bart's.

And so he made his way to St Bartholomew-the-Great, arriving just in time to hear the bells chiming the hour. Visiting time at the hospital must have just ended, for families began emerging to make their way home, their faces showing a mixture of sadness at leaving their relatives and relief at escaping the smell of antiseptic and the clinical atmosphere of the wards.

As he tried to marshal his thoughts into some kind of order, he wandered aimlessly towards Pye Corner where, high up on the wall, a small gilt statue of a cupid marked the furthest extent of the Great Fire of

London. It was supposed to be a warning against the avarice that tub-thumpers claimed had caused the fire in the first place: punishment for gluttons.

He turned into Cock Lane – London's first red-light district – where prostitutes had once plied their trade outside the City walls. It was certainly dark enough for a knee-trembler in a doorway, even at this time in the afternoon.

The road curved downhill, past the back of Snow Hill police station. Number 33 was supposed to be haunted and had been since 1762 when crowds – including Dr Johnson, Oliver Goldsmith, Joshua Reynolds and Horace Walpole – had flocked to hear the ghost of "Scratching Fanny", the late sister-in-law of William Parsons, the officiating clerk at nearby St Sepulchre's. She had died of smallpox, but it was claimed the scratching was a sign that she had been a victim of arsenic poisoning. The noises had stopped when Parsons' eleven-year-old daughter, the first person to have heard them, was moved to the home of the rector of St John's, Clerkenwell. But by the time the fraud was exposed, local taverns had already made a fortune from supplying the ghost seekers with liquid refreshment.

Johnny felt as if he was haunted by a deception where someone was trying to create a smokescreen to hide the true cause of a young person's death. Only whereas in Scratching Fanny's case the cause of death had been natural and the suspicious circumstances invented, the corpse delivered to Bart had a death certificate that read "hypothermia" and injuries that could only have come about as the result of foul play. Or possibly an accident – but if that were the case, why dump the body anonymously?

Who was the cop that, according to PC Vinson, had been transferred "for personal reasons"? Could Vinson's unnamed wolly and Matt's old team-mate Aitken be the same man? Or was Vinson deliberately sending him down a blind alley?

It was eerily quiet. Johnny stopped and listened. Not a sound. His nerves were constantly on edge since finding Harry's butchered corpse. He was forever looking over his shoulder, wondering if he was being followed. He waited a moment, steeling his nerves, and then walked on.

And what of Harry? Why had he been mutilated in such a fashion? He was a cock-sucker, to be sure, but there was real malice in his emasculation and it suggested the murderer had taken his time in wreaking his revenge. It was all right for naked boys to be mounted on walls in the name of history, but mounting them in private for pleasure was against the law. The same law that didn't really give a toss about the killing of a pervert; there was no way Harry's murder would be given priority by the murder squad.

Harry died because he'd been about to tell him something. He had to find out what. Who else might know? His lover? Perhaps he had been too soft on him. Johnny had been so unnerved – some might say unmanned – by the surroundings he had not been thinking straight. He needed to see the boy away from the shop.

"*En garde!*"

Johnny gave an involuntary yelp as his heart leapt into his mouth. A figure emerged from a doorway, assumed the fencing position, and pointed his epée at him. It had a cork on the tip of it so it could not be classified as an offensive weapon.

The would-be assailant also happened to be entirely unclothed.

Johnny relaxed. "The Naked Swordsman" was a Smithfield regular, a harmless lunatic who refused all attempts to help him. He was rumoured to be the illegitimate son of George V.

"What the hell are you doing?" said Johnny. "You'll catch your death out here."

How he had not already done so was a perpetual mystery.

"And I wouldn't be the first one either. Only a week ago, dear sir, I saw something that would make your blood run cold. Get thee hence. This is a place of evil."

"Then why are you lurking here?"

"I intend on getting arrested and spending the night in a nice warm cell." He nodded at Snow Hill station.

A light suddenly shone down from the top floor. The madman removed the cork and stuck the ice-cold tip under Johnny's chin.

"Thus far and no further. If you wish to live to see me in the dock again, newspaperman, look elsewhere for a story. The boy would have died hereafter. And others will do so if you insist on ferreting around this dung-hill. Move on, I say, move on."

Johnny backed away a few paces, then turned to climb

the hill to Giltspur Street. There was no point in questioning a fruitcake. Which boy was he talking about? He couldn't mean Harry – that was less than a week ago. Was he referring to the dead cop? His body turned up at the morgue early on Sunday. Could it be that the poor lunatic had glimpsed the aftermath? If he had seen something at the back of Snow Hill station that night, his insanity had probably saved his life.

Who would believe the naked wretch, even if he were telling the truth?

Matt took off his helmet and rubbed his forehead where it always left a red mark. His hair was damp with sweat. He escorted the now docile Frank Bundock – aka Frank Wilson and George Wilson – down to the cells where the custody sergeant booked him before banging him up with the regular haul of Saturday-night drunks trying to sleep off their hangovers. Matt had spotted the habitual criminal picking the pocket of an American sightseer in Cannon Street. It had not been difficult: not many dippers had a deformed left arm. Although Bundock had tried to do a runner, Matt collared him in Red Lion Court. There were times when he felt like a glorified street-cleaner: Bundock would be back thieving after six months inside. Birching was too good for him. Still, the grateful Yank had got his money back – and even tried to give Matt a tip!

He had fifteen minutes to write up his report before returning to his beat. Apart from the kitchen staff, the canteen on the first floor was almost deserted. It was too early for the night shift to gather before going on duty, and those on the morning shift had long since left. The officers had their own mess on the floor above. He was glad of the chance to rest his feet and grab a quick cup of tea. His own hangover had still not quite dissipated.

Herbert Watkiss came slouching in. The handsome constable looked peeved.

"What's up with you?" said Matt. "Still feeling sore about last night? On the sheet again?" Watkiss' beat was one concentric circle closer to the station than Matt's.

"Looks like it. Rotherforth called me in. I probably failed to break one of his bloody pieces of cotton." The inspector was known to tie pieces of black cotton across alleyways and doorways to check that his men were hitting every mark.

"So, come on then. What did you say to Vinson to make him hit you?"

"I didn't *say* anything." He lowered his voice. "I didn't mean any harm. It was a joke, that's all."

"What was?" Matt rolled his eyes. It was like pulling teeth.

"I just held up a sprig of mistletoe."

Sergeant Philip Dwyer was on desk duty when Matt got back down to reception. Seeing Matt, he put down the second-hand copy of *Hogarth's London* by H.B. Wheatley that he should not have been reading, and nodded to a pretty girl clutching her handbag by the frosted-glass doors.

"Someone to see you, PC Turner." He managed not to wink. "Make it snappy."

"Thanks, Sarge."

Matt went over to the young lady. She looked up at him and smiled nervously. He studied her features, wondering if he should recognise her. She had enormous hazel eyes: he could almost see himself in them. An Alice band kept her unruly auburn curls in check. She licked her lips with the tip of a very pink tongue and held out her hand.

"How d'you do."

As they shook hands he could feel the girl trembling. She looked round. "Could we go outside?"

The bored Dwyer could contain himself no longer: "Now there's an offer you can't refuse."

Matt ignored him and pushed open one of the doors. Cold air hit them in the face, making their eyes water.

They paused underneath the blue lamp. Still she seemed too nervous to speak.

"I've got to go back on the beat." Matt nodded up the hill towards the Old Bailey. "Why don't you walk with me?"

"Thank you. I don't know who else to turn to: no one will give me a straight answer." She took a deep breath as if composing herself and then said, "My name is Lilian Voss. George Aitken is my fiancé. I'm so worried about him. He seems to have disappeared . . ."

FIFTEEN

Monday, 14th December, 9.30 a.m.

Bill was most put out.

"Come on then, Coppernob. Spill the beans. What's so special about this assignment? 'Life on the Beat' doesn't sound at all special to me. Sounds like a cover story for something else." His eyebrows formed themselves into circumflexes.

"I can't tell you," said Johnny. "Stone's orders. Sorry."

He did not want to involve Bill unless it was absolutely necessary. He wanted his name – and no one else's – on the byline.

The seasoned hack regarded him quizzically. "I could help, you know. A week is not a long time. No one likes to see a cop-killer go free."

It was no good. Bill knew him too well. "I've nothing to tell you – yet."

"My dear Johnny, it's me you're talking to. You're not the only one with friends at Snow Hill."

Johnny looked round anxiously, hoping Patsel was not in the vicinity. The last thing he needed was advice from the bossy buffoon. "If you trust me, you'll keep your lips sealed."

"Afraid I'll steal your glory?"

"Not at all. I wish I could call on your expertise." A little flattery never went amiss. "I haven't even been able to establish if a murder has taken place."

"You mean apart from that boy-whore last week?"

"Yes."

"That's not going to provoke a tidal wave of moral outrage, is it?" mused Bill. His chair complained as he leaned perilously backwards. "Who cares about a dead catamite?"

Johnny was going to say he did but bit his lip. Catamite? They were not in Ancient Greece. The sooner the conversation came to an end the better. "I've got to go."

"If you say so. I'll let you know if any more telegrams turn up." He winked.

Johnny had the distinct impression Bill knew more than he did. He grabbed his mackintosh.

Sighing in defeat, Bill swiped the return lever on his battle-scarred typewriter. "Watch your back, Coppernob."

The only reason Johnny had gone into the office was to find out if any more messages had been delivered. However, his pigeonhole was empty. It looked as though his informant was maintaining his silence. It had to be someone at Snow Hill. Unless . . .

Had Bill got there first and removed a third telegram?

Johnny shook his head. He was becoming paranoid.

In the eighteenth century, Honey Lane had been the site of the City's smallest meat market but its hundred or so stalls had long since disappeared. However, if you knew where to look – or rather knock – it was still home to a meat-rack of sorts.

The house in question was just off Milk Street, with an emergency exit that led through the building at the back and out on to Russia Row. It was the only male brothel in the City – and the cops, who accepted back-handers if not hand-jobs – discreetly ensured it remained so.

Johnny approached it via a passage off Cheapside between a pub and a cobbler's and, as though he had not a care in the world instead of a stomach full of butterflies and an urgent desire to empty his bowels, grasped the brass lion's head and hammered on the glossy black front door.

A bloodshot eye appeared at the peep-hole. There was a pause as it sized Johnny up, then the door swung open and an unshaven thug – who resembled one of Oswald Mosley's myrmidons – stood aside to let him in.

"After an audition are we, sonny?"

Johnny, unsure whether to be insulted or flattered, decided on the former.

"Don't be so impertinent. Do I look that desperate for a job?"

"Some do it for the pleasure as much as the pay." The human guard-dog sniffed as if he couldn't care less either way. "Anyway, you're a bit keen, aren't yer? Not all the boys are 'ere. Won't be till midday."

"Lunch time your busiest period then?" asked Johnny.

"Why d'you want to know?"

"Just asking. It's my first time."

"If you say so," said the bouncer in a tone that implied disbelief. Then, looking over Johnny's shoulder, added: "Sir."

"And what do we have here?"

The high-pitched voice right behind him made Johnny jump. It belonged to a portly middle-aged woman in a sequinned dress that was at least a decade out of date. Her heavily powdered jowls were the colour of junket. A chihuahua quivered in the palm of one hand. She held out the other. There were rings on every finger and the way the gems sparkled suggested they were not costume jewellery. The lap-dog yapped.

"Cecilia Zick. How d'you do?"

"Julius Handford." They shook hands. "A mutual friend suggested I visit when next in town."

Johnny was certain she would never recognise the character from Dickens' novel. It was the name John Harmon gave when viewing the drowned body supposedly his own.

"And who might this 'friend' be?"

"John Gielgud. I was told that discretion was guaranteed."

"It can be. I run a top-class establishment and it costs me a lot to keep it running, if you know what I mean. Palms to grease as well as arses."

"I'm not a policeman," said Johnny, with an attempt at a smile.

"I can see that, Ducky. Way too short. Hope your little man is bigger." She tittered. The doorman guffawed – out of duty rather than delight. She nodded to the left. "This way."

The sequins shimmered on her plump posterior as she opened a door into an ornately decorated parlour. There was a faint smell of stale cigar smoke and Ronuk's Furniture Cream. A fire, which appeared to have just been lit, crackled in the grate. A pair of leather armchairs either side of it, and a chesterfield that had clearly supported thousands of backsides, lent the room the air of a gentleman's club – for gentlemen who liked gentlemen. Oil paintings of naked youths covered two of the walls but the one facing the shuttered windows had a large curtained aperture. Zick pulled the golden tassel that dangled at one side and the drapes swept back to reveal an internal window.

"Don't worry, love," said the madam. "They can't see you. It's a one-way mirror. That's why they keep looking at it. They'd eat themselves if they could." She laughed. "But that's why you're here."

Johnny could not believe his eyes. He had reported on brothel raids, seen prostitutes of both sexes in the dock, but the casual way the boys presented themselves was somehow obscene. Some wore nothing but their drawers; others were in uniform. There was an army cadet, a sailor, a policeman – Zick certainly had a sense of irony – and a lad from the District Messenger Company. Its young employees in their smart, close-fitting uniforms were notoriously available. Rumour had it that DMC actually stood for *Devour My Cock*. There was no smoke without fire.

"Take your time," said Zick, watching him closely. "If you fancy someone older, they'll be here later on – earning a bit of extra in their lunch-hour. I've got a couple of bankers if pinstripes are your thing."

"I'll have him," said Johnny, pointing to the DMC boy.

"An excellent choice, if I may say so. Our Stan's very popular. Or should I say, *accommodating*? I take it that's what you're after?"

"What d'you mean?" asked Johnny.

"You want to fuck rather than get fucked?" Johnny reddened. Such matter-of-factness about unspeakable acts embarrassed him. And he thought he was a man of the world.

"Er, yes please."

Zick eyed him shrewdly. "Sure?"

"Absolutely."

"Tip-top. That'll be a guinea then for half an hour." Johnny was amazed. He barely had enough. If Stone refused to allow him to claim it on expenses, Stan would not be the only one supposedly getting fucked.

He followed Zick out of the parlour and waited while she went into the room next door. The dog yapped at him again. Johnny hated such excuses for pets.

A moment later Stan emerged, gave Johnny a cheeky grin, and started climbing the stairs. Johnny felt as though he were ascending the scaffold.

The room was on the top floor of the building under the roof. Johnny smiled to himself: in Cockney rhyming slang "up on the roof" meant "poof". Its sloping sides would have troubled anyone taller than him. Stan stripped with practised rapidity and lay on the bed. His big, brown eyes met Johnny's.

"What you waiting for, lover boy?" He frowned, sensing the lack of interest. "Don't you like what you see?" Stan stretched out his pale, sleek body like a Siamese cat.

"I'm not here for sex. I'm a reporter."

Stan immediately leaped to his feet and grabbed a handbell from the nightstand.

Johnny grabbed it off him. "Keep your hair on. I'm not going to get you into trouble. Look, you're being paid to do nothing. Where's the harm in that?"

Stan pouted – apparently injured at being turned down. "Keep your voice down then." He started rolling around on the bed to make the springs squeak, unabashed in his nudity. "What d'you want to know?"

"Did you deliver a message to the *Daily News*, addressed to John Steadman, last Monday?"

"Can't remember. I deliver dozens of messages to all the papers everyday. This is just a sideline." He winked.

"Sure you don't fancy a quickie? You're just the way I like 'em. The shy ones are the best. So randy, so grateful, so quick. Except some of them cry when they come."

"No, thank you. The message might have come from Snow Hill police station."

Stan got up with a sigh and began to get dressed. "Okay. I remember now. I did collect one from the cop-shop and take it to the *News*."

"Who gave it to you?"

"The desk sergeant." So the whistle-blower was an insider.

"Ever heard of someone called Harry Gogg?"

"Everyone knew Harry. He was an angel. A favourite with the clients."

"You know what happened to him?"

"Course I do. And I don't want the same thing happening to me, so do me a favour and mind your own beeswax."

"Don't you want his killer to be brought to justice?"

Stan laughed. "Jesus, get you! The likes of us don't get justice. There's those that do bad things and get caught, and those that do bad things and get away with it. Believe me, Gogg's killer ain't never going to swing. Now, I've got to get back to work. If I tell Zick you're a reporter, Alf'll make –"

"There's no need to tell me anything, dear." The door flew open and Zick stood there, her white cheeks now florid – from rage and no doubt the exertion of climbing three flights of stairs. She grabbed Johnny's left ear and twisted it, hard. "I knew you were a wrong 'un. Julius

Handford, indeed! I wasn't born yesterday. Stan, get back downstairs at once. I'll speak to you later."

Stan shot through the door, his face full of fear.

Zick twisted Johnny's ear again.

"Ow! Will you please stop doing that?"

She dragged him out on to the tiny landing and kicked him down the stairs.

"Get out of my establishment, you dirty little muck-raker. You breathe a word of this to anyone and you'll regret it. If you think Harry had it bad, believe me it can be worse. Much worse. The fucking nerve of it! Not much of an undercover journalist, are you? Didn't even get into bed with your snitch. What's the matter? Can't get it up? Alf! *Alf!* Where the fuck are you?"

Dazed and bruised from his headlong fall, Johnny felt the chihuahua nipping his ankle. Instinctively he kicked out at it, which only served to increase Zick's fury.

"Stop that! Don't you dare take it out on an innocent creature, you big bully. If I ever see you again, you'll be sorry."

Johnny felt a pair of giant paws haul him to his feet. Alf dragged him down the remaining stairs, past the gaggle of staring boys in the hall, opened the front door and flung him down the steps. The door slammed so hard the lion's head gave a single knock that seemed to say *and good riddance*.

Slowly, Johnny got to his feet and patted himself down. Nothing seemed to be broken. His head ached, his ear was burning and his healing hands, still sore from the floor of the freezer, were scuffed and red raw again. He brushed his coat off as best he could and leant against the area railings, trying to compose himself. This proved impossible. A familiar voice rang out:

"Enjoying yourself?"

It was Henry Simkins.

SIXTEEN

Johnny could not be bothered to resist as Simkins led him out into Cheapside, hailed a cab and took him to his club in Watling Street – even though it was only a two-minute walk away. It was obvious he did not need to worry about expenses.

A white-jacketed waiter placed two brandies and a bowl of nuts on the highly polished table between the winged-back armchairs and retreated noiselessly. Johnny examined his surroundings: it was like being back in Zick's parlour except everything was on a grander scale. His whole house would fit beneath the distant cloud-painted ceiling.

"Come on!" Simkins picked up his glass. "Your very good health."

He downed his in one go. Johnny sipped at the resinous liquor and felt the healing fire spread through his veins.

"Congratulations, by the way, on breaking the story of the slaughtered butcher's boy. I bet Herr Patsel loved that: degenerate scum swinging from a meat-hook. Must have made him feel homesick." He took another swig of the expensive alcohol. "So did you discover anything useful before you were slung out?" Simkins tried – and failed – not to smile.

"I've been thrown out of better places," said Johnny. It was true. Somehow his rival always succeeded in catching him at a disadvantage – and yet he was not an unkind man. This did not mean he had to like him, though.

"Am I to take it then that Miss Zick was less than forthcoming?" Simkins raised an eyebrow. "Sample any of her wares?" He laughed. "Just in the name of research, of course."

"Hear that?" said Johnny. "It's the sound of my sides splitting."

"Ah, but the subject is *rump*-splitting, isn't it?" Simkins leaned forward. "Harry Gogg was one of Zick's boys, wasn't he? She can't be very pleased at losing one of her most popular employees. I'm told he could be very enthusiastic. Really put his back into it."

"Who told you that? And why are you so interested?"

"As if I'd reveal my sources to you! Murder holds its own fascination, doesn't it? Some might say the death of a male prostitute is of little consequence. In some ways, I have to say, I agree. However, *who* killed him and *why* is tremendously important, don't you think?"

"I do," said Johnny. The brandy was soothing his

aching body but not his racing mind. He had taken a lot of punishment in the past few days. "So once again we're chasing the same story. Well, good luck. You'll need it."

It had been some time since Johnny had beaten Simkins into print. Of course, he was at a disadvantage, thanks to Patsel: the Old Bailey was where stories ended not began. Nevertheless, in the two years he had been reporting from the Sessions House he had managed to pick up and run with a few leads, and three months earlier he had pre-empted Simkins in revealing a case of jury nobbling.

The fact that Simkins had not yet asked him about discovering Harry's body suggested the dandy was unaware of his involvement – or the possibility that a cop had been killed. And he probably did not know that Harry's partner worked in the Urania Bookshop. Johnny felt certain that, for the moment at least, he was ahead.

"Have you tried talking to Gogg's fellow bummarees?" said Johnny. The thought of Simkins surrounded by the blood-spattered brutes was strangely amusing.

"Indeed. As expected, it was an utter waste of time. Bunch of taciturn ruffians," sighed Simkins. "They actually seemed glad to be rid of him. Bet you a pound to a penny, though, one or two of them had availed themselves of his special skills. It's the ones who boast about being family men you've got to watch out for." He switched to stage Cockney. "Know what I mean, guvnor?"

He rattled on, switching accents with the greatest of ease. Everything seemed to come easily to him. When the waiter appeared to replace their empty glasses with new ones it occurred to Johnny that Simkins' whole life had been presented to him on a silver salver.

"Penny for them." Simkins tossed back his floppy, chestnut locks and crossed his legs.

Matt, half in jest, had once told Johnny that only effeminates did that. Real men sat with their legs apart.

"I was thinking how lucky you are – and wondering why it is you do what you do when you could do anything you want," said Johnny.

"But I *am* doing what I want," said Simkins. "There are too many doctors, lawyers and MPs – the majority of them less than mediocre. I've no doubt I could have made a name for myself in any of those professions, but I prefer the thrill of the chase, exposing crime and shocking my millions of readers. I also like enraging my father. Tell me, do you hunt?" Johnny snorted. "A thousand apologies. Stupid question. You should come down to the country one weekend, Steadman. See how the other half live. You might even enjoy it."

"I'm sure I would, but I'm not sure why you'd want me as a house guest. Someone to entertain your toffee-nosed companions? A boy from the back streets set up to be bamboozled by the display of so much ostentatious wealth?"

"No wonder you didn't grow any taller with such great big chips on both shoulders! Don't be so suspicious, Steadman. I'm not being patronising when I say you amuse me. There's a whole other world out there – and if you let me, I'd be happy to show it to you."

Was he lonely? Simkins was always boasting of his hectic social life, but his impressive poise could be an act. Perhaps they had more in common than Johnny had realised. He became aware Simkins was studying him, as if trying to read his mind. Suddenly he scowled.

"Oh Christ. Speak of the devil."

A distinguished-looking gentleman with swept-back silver hair and hawkish eyes, passed by their table. His handmade suit failed to disguise a sizeable paunch.

"Shouldn't you be in a gutter somewhere?"

Simkins stood up. "Father! What a delightful surprise. As a matter of fact, I've just fished my luncheon companion, Mr John Steadman of the *Daily News*, out of one."

Simkins Senior made no effort to shake his hand. Seeing his presence acknowledged with only the merest hint of a nod, Johnny was glad he had remained seated. You only got to your feet for ladies – certainly not Tory MPs who were already enjoying the Christmas recess.

What was Aubrey Simkins doing here? Taking the opportunity to cultivate lucrative City connections? Perhaps he was missing the House of Commons. Mr Twemlow, in *Our Mutual Friend*, called it "the best club in London".

The brusque back-bencher gave one last shake of his head, muttered loudly, "the boy's a buffoon", then headed for the dining room without a backward glance.

"He's always saying that," said Simkins bitterly. It was the first time Johnny had seen him lose his composure. "When I was five I got diphtheria and passed it on to Augustus, my older brother. There was no vaccine in those days. I survived, as you can see, but Augustus didn't. My father has never forgiven me."

"I'd have thought he'd have cherished you all the more," said Johnny. "Have you any other siblings?"

"A younger sister, Victoria, who was only too happy to take on the role of favourite. She's daddy's girl all right." His tone was almost envious.

For the first time Johnny was seeing that Simkins did indeed have a vulnerable side. Everybody was hiding something, it seemed.

"I never knew my father. He died at Passchendaele."

"Count yourself lucky," sighed Simkins. "If you don't know them, you can't hate them."

"Hate is only the flip-side of love."

Simkins sniggered. "You sound like Patience Strong, Steadman. Come on, let's eat – as far away from the Right Honourable Member for Orpington as possible."

After generous helpings of steak-and-kidney pudding and spotted dick, washed down with a bottle of claret – most of which Simkins consumed, downing it in great long draughts – Johnny thought it wiser to walk. Besides, he did not want his companion to know where he was going.

The knowledge that he was on to something put a spring in his step. The skin covering his cheekbones tightened as his face met the freezing, sooty air. He had worked hard not to give anything away during the meal and in the end resorted to telling the toff about Daisy – but not, of course, Matt's photograph – to divert him.

Once Simkins, his offer of a lift spurned, had disappeared in a taxi, Johnny was finally free to head back to Smithfield. He marched up Friday Street to Cheapside then cut down Roman Bath Street alongside the General Post Office en route to Little Britain.

As it turned out, he had more than just a fortifying meal to thank Simkins for. His fellow diner, slipping into and out of accents as he regaled Johnny with Fleet Street gossip, had reminded him of Sloppy in *Our Mutual Friend* who gave Mrs Higden "the Police-news in different voices". Dickens would no doubt have known that "slop" was old back-slang for a policeman.

Matt said that George Aitken had telephoned him at Snow Hill. He had not actually seen him. Anyone could have been impersonating the cop. He must check whether the call came through on an internal line – which it would if Aitken were still a working policeman – or through the local exchange.

Johnny also needed to get hold of a photograph of Aitken – and he knew exactly where to lay his sore hands on one. Back in the spring, all officers serving at Snow Hill had been photographed on the steps of the Old Bailey – and the *Smithfield Sentinel*, a local rag, had published it. He remembered Matt proudly showing him a copy at the time.

The offices of the newspaper were in Long Lane. It took Johnny an hour to find what he was looking for in the back-issues department and by the time he was done his fingertips were black with ink.

Twenty tall, tough men, their whistle-chains shining as brightly as their boots, stood staring into the camera. Johnny's eye was immediately drawn to the middle of the front row, where Inspector Rotherforth – the only officer, distinguished by his flat, peaked cap – was flanked by four men on each side. Matt was in the second row, next to Aitken, a half-smile playing on his lips. There were three constables in the back row, one of which was Vinson. Johnny recognised most of the men. He had seen them on points duty, giving evidence from their notebooks in court and cheering on Matt at boxing matches. A caption underneath the photograph identified each officer.

Johnny looked at Aitken again. He could not recall having met him. The wolly appeared to be the youngest of the group but seemed remarkably self-possessed, calmly meeting the camera's gaze.

Perhaps he was alive and well – Johnny truly hoped so – but instinct told him otherwise.

And the man who could give him final confirmation was only round the corner.

"Now what d'you want?"

"And it's lovely to see you too, Percy. Coast clear?"

"Looks that way, don't it?"

Johnny was relieved to see that the slabs were unoccupied. Once again the disinfectant in the air pricked his nostrils. He produced the old newspaper and showed the photograph to the mortuary assistant.

"Recognise anyone?"

Percy turned white and groaned.

"I knew I should have kept my gob shut." He pointed to Aitken. "He's the one they brung in."

"Thank you." Johnny gave him half a crown.

Pity for the young policeman instantly gave way to exultation: he had been right all along. There *had* been a murder – and someone was trying to cover it up. He needed to tell Matt straight away.

Slipping the *Sentinel* back into his pocket, he started towards the swing doors.

"Don't you want to know who was with 'Arry, then?"

Johnny froze.

"He's in the picture as well?"

Percy nodded. Johnny retrieved the paper and held it out.

"Show me."

Percy held out his hand too. Johnny, tutting with impatience, produced his last half-crown. Surely he was not going to finger Matt?

"Ta very much," said Percy with a smile of satisfaction. He pointed to one of the trio on the back row.

It was PC Tom Vinson.

The cold and dark streets of Smithfield matched Johnny's mood. As always his route back to the office bypassed the main roads whose slimy pavements were clogged with exhausted workers making their way home or to the pub. But whereas normally he thought of his backstreet shortcuts as steeped in history and literary associations, tonight he passed through Shoe Lane and Gunpowder Alley weighed down by the knowledge that something evil lurked here. Something the Smithfield Market police force, sworn constables answerable to the City of London Corporation, were powerless to check.

Right now he needed to see Matt and he needed to think. But first he had to put in an appearance at the offices of the *Daily News*.

"I've been looking for you," said Patsel, before Johnny had even had a chance to take off his coat.

"Well, you've found me," said Johnny.

Bill, flicking through a copy of the final edition, its ink still wet, made a surreptitious gesture to warn him that this was not a good time for backchat.

"Where have you been?" His superior's spectacles glittered in the light. It was impossible to see his piggy eyes and thus gauge what he was thinking. How Patsel always managed to find the perfect angle to achieve this effect was a much-discussed mystery.

"Smithfield. Why? Stone told you that I'm on special assignment, didn't he?"

"He mentioned something along those lines, yes." Patsel smiled – a sure sign that trouble was coming.

Johnny's colleagues, sensing a confrontation, stopped what they were doing and eavesdropped.

"I've had a complaint," continued Patsel. "You're interfering in a police investigation."

"What investigation? I've been to a queer brothel, Trump's, Bart's and the offices of the *Sentinel.* I wasn't aware that any of those venues were under suspicion – or surveillance."

Patsel remained silent. Johnny tried to stay calm. "Are you pulling my leg?"

"No."

"Who made the complaint?"

"They said they were from the press bureau. He didn't give a name."

"Did you ask? It would have been useful to know. I might have unwittingly stumbled on to something. The day-to-day life of a City cop is hardly top secret – unless they're in league with white slave traders."

Everyone laughed – except Patsel. There were constant stories in the yellow press that young women were being chloroformed in cinemas and spirited away to serve in the harems of the east, but no evidence to corroborate this had ever been found. Laughter unsettled the humourless Patsel. If someone cracked a joke he would always be the last to laugh.

"Watch your step, Steadman," he huffed. "No more complaints, if you please. Keep me informed." He retreated to his dugout.

A paper aeroplane, thrown by Louis Dimeo on the sports desk, dive-bombed Johnny.

"A queer brothel, eh? When d'you start?"

"Why? Fancy being my first customer?"

Louis, by way of reply, grinned and gave him the finger.

"What was that all about?" Johnny asked Bill when

the spectators had turned back to their typewriters and telephones.

"He doesn't like being overruled. He'd prefer you to stay at the Old Bailey where you can't cause as much trouble."

"The sooner he slings his hook, the better."

"Santa may come early this year." Bill winked. "Anyway, how are you getting on?"

"It's been an interesting day."

"What were you doing at Zick's?"

Johnny paused.

"How come you know I visited that particular knocking-shop?"

"Let's call it an educated guess."

Johnny looked into his mentor's rheumy eyes. Had he been following him? Or had Simkins been in touch? Could he still trust Bill?

Putting his suspicions to the back of his mind, Johnny asked, "D'you know the place?"

"I know of it. Know that it has police protection."

"I gathered as much." He would have liked to run a few ideas past Bill, and he had a whole list of questions forming in his mind, but in light of the mystery complaint it occurred to him that it might be better and safer to keep his thoughts to himself. Harry Gogg had been killed after Johnny had approached him – he did not want the same thing to happen to Stan.

Bill was looking at him expectantly. Johnny was searching for some flippant remark to ward him off when his telephone rang.

"There's a young lady here to see you, Mr Steadman. Should I send her up?"

"No, that's all right," said Johnny, glancing at Bill. "I'll come down."

A mousy girl, huddled inside a thin, black coat, was standing underneath the giant four-faced clock that dominated the foyer. Each time the lift doors opened, a stream of secretaries, copytakers and advertising salesmen flowed round her, heading for the nearest Tube station or watering hole, but she stood her ground.

Johnny spotted her immediately. She seemed intimidated yet defiant.

"Hello. I'm John Steadman. What can I do for you?" They shook hands.

"Thanks so much for seeing me. Your friend PC Turner suggested I get in touch with you. My name is Lilian Voss. I'm trying to trace my fiancé George Aitken."

It was as if she had punched him on the nose. He stepped back, his mind in a whirl. His heart went out to her, and his first impulse was to tell her the truth – but his head told him that he had to lie. If she knew too much, her own life might be in danger. And even assuming he could come up with a way to keep her safe, there was no telling what she would do in her grief. If she were to start screaming blue murder, it would alert every newspaper in the land. Somehow he had to protect her *and* his scoop.

Johnny led her to one of the green leather banquettes

that would not have looked out of place in the House of Commons. People on the top floor of double-deckers – which stretched down Fleet Street nose-to-tail like circus elephants – stared through the windows at them.

"When was the last time you saw George?"

"You know something, don't you? I can tell." Tears sprang to her eyes. "Please say he's safe. I can't bear not knowing what's happened to him. The police wouldn't tell me. Said it was against regulations to discuss staff movements. But he'd have let me know if he was going to be transferred. We're in love." She rummaged in her handbag for a handkerchief. "We're going to get married in March."

"I don't know what has happened to George," said Johnny – which was true, in a way. "But I promise you I'm going to find out." He gave her a moment then gently tried again: "When was the last time you met?"

"A week last Friday – the fourth. We saw *It's Love Again* at the Paramount in Tottenham Court Road. I adore Robert Young and George likes Jessie Matthews. He was going to be on duty all weekend, so we arranged to meet on the following Monday evening. But he never turned up." She dabbed at her eyes with the handkerchief. "I'm a trainee nurse at Bart's. We used to see each other in the Red Cow – it took him ages to pluck up the courage to ask me out. It was good to know that he was literally round the corner at Snow Hill while I was on the ward."

"The last confirmed sighting of him I have is Monday the seventh."

"Where?" She grasped his hand with both of hers.

Johnny hesitated.

"At Bart's."

"Oh!" She suddenly smiled. "Was he looking for me?"

"I don't think so." The disappointment on her face made his heart ache. "He was with another cop."

"Who? Not PC Turner?"

"No. Someone else. At this stage I can't tell you anything else, but I promise you as soon as it's safe I'll explain everything. I can't go into details now. George may have seen or done something he shouldn't and gone into hiding. Trust me, I'm going to do everything I can to uncover the truth."

"I trusted George – and now look at me." She wiped her eyes again and put the handkerchief back in her bag. Then she stood up.

Johnny got to his feet as well. "I'm sure he'd get in touch if he could."

Her hazel eyes, now bloodshot, searched his face for clues but found none.

"Thank you for seeing me. PC Turner said if anyone could help, you could."

He was flattered by the recommendation. He wondered how much she had told Matt, and what he'd made of her story. It remained to be seen how he would take the news of Aitken's death.

"Is there somewhere I can call you?" He retrieved his notebook from his pocket.

"We're not allowed to receive calls at work, but there's a telephone in the nurse's home."

"The one in Little Britain? I think I have the number somewhere."

"I bet you do – but this will save you time." She took the pencil and neatly inscribed her name and the number. "I hope to hear from you soon."

He watched her disappear through one of the three sets of double doors. He was not looking forward to the moment when he would have to break the bad news to her.

SEVENTEEN

Monday, 14th December, 7.30 p.m.

"So why was there a bloody knife in your pocket then?" Stella's emerald eyes sparkled with mischief. He could not stop staring into them.

"I'd just killed someone who asked too many questions."

The conversation at the next table in L'Amuse Bouche resumed as the pair of bankers pretended not to be eavesdropping. You needed to be in a Savile Row suit to afford to dine in such an establishment, but Johnny was out to impress. Silver service joints, like this one in Walbrook, made him uncomfortable. Simkins would be right at home here. Johnny grinned when he thought how furious his rival would be when he learned that it was his gift for ventriloquy that had given Johnny his big breakthrough.

"Do you ever give a serious answer?" She dabbed

her full red lips with her napkin before taking another sip of wine.

Daisy preferred to drink Mackeson stout and orange unless champagne was on offer – which it never was with Johnny. She hated foreign food too: "All that oily muck's too fattening." The thought of ramming Matt's photograph down her throat made him smile. Although she did not know it yet, he had a date with Daisy later.

"I'm at my most serious when being playful," said Johnny. "There's no great mystery with the knife. I'd just found it."

"Where?"

"Passing Alley."

"And what were you doing down there at that time of the morning?"

"Looking for a policeman."

"They're never around when you need one."

Johnny leaned forward. Stella did the same. She really was beautiful: almond eyes, slender nose, unusually white teeth. No wonder her father had fixed him with a glare – the kind that meant *keep your hands off!* – when he picked her up.

"My best friend works at Snow Hill. I was waiting till he came on duty so that I could hand it over," said Johnny. "I wanted him to get the credit."

He had called the station to tell Matt about Aitken but had yet to receive a reply to his necessarily cryptic message.

"What's his name?" asked Stella, sitting back and checking automatically that the cameo brooch, borrowed from her mother, was still pinned to her royal blue dress. It showed off her creamy skin to perfection.

"Matt Turner."

"It doesn't ring a bell – which is a good sign. Our family doesn't have too high an opinion of the Snow Hill mob."

"Why's that?"

"They're as bent as you can get." She lowered her voice. "When my father refused to contribute to the local police benevolent fund, he was threatened with the loss of his licence. A week later he was beaten up by a couple of heavies just after closing time. After that he started to pay up. Now one or other of them comes round every Friday to collect – and knock back a double malt."

"Well, I'm sure Matt isn't one of them."

"What's he look like?"

"Tall, blond, massive shoulders. He's a talented boxer, but only violent in the ring. You couldn't wish for a better mate."

"I don't think I've seen him. I'll certainly keep an eye out for him now though." She winked.

"He's married to a wonderful woman called Lizzie." He paused and took a swig of Chablis, larger than intended. It went down the wrong way. Trying to stop the coughing only made it worse. Tears sprang to his eyes. Stella got up and slapped him on the back.

"Better?"

"Yes, thanks." His breathing slowly returned to normal. He wiped his eyes with his napkin.

"The tears usually come after I've said 'no'."

"I don't doubt it." He sighed. "Why aren't you married?"

"Haven't met the right chap – although plenty have asked. Besides, I'm only twenty and don't intend to pull pints for the rest of my life. I'm taking a secretarial course as well. I'd rather be behind a desk than a bar. What about you?"

"Same as you."

"Haven't met the right chap?"

"Ha, ha, ha. Very droll." Johnny tried not to show he was hurt. That damn kiss in the alleyway had raised all sorts of difficult questions – most of which he had no intention of answering.

"It's not true, though, is it?" Stella stared at him. "I know heartbreak when I see it."

"I know you'll break mine if I let you." For a moment they gazed into each other's eyes. Johnny was the first to look away. "You're right. There was someone, but she chose another bloke. I've been on my own since then."

It was not a real lie: he and Daisy had never been together. Their relationship, to dignify it with a word it did not deserve, was a meeting of bodies, not minds.

"You'll get over it," said Stella. "Men always do. You must come across plenty of available girls in your line of work."

"It depends what you mean by available."

"Enjoy your freedom while it lasts. People are so desperate to handcuff themselves to each other. I call it holy padlock." She sighed. "I wish I lived by myself, had only myself to please, had no one to answer to except my conscience."

"It's reassuring to know you have one," said Johnny. "Harry Gogg's killer clearly hasn't. How anyone could do what they did . . . I presume you heard about it – or even read my exclusive report."

"As a matter of fact, I did. Ma showed me the *News* on Friday and said you'd been asking after Harry. The whole market's been talking about nothing else. That's why I asked you about the knife."

"It was used in his murder."

"I thought he'd been found hanging," said Stella.

"He was," said Johnny. "On a meat hook." He added in a whisper: "His crown jewels were in his mouth."

"Ugh!" The bankers turned to look at her as she involuntarily raised her voice. She had another sip of wine. "I was always glad to see him in the Cock. He was a sweet lad, full of juicy gossip – that's why he was so useful to the cops. They would send him into the underground conveniences opposite Bart's, wait a few minutes, call Harry's name and then hammer on the appropriate cubicle door. The culprit would do anything – pay anything – to be let off. Nicking perverts is a useful way of boosting the arrest figures – the same jar of Vaseline has been used as evidence in a hundred cases – but sometimes, just for a laugh, they would chuck a paper bag filled with water into the cubicle. Harry and his client would come out soaking. There was nothing Harry could do. He was terrified of being arrested too."

* * *

Johnny helped Stella into her coat. Her cheeks were still flushed from the alcohol-soaked *crepes suzettes*. As they turned into Bucklersbury she slipped her arm through his.

"Thank you. It was a wonderful meal. I don't get to eat in such places that often."

"I don't believe you," said Johnny.

They turned into Cheapside. The only living creature in view was a skinny stray – a cross between a greyhound and a Dalmatian? It began slowly wagging its tail, in hope rather than expectation. Johnny stopped to stroke it but as soon as it realised that he had nothing on him that it could eat the rejected pet trotted on. Sometimes it seemed the whole world was hungry.

Johnny, with Stella by his side, was walking on air. He was in no way disappointed that the evening was ending with a walk back to Smithfield. He had known that she was not the kind of girl to put out on a first date but had still worn his lucky green tie – surely enough to win him a goodnight kiss. Just the thought of it was enough to warm him.

High above them, the golden dragon atop the steeple of St Mary-Le-Bow, its wings outstretched, swung round to face the freshening northerly.

EIGHTEEN

Tuesday, 15th December, 7.40 a.m.

Just five more minutes. Johnny turned over, revelling in the warmth of his bed, reluctant to brave the glacial bathroom. There were still traces of Daisy's make-up on the other pillow. He must do some laundry at the weekend. Stella would not have been impressed – had she agreed to come home with him.

Although aroused, he had not been stupid enough to ask.

They'd arrived back at the Cock just as her father was booting out the last of the boozers. Stella had pulled him into the shadows and treated him to a long, lingering kiss that took his breath away.

"I've been wanting to do that all evening," she said. Johnny could not believe his ears. She was so out of his league. What did she want? Bill's cynicism was contagious.

"I've been hoping you would all evening. Can I see you again?"

"Of course. Call me." She seemed to find his boyish eagerness endearing. "And let me know what you find out. Sweet dreams."

"All right, love? Have a good time did yer?" Her father's voice was followed by the sound of the door being bolted behind her.

For a moment, Johnny stared at the door. Should he try and pump the publican for information about his beating and Snow Hill? There was no time. Besides, he did not want to get on the wrong side of him – or his daughter. He ran for the last tram to Camden Town.

Daisy's digs were in a dead-end off the High Street. Her landlady, a typical theatrical battle-axe, locked the front door at midnight: *I run a respectable establishment* was the widow's constant refrain. Gentlemen callers, no matter what the time of day, were frowned upon and never, ever, admitted. She liked to think of herself as a mother hen, clucking and caring for her clutch of young actresses and dancers, vulnerable girls at the mercy of hard and unforgiving businessmen. On the one occasion that he had met her – seeing Daisy home after another expensive date – Johnny could tell Mrs Osgood was nothing of the sort. She was simply a money-grubbing old cow.

He stared up at the narrow terraced house. Its soot-encrusted stucco gave it the appearance of a mouldy wedding cake. The hall-light was on but the rest of the building was in darkness. Johnny quickly and quietly went down the area steps and stood against the basement door. He would not have long to wait.

The cold soon seeped through the soles of his shoes and into his bones. Fighting the urge to light a cigarette – it might give him away – Johnny strained his ears. A whistle shrieked as the last sleeper train of the night from Euston began the long, slow climb north.

The short cul-de-sac was lit by a single gas-light fixed to the wall at the end of the street. A pair of boots suddenly appeared through the area railings. Johnny looked up. They belonged to a policeman.

"Get yourself up here now." Johnny had no choice. Feeling foolish, he joined the cop on the pavement.

"Good evening, officer."

"Name?" The fresh-faced constable – who looked about the same age as he was – shone a red torch into his eyes.

"John Steadman."

"Done this kind of thing before?"

"What kind of thing? I was waiting for my girlfriend."

"Peeping Toms always say that."

Johnny bridled. "What exactly am I supposed to have been peeping at? I was facing the street, not the window – which, if you care to look, is shuttered."

"I don't like your tone," said the man from the Met, producing a notebook from his greatcoat. "You were acting suspiciously. Give me one good reason why I shouldn't arrest you."

Johnny could feel his temper rising with his heart

rate. He had to stay calm. The last thing he needed was for Daisy to find him in this position. A face appeared at a first-floor window.

"I beg your pardon. No offence intended. Honestly, I was doing nothing wrong. I'm a journalist." He handed over his press card. This was a risky move. Most coppers distrusted reporters. "My best friend is a City cop."

"Where's he stationed?"

"Snow Hill." Both men turned at the sound of footsteps. Johnny's armpits began to prickle. So much for ambushing the minx.

"What are you doing here?"

Johnny could see she had been drinking. Her powdered cheeks were flushed and her kohl-rimmed eyes were shining. However, the expected barrage of insults did not come. Daisy looked scared rather than angry. Of course: she thought that he and the cop were waiting for her! After all, she had stolen something from him.

"Waiting for you. What else?" He gave her a kiss on the cheek. Fortunately, she did not shove him away. If she had screamed *Get off me you pervert*, or words to that effect, he would have been in real trouble.

"Do you know this man?" The PC stepped towards them.

Johnny, seizing his chance, put his arm round Daisy's waist as if to reassure her. When she glanced at him in alarm he winked. He was beginning to enjoy the situation.

"Yes, yes, I do," said Daisy, trying unsuccessfully to keep the quaver out of her voice.

"What's his name?"

"Johnny Steadman."

"He says you're his girlfriend. Is that true?"

She looked at Johnny, confusion and fear flitting across her face. He smiled encouragingly.

"Yes, officer. I am."

"Very well then. I'll leave you two alone." He handed back the press card to Johnny. "Careful how you go." He held Johnny's gaze for a moment too long – as if to say *you don't fool me* – and resumed his beat. They watched him in silence until he turned into the High Street.

"What the hell are you doing here?" She shoved off his arm.

"I need it back."

"What?"

"Don't play the innocent with me. Or are you saying you stole more than one item?"

She sneered at him.

"Couldn't face me by yourself? Needed a big man to hold your hand? I told you to stay away from me."

"I could have had you arrested."

"Oh, yeah? What for?" She had thought it through now. "If your friend in blue had found anything, you'd have been arrested for possessing indecent material. I'd have said it was yours – which it is. You could have left it in my room to frame me."

"Except men aren't allowed in this flop-house, are they?" He was beginning to lose his temper. The explosive combination of alcohol and tiredness was taking its toll. "Don't try to out-think me. You're just a pretty face. Give me the photograph and I'll be gone."

"What's going on?" The landlady, wrapped in a thick woollen dressing gown, stood on the top step, light – but not heat – streaming out behind her. Her head, covered in curlers, looked like a frightened hedgehog.

"Nothing, Mrs Osgood. I won't be long," said Daisy.

"I should hope not. Two minutes and this door will be bolted." She went back inside.

Daisy made as if to follow. Johnny grabbed her arm.

"Let go of me, you little queer. I haven't got your precious photograph."

"Where is it?"

"I burned it. I was afraid she'd find it." Daisy nodded towards the doorway, which, instead of causing her spirits to sink as usual, now held out the promise of safety.

"You had no right! It didn't belong to me. I was looking after it for someone."

"Who? Your boyfriend?"

Church bells began to chime the end of the day. If the front door of number six had not opened again he would have slapped her. Daisy ran up the steps. Mrs Osgood, choosing not to say good night, merely sniffed in his direction and shut the door. He heard the key turn in the lock and the bolts slide into their brackets. There was nothing more he could do. He had a long walk ahead of him.

* * *

As Johnny trudged back to Islington, Daisy sat on her single unmade bed with its stained and sagging mattress.

She had not burned the photograph.

The naked man in the foreground was a real dreamboat. She had recognised him straightaway. She had danced with him once, while Johnny was mooning over his wife.

It had taken a while for her to remember the woman's name, but she knew where she lived, if not the number of the house: Devonia Street, round the corner from Johnny's place. She was sure the GPO would have little difficulty in ascertaining the full address.

It was about time Lizzie Turner got to know Matt and Johnny's dirty secret.

His fury had worn off by the time he closed the front door of his cold, dark house.

He was not queer. He did not care what Daisy thought – he would never see the hard-nosed floozie again if he could help it – but the idea that anybody could think he was unsettled him.

It was at times like this that he missed his mother most – not that he could have discussed such a subject with her. Having lost a father he had hardly known, it was inevitable that he had become closer, perhaps too close, to his remaining parent. Stella did not realise how fortunate she was to be the centre of a loving family.

Worse than losing the one piece of evidence that Matt was being blackmailed was the knowledge that he had accidentally betrayed his friend's trust. And there was no one he could talk to: Matt was the only one he could share such secrets with.

It seemed his head had barely hit the pillow when he was awoken by the sound of someone hammering on the door.

Whoever it was kept on hammering until Johnny had pulled on his dressing gown, hurried down the stairs – who the hell could it be at this unsocial hour? – and opened it.

"Matt!"

He did not wait to be invited in.

"You idle so-and-so. Glad to see you're taking things easy while on special assignment. It's good to know that someone's sleeping well."

"I had a late night," said Johnny, judging from the thunderous look on Matt's face that now was not the moment to tell him about Stella. "Still having nightmares?" Matt nodded. "Let me find my slippers and I'll make us some tea. As it happens, I was going to come and see you today. I've loads to tell you."

"Save your breath," said Matt. "I've just received another picture – posted to Devonia Street."

Once he had filled the kettle and left the lit oven open to warm the kitchen, Johnny sat down at the table opposite his seething friend.

"Let's see it then."

"No," said Matt. "There was a message on the back: *Tell your friend to stop sticking his nose where it's not wanted – or Lizzie gets the next one.*"

"It's just as well she's not the sort of wife who opens her husband's letters," said Johnny.

"Well, I wouldn't open anything addressed to her," said Matt. "Besides, she'd get in a right tizzy if I did."

"True." Johnny stifled a yawn. "You realise this proves I must be getting somewhere."

"For fuck's sake!" Matt thumped the table. "Will you pay attention: you've got to stop digging around."

For a moment Johnny thought he was going to thump him as well. He forced his sleepy brain into action. He had to tell Matt what he'd learned, but there was no need yet to say who from. He was sure the terrified Percy was holding something back, and he knew he'd never get it out of him if the police started asking questions.

"Matt, I'm convinced a cop has been killed. You haven't seen George Aitken – only spoken to someone impersonating him. And guess who took the body to Bart's with Gogg: your mate Vinson."

A look of confusion crossed Matt's face – there was no doubt Johnny had managed to surprise him – but he refused to be distracted.

"That's as maybe," said Matt. "Nevertheless, you have got to stop snooping round the station."

"Why send Lilian Voss to see me then?"

"Ah. She's already been to see you, has she?"

"Yesterday evening. She's at her wit's end. No one at Snow Hill will tell her where George Aitken is, and it can't be a coincidence that the original tip-off came from there."

"How d'you know?"

Matt, scrubbed and in uniform, studied him. Johnny, hair tousled and with sleep still in his eyes, felt self-consciously grubby.

"I spoke to the messenger boy who collected it from the desk sergeant last Monday. He just happens to be a part-time whore who works at Zick's place – as did Harry Gogg."

Matt seemed uninterested in these revelations. Had he known all this already? Johnny got up to fill the teapot.

"I hadn't received this new picture when I saw Miss Voss. It changes everything. Perhaps it was sent because I spoke to her." He scratched the side of his head – a sure sign that he was agitated. "Promise me you'll kill the story. It's not just my career on the line."

"What d'you mean?"

"We have a prime suspect for Gogg's murder. He was seen leaving the cold-store in Green Hill's Rents on the night in question. And the same person was seen in and around Smithfield asking after Gogg the previous day. He left his hat behind. We have the murder weapon – a butcher's knife . . ."

"Which I gave to you!" said Johnny.

"Precisely," said Matt. His sky-blue eyes blazed in triumph. "So whose fingerprints, the only set of prints, d'you think we found on it? So far the owner of them has not been identified."

Johnny sat down. "You wouldn't. You'd actually see me hanged? No, you're bluffing."

"Try me," said Matt.

Johnny could not believe his ears.

"But I didn't do it! You know that! D'you want the real killer – or killers – to go free?"

"I don't care. Nothing we do can bring Harry back. Besides, I'm not going to lose Lizzie just because of some cocksucker."

"She'd understand," said Johnny. "She knows you're not a pervert."

"She would not. Put yourself in her place," said Matt. "She'd never be able to get the images out of her head. I can't get them out of *my* head. She'd never trust me again. Every time we went to bed, every time we . . . Whoever's sending the pictures could destroy my marriage, destroy my job and destroy me – but I'm not going to let them." He wiped away a tear angrily. "Promise me."

Johnny could see that Matt was right: in one way. Despite all that he had been through, despite all his efforts that were just beginning to bear fruit, their friendship was not worth the story, no matter how big it might turn out to be. Matt must be truly desperate if he was prepared to frame him.

Misinterpreting his silence as refusal, Matt said, "If you won't do it for me, then do it for Lizzie. She's pregnant again."

"Okay, okay," said Johnny. "Congratulations. I was going to say yes anyway. You saved my life last Friday. How could I refuse?"

Matt did not bother to look relieved.

"You knew, didn't you, Johnny?"

"About what?"

"Don't play dumb with me. The baby!"

Johnny had a glimpse of how terrifying Matt would one day be in the interview room.

"No, I didn't." Johnny swallowed nervously. This was not the way he had imagined the day would be. Instead of impressing Matt with his findings, he was in danger of finding his head in a noose. "Sorry if my congratulations sounded insincere. I was just thinking of myself, as usual. I suppose I'll have to go back to the Old Bailey, unfêted and unpromoted."

"There'll be other stories," said Matt, suddenly mollified. "I'll keep my ears open."

A heavy silence descended on the table. Johnny could hear Matt's breathing slowly returning to a more normal rate. His own heart was still thudding in his chest.

"Why don't you get the first photo while I pour the tea?" said Matt eventually.

Johnny, mentally cursing Daisy once again, struggled to hide his dismay. He dare not tell the truth – in his current state of mind Matt might really hit him – but the trick about lying was to stick as close to it as possible.

"It's not here."

"I assume you're having me on."

"It's at the office. I thought it was safer locked in my desk there than lying around here."

Matt observed him for a moment then a half-smile formed on his lips.

"Sure you're not just keeping it to wank over?"

"Why would I do that when I could have the real thing?"

They stared at each other in silence then burst out laughing and, having started, found it hard to stop. The tension in the room finally evaporated.

"So," said Johnny, wiping his eyes, "who's going to be the godfather?"

NINETEEN

Tuesday, 15th December, 5.40 p.m.
"Don't tell Matt you've seen me," said Johnny, attempting, unsuccessfully, to keep out of the way of the stream of shoppers who had popped into Gamage's on their way home. Lizzie, armed with a perfume bottle as usual, shot him an angry glance. If he was hoping for her blessing as he went behind her husband's back, he was going to be disappointed. It was her fault for asking him for help in the first place. And yet, and yet . . . if anyone could get to the bottom of Matt's problems it was Johnny. Only she knew Matt better.

"As if I would. He's got enough on his plate without fearing that he can't trust his friends."

"That's not fair. I never actually promised that I would drop the case," said Johnny. "I agreed to stop snooping around Snow Hill. I'm trying to help."

"Well, he's under the impression that you did drop it."

Lizzie stepped into the path of a highly coiffured, smartly dressed woman. A tyrant of the typing pool was Johnny's guess.

"Would madam care to sample Summer Meadow?"

The matron pulled back the arm of her coat to bare her wrist, sniffed delicately at the dab of scent – "Very floral, I must say!" – and kept on going.

Lizzie sighed. "My feet are killing me – and you're bad for business."

Johnny watched her black bob swaying as she scanned the aisle for prospective customers. It was the men who slowed down, not the women.

"Have you ever met someone called Tom Vinson? He works with Matt."

"No, I can't say I have. Matt's mentioned him though. If they're on the same shift they often have a drink together after work. Why d'you ask?"

"His name came up. That's all." The less Lizzie knew the better. "Did Matt tell you why he wanted me to stop?" Johnny chose his words carefully: he was on dangerous ground. He must not provoke any further disapproval. Why had the second photograph had so much more effect than the first? Was it just the threat to tell Lizzie, or something in the photograph itself?

"Of course. Why d'you ask?" Lizzie looked at him quizzically. "Are you suggesting he was lying?"

"Not at all. It's just that he said it was hush-hush and I know he'd never jeopardise an ongoing investigation by revealing operational details."

"Precisely. The fact that the internal affairs squad are involved shows they are taking the boy's death seriously."

Johnny presumed she meant Harry Gogg, not George Aitken – who would be the real reason for the rubber heelers to interfere. All transfers had to have the written consent of the Commissioner. Why would he agree to transfer a dead man? So, it was likely Lizzie did not know about Aitken or the incriminating photographs. Good. It was time to placate her.

"You've told him about the baby then?"

"I thought it might cheer him up. Of course the first thing he said was that I should stop work – and at times like this I feel as though I might as well. Anyway, as soon as the baby begins to show I'll be shunted off to the stockroom or the zoological department – the ideal place for a brood mare."

Johnny laughed. "Okay. I'll leave you to it. Just remember I want Matt's nightmares to end as much as you do."

"You don't have to sleep with him." Lizzie smiled thinly. "Be careful. You know what Matt's like when he doesn't get his own way."

"A mule and a brood mare: what a pair!" Matt's obstinacy and tenacity stood him in good stead in the ring. "See you soon."

He could not kiss her goodbye here. As he made his way out of the huge department store, Johnny imagined it a microcosm of the capital itself. Like London it had started small – a shop with a five-foot frontage in High Holborn – and grown piecemeal by slowly absorbing its surroundings. Now the place was a maze of showrooms connected by passageways, ramps and steps. It contained everything under the sun – but finding what you wanted was something of an art. The motto of the founder, A.W. Gamage, could still be read above the main entrance: *Tall Oaks from Little Acorns Grow.*

Lizzie watched him weaving through the tide of shoppers, his shoulders hunched in determination.

Should she have told him?

She could not get the sickening photograph out of her mind. Who had sent it? Why address it to her? Was it some kind of twisted joke?

There was no doubt that it was her husband yet, at the same time, she was sure that it must have been taken against his will. But how? She could not imagine the circumstances. Matt had no interest in other men's bodies. He worshipped her body with an ardour and tenderness that could not be feigned.

She was skewered on the horns of a dilemma. The events caught on camera must be the cause of Matt's nightmares. Did he know what had happened and was keeping silent to protect her? Or was he suffering in ignorance? Would telling him only serve to increase his torment?

Johnny would have known what to do. He would never sacrifice their friendship for the sake of a story. He had a heart of gold.

Somehow she had to preserve Matt's dignity and the only way she could do that was to pretend she had never received the disgusting thing. That did not mean she would give up trying to think of a way to find the culprits.

Perhaps Inspector Rotherforth could help – in the strictest confidence, of course. He was someone she could trust, he appeared to have a high opinion of Matt, and Matt looked up to him.

But would Matt thank her for interfering?

It was too risky to take the most direct route to the Urania Bookshop – across Holborn Viaduct, past the end of Snow Hill and along Newgate Street – because he might bump into Matt.

Instead, jostled by the tide of careless commuters, their black umbrellas a forest of mushrooms, Johnny approached Amen Corner from Ave Maria Lane rather than Warwick Lane. St Paul's, its dome slick with rain, loomed in the gloom.

He had spent the day torn between conscience and desire. It was true that he had led Matt to believe that he would drop his investigations. However, although he wanted to protect him and Lizzie, he also wanted to nail the killers of Harry Gogg and George Aitken.

He wished he knew which story the sender of the pictures was so anxious to spike – perhaps it was both. It seemed increasingly likely that the two murders were part of the same case.

Where was the harm in finding out more about them? Such research certainly fell under his remit for the series on the life of a City cop. Maybe he was blinded by ambition – but the figure of Justice that presided over the Central Criminal Court was blindfolded too.

Johnny could fully understand why Matt had decided

to shirk his professional responsibilities: he had personal ones too, and Lizzie was more important than any job. But the fact that his friend was being blackmailed only made it all the more vital that Johnny did his duty and exposed the evil-doers. They had to be stopped. The fact that doing so would make a great story was merely a bonus . . .

Somehow he would find a way to keep Matt's name out of it.

He turned into Amen Corner and ducked beneath the entrance to Stationers Court to get out of the rain. The shop was directly opposite. Its lights were still on, the last few Greek lovers choosing their entertainment for the evening. Johnny lit a cigarette and waited. A customer emerged, looking anxiously round him before heading quickly for the anonymity of the crowds in Warwick Lane. A few minutes later a second man came out with his collar up and his hat tilted at an angle to conceal his eyes; he too wasted no time in leaving the vicinity.

It was almost six o'clock when the door opened a third time. Bill Fox came out.

Johnny stepped back into the shadows. What the hell was Bill doing here? Surely he was not one of them? He was a widower! It was far more likely that he was trying to steal Johnny's story. But why? He had never done anything like that before.

Matt would go mad if he heard that yet another journalist was sniffing around. And what about Simkins? Neither of them knew about the naked photographs though.

Church bells across the City began tolling the hour. Johnny sprang into action. He crossed the road and managed to get the door ajar before Harry's boyfriend blocked his way.

"Sorry, we're closed." To emphasise the point he turned the sign hanging in front of the blind around. Johnny stuck his foot in the gap. Stalemate.

"Remember me?" Johnny pushed.

The shop assistant pushed back.

"Fuck off! I've got nothing more to say to you." His blood-shot eyes were full of anger and pain.

"Don't you want to know who killed Harry?"

Johnny pushed again – and almost fell into the shop as the boy stood back. The door was locked behind him.

"Men are always falling for me," said the boy with a laugh. Johnny, trying to regain his dignity, realised he did not even know what the boy was called.

"What's your name?"

"Joseph Moss – but everyone calls me Jo."

"Well, Jo. I need your help. Harry, as you're no doubt aware, was forced to work for the cops, helping to snare sad souls like your customers. He was an informer too. There must have been lots of men who wished him ill, but can you think of anyone in particular who would want to shut him up for good?"

"Harry had no choice. He hated tricking folk like us."

"Like *us*? I'm not queer."

"If you say so. I meant meself and Harry."

"I'm sorry." He really must stop being so defensive. People would think he was protesting too much. "Go on."

"Not last Sunday but the Sunday before, Harry didn't come home. We lived together, upstairs." The simple statement was said with pride – and defiance. "He said he'd had to do a job for the cops and gone straight to work afterwards. He started at four."

"On a Sunday? The market's closed. Did he say what he'd been doing?"

"No. He was scared. He said it was better for me if I didn't know. Ignorance being bliss and all that. He always looked out for me."

Johnny was afraid the boy would start crying again.

"Well, I can enlighten you. He helped take the body of a dead cop to Bart's."

Jo gasped.

"He wasn't a killer!"

"Of course not. I don't think he knew that the cop had been murdered. He might not have even known that the body was that of a cop. However, he was with another cop called Tom Vinson. Have you heard of him?"

"Yes. Harry said he was a good egg. Never clipped him round the ear or demanded a free gobble – unlike the others."

"Do you get much hassle from the cops?"

"Only if we don't pay up on time. They call it insurance. Ha! Protection money, more like. Even so, the owner is prosecuted from time to time – to protect the reputation of the cops." He laughed at the irony. "Glad it's not my lolly."

"Who collects the cash?"

"I'm not that stupid. I don't want to die like Harry."

"How d'you know they're not responsible for his death?"

"Why would they kill someone so useful to them? It don't make sense."

"Maybe." He had some serious thinking to do. "Has anyone been round asking questions since Harry died?"

"Only you. Why would anyone ask me? Only the cops know about me and Harry."

"Remember the photograph I showed you?"

"How could I forget?"

He searched Johnny's face for a clue to what was coming next.

"Have you got any more of the same man?" He needed the evidence.

"Sold out." Very convenient.

"How about that bloke who was in just before me – have you seen him before?"

"Course. He's a regular."

Johnny was shocked. How could he have worked with Bill for so long and not suspected anything? Naturally he understood why Bill had not told him, but what else had he kept from him? Perhaps Joseph was lying again.

Mistaking his silence for disappointment, the boy said, "If you're normal, why are you so interested in the big, blond guy? I've returned the negatives to the photographer, but he's probably still got them . . ."

Before Johnny could reply there was a knock on the door. A flash of panic flitted across the boy's face.

"Quick! In here." He led Johnny round the counter

and into the room behind it. "Keep quiet if you know what's good for you."

Johnny pressed his ear to the door but could only hear low murmurs. Then a door creaked at the far side of the shop and heavy footsteps climbed the stairs. He followed their progress as they crossed the ceiling above him.

When he tried to open the door of the stockroom he found it locked. The only window was barred. He was trapped.

A few minutes later the voices suddenly got louder. Joseph was shouting. Johnny was sure he heard his own name. The newcomer's voice was much deeper. A sudden thump – that made the bare bulb above him sway – startled him. An eerie silence descended. The hairs on the back of Johnny's neck stood up. He turned out the light.

Something was dragged across the ceiling. Johnny waited. He could probably break his way out – but he didn't want to make any noise until he was sure the man had gone. Whoever it was could be heard coming down the stairs now. Johnny held his breath until the ring of the shop-bell was followed by the sound of the door closing quietly. Was it a trick?

He listened for movement from upstairs but there was nothing. What was Jo playing at? The ominous silence continued. Then he smelled smoke.

He smashed the lock with a heavy, newfangled, adhesive tape dispenser and wrenched open the door. The shop was in darkness. An orange glow outlined the door to the stairs. Johnny opened it and ran up them. Jo lay on the first-floor landing. Blood was oozing from a gaping head wound – but that was not what had killed him. A piece of knotted garden twine encircled his neck and bit deep into the skin.

Knowing it was futile, Johnny nevertheless checked for a pulse.

From where he knelt he could see along the landing to a living room at the front of the building. A paraffin heater had been overturned on a rug. An old armchair was already ablaze, tongues of flame licking the flimsy curtains. Seconds later, they were alight. Smoke came billowing towards him.

Johnny got to his feet. The kitchen was unoccupied but, entering the room, he immediately saw that the oven door was wide open. The bastard had left the gas on but not lit it. Johnny ran over and turned it off. He opened the window; it overlooked a grim light-well. A pigeon fluttered its wings in panic. Johnny could see no way out from here.

As he turned to flee he heard someone – it sounded like a man – coughing. It came from what was presumably a bedroom next door to the living room, which was now – fed by the inrush of cold air – a multi-coloured inferno.

He almost made it. However, as he got his hand on the door-knob, a flashover blew him off his feet and, with a roar, sent him hurtling back along the landing. There was a scream as the ceiling came down and the floor where he had been standing collapsed.

The stairs leading to the ground floor were now blocked with fallen masonry and burning wood. Instead of going down, he would have to go up.

The air was slightly clearer in the attic – which seemed to have been converted into a makeshift cinema. A magic lantern faced a small, portable screen which stood in front of the bare-brick chimney breast. An aisle bisected four rows of six bentwood chairs. There was no skylight. He would have to smash his way through the roof. Smoke came snaking up through the floorboards.

Johnny coughed so much he threw up, the stench of his vomit on the hot floor making him retch. The screen was his only weapon. It rolled up into a metal canister which he could use as a battering ram. He aimed it at the unplastered slope and, with all his strength, slammed it into the tiles. They hardly cracked. He tried again and again, his energy draining away, only adrenalin keeping him going. At any moment he expected the whole house to explode.

Finally, the impromptu torpedo broke through, producing a hole about six inches in diameter. The smoke poured out through it.

Widening the hole was comparatively easy, although there was so much smoke he could hardly see what he was doing. He switched to using his hands to pull the slates apart, wincing as his healing skin was ripped apart once more.

One minute later, as he was wriggling through the hole, the floor of the attic dropped away, the projector and chairs plummeting past the charring corpse of Joseph, and landing in the shop below.

The nude statues remained aloof, maintaining their poses, their sightless eyes unaffected by the smoke.

A great night's work: two for the price of one.

Moss sealed his own fate when he spoke to Steadman again. I think he was beginning to suspect I'd killed his fellow sodomite anyway. Soon as he heard about Gogg delivering a dead cop to Bart's it must have confirmed all his suspicions. He was quite a bright boy, Jo; knew how to make himself useful. Shame he had to die, really.

Perhaps he and Gogg will now be running across the burning sands together in the seventh circle of hell.

Steadman will never know who killed him. He had enough warnings, but the silly bugger just couldn't take a hint. Persistent as he was, he'd have got to the bottom of things in the end.

The others won't be too happy when they learn about the bookshop. I'll soon put them right, explain what's at stake. It won't take long to find new premises.

In the meantime, there's still the bordello. It brings

in far more money anyway. The real thing is so much more exciting than pictures.

That just leaves Turner to keep an eye on now. The second picture seems to have done the trick.

Let's just hope Steadman didn't confide in anyone else – for their sake.

TWENTY

The roof was treacherous, the earlier rain having frozen. Johnny, wheezing from the smoke, scrambled up the slippery slope till he could sit astride the apex. Flames were already flickering out of the hole he had made. The frost was melting rapidly. He worked his way along the ridge then, holding on to the chimney stack, moved round on to the neighbouring property.

When he reached Warwick Lane the roof-line changed. Each roof was now V-shaped with a gutter running down the middle, so he had to scrabble up one side and slide down the other. It was not until he came to Warwick Square that he discovered a flat roof with an iron ladder leading down to a fire escape.

The dome of the Old Bailey came into view. The distant bells of a fire engine grew louder.

He gave a prayer of thanks as his feet touched the ground. His legs were shaking, but Johnny forced himself to continue. There was only one way out of the square. He crossed Warwick Lane as the engine sped past and hurried down White Hart Street into Paternoster Square. He took the southern exit by the library into Paternoster Row and went into the Bookbinders' Arms on the corner of Paul's Alley. When the publican saw his soot-smeared face he refused the proffered shilling and let him use the telephone for nothing. The drinkers lowered their glasses and voices, keen not to miss any potential excitement.

There was only one person he could call: his editor.

Johnny had enough wit left not to mention his name. He virtually whispered into the receiver. His throat was painfully parched from the toxic fumes he had inhaled.

"This could be a blessing in disguise," said Stone. "If you're supposed to be dead then we must somehow convince the world that really is the case. Don't go home. Come to my humble abode."

He gave Johnny the address and told him to hail a cab. Johnny was intrigued by the idea of playing dead.

After all, he was accustomed to being under six feet.

Victor Stone lived in Bedford Gardens off Kensington Church Street. There was nothing humble about it. The five-storey stuccoed terrace gleamed white in the crescent moonlight. His wife Honoria tended to Johnny's wounds – *We have been in the wars, haven't we?* – while her husband interrogated him.

"So we now have four dead bodies: Harry Gogg;

Joseph Moss, the boy who lived with him; George Aitken, the young copper; and the unknown person in the shop."

"And it could so easily have been five," said Johnny. "I'm sure I was meant to die as well. Whoever it was probably locked me in the freezer the night Harry died as well."

"And your evidence?"

"I haven't got any." Johnny coughed out of embarrassment then necessity. "All I do know is that the man who took Aitken's body to Bart's with Harry is a policeman called Tom Vinson. He works at Snow Hill. However, the morgue attendant who identified him would be very reluctant to confirm this officially. I also found out that Harry was a male prostitute and police informer who worked at the same brothel in Honey Lane as the boy who collected the first tip-off from Snow Hill and delivered it to me."

"Nobody's likely to spill the beans while the killer – or killers – are still on the loose. It's all hearsay," said Stone. He sounded unimpressed. "You can't accuse Vinson of anything without proof." He paced up and down, thinking out loud: "The unknown man in the shop is intriguing and could prove to be a godsend. Moss's killer may have been unaware of his presence, just as you were. If you're right about his intention to kill you, he'll be expecting two bodies to be found in the wreckage. That could work to our advantage – and it would be much easier to maintain the illusion of your death."

* * *

When Johnny eventually came down to breakfast the next morning – his boss had left for the office hours before – he found an article in the *Daily Chronicle* ringed in red on the table:

> Two people are suspected to have died in a fire that completely gutted a bookshop in Amen Corner last night. The City of London police named the first victim as Joseph Moss, who worked in the shop, and the second as John Steadman, a journalist thought to be investigating the recent murder of Harold Gogg, a friend of Moss who worked at Smithfield market. The cause of the fire has yet to be established. The blaze was so fierce that fire officers are still searching for remains of the bodies.

The byline read Henry Simkins. Once again he was unwittingly doing Johnny a favour. But how had he got hold of the story so quickly? And how did the police know that he was in the shop last night?

Simkins must have been following him. He'd been lying in wait outside Zick's, so perhaps he'd been in Amen Corner too. Perhaps he had raised the alarm. If Simkins had been tailing him, then he must have seen the killer leave the shop.

Johnny, much to his sudden frustration, realised that a dead man could hardly demand answers from Simkins. It was going to be harder than he had originally thought.

Stone had told him to keep a low profile, which meant that he was in effect under house arrest. The events of the past few days had taken their toll – the inside of his lungs felt as if they had been sandpapered – so Johnny was content to lie around on a sofa and avail himself of Stone's extensive library.

The palatial residence was more like a luxury hotel. Its staff had been told that a nephew had come to stay. However, Johnny found it hard to concentrate on anything other than the killings. Three men – four, if Aitken were included – had been murdered. The injustice of it made his blood boil and – much to his surprise – the fact that Harry and Jo had been lovers made it feel all the more tragic.

Honoria took great delight in dyeing his hair and eyebrows black. This was only the first stage in a transformation that called on all the expertise she had gained in amateur theatricals. A false Roman nose – made out of thin rubber and stuck on with gum Arabic – totally changed the shape of his face. Lifts in his shoes gave him a couple more inches in height.

"There!" said Honoria, pleased with her efforts. "The next time you set foot outside, that's who you'll be."

It was a bizarre feeling, looking at his new self in the mirror. The stranger staring back was and, at the same time was not, him. It highlighted how much his ginger hair formed part of his identity. Darker hair made him seem older and more serious – or maybe it was just the events of the past week. Whatever the cause, no one was likely to recognise him.

However, wearing the pancake used to disguise the prosthesis made him doubly uncomfortable: it was hot under the extra layer and, more importantly, only women (and pantomime dames) wore make-up. Honoria assured him that it was virtually invisible then produced a bottle of surgical spirit to remove the glue.

His new look added to his sense of dislocation: as far as he was concerned he might as well have been abroad. West London was a different world to Islington and the City. The air was clearer and the wide streets were cleaner. It was where the other half lived. Watching life going on as usual through the huge sash windows, Johnny relished the fact that it was a scene that he had not been meant to see.

Stone returned home with the final editions of all the newspapers and a copy of the premature obituary that would appear in the next day's *News*. Johnny was delighted to see that it painted a flattering portrait of a dedicated journalist whose promising career had been cut tragically short.

"Thank you, sir. I hope I can live up to such a death notice!"

"So do I," said Stone. "Consider yourself honoured: I wrote the piece myself."

The fatal fire filled many column inches. Simkins had followed up his earlier report with an exclusive which claimed that a suicide note had been found on the grave of Harry Gogg along with a red rose. Johnny read it in disbelief:

I am sorry. I loved Harry more than anything in the world but I could not stand his unfaithfulness any more. When he said that he was leaving me I snapped: if I could not have him then no one could. I killed him – and I killed John Steadman when he accused me of doing so. I realised then that sooner or later I would be arrested. It is better this way. I deserve to drown in hell-fire. Forgive me.
Joseph Moss

The police declared the case of Harry Gogg's murder closed and confirmed that they were not looking for anyone else in connection with Mr Steadman's death.

Simkins, in an apparently affectionate tribute to his fellow reporter and "friend", still managed to sling a little dirt by implying that it was not the first time that Johnny had visited the pornographic bookshop. How could he have known that if he hadn't been following him?

"This is all nonsense," said Johnny. "The killer must have written the note, but the scenario it suggests is incredible."

"I agree," said Stone. "Moss is hardly likely to have killed you, written the note, then visited his lover's grave one last time before returning home to set fire to himself and the shop."

"And how did Simkins find the note? He must have been tipped off by the killer – or the police. He must be in cahoots with one or the other. Unless, unless . . . they are one and the same."

Stone looked at him with amusement.

"That is the conclusion I've come to – which is why I've told Bill Fox to continue investigating the circumstances surrounding your death. He's not at all convinced that Moss was responsible for the blaze. He's most distressed by it."

"I bet he is," said Johnny wryly. Where would he obtain his one-handed reading now?

"What's that?" His superior's eyes bore into him. "Is there something I should know?"

"Not at all, sir. I . . ." He shut up. Whatever he said would only complicate matters.

Bill, despite appearances, might be entirely innocent.

"You better not be keeping anything back, Steadman. I've gone out on a limb for you. It's a very serious business deliberately misleading our readers – their trust, once broken, can never be regained." His voice softened: "Fox thinks the world of you. It would have looked suspicious – and heartless – to refuse his request. Our competitors are showing an unhealthy interest in the case, so it's only right that we should continue to report on any developments. It would look odd if we were seen to be doing nothing. The fact that you are still alive gives us the edge, though." He fixed Johnny with his penetrating eyes. "I know you're not happy about sharing your story but just think of Fox as, ahem, a smoke-screen. He doesn't know that someone else died in your place. You need to concentrate on finding out who it was, as well as the identity of the killer."

Johnny was ashamed that he had failed to save the

man's life. It must have been terrifying: crushed by falling debris, waiting for the flames to consume him. He would have been a vital witness. But what was he doing in the flat above the bookshop? And why had no one reported him missing? It was yet another mystery.

The next day, Thursday, 17th December, in a rare – if not downright suspicious – example of bureaucratic efficiency, the City of London coroner was informed that the remains of two men had been retrieved from Amen Corner.

The pathologist's report stated that asphyxiation due to smoke inhalation was the likeliest cause of death but, due to the lack of evidence – namely a couple of charred incomplete skeletons – this could only be an educated guess. As the police had only the note purported to have been written by Joseph Moss to go on, an open verdict rather than one of murder/suicide was duly recorded. The next of kin were informed.

Stone quickly made the necessary arrangements.

His funeral took place on Friday, 18th December. It was too dangerous for him to attend the service in St Bride's, the journalists' church in Fleet Street, so instead he had to make do with taking the Tube to East Finchley for his funeral.

As he walked up the hill to St Pancras & Islington Cemetery, marble headstones, moss-covered memorials and tilting obelisks stretched as far as the eye could see. So many people lay mouldering underground – including his mother. If he had really been dead then he would have been interred with her, but Johnny had been adamant that her grave not be disturbed. Stone had understood and arranged for his reporter to be buried in a new plot near Coldfall Wood.

Johnny had wanted to place some flowers on his mother's grave but was afraid that the gesture would give the game away. He was the only person who ever did so.

He wandered round the vast necropolis, the lifts in his shoes promising blisters. On the other side of the bone-yard another body was being laid to rest in Strawberry Vale. This funeral was a swanky affair. The glass-sided hearse, now empty, rolled forward as the horses that pulled it, each with its own plume of black ostrich feathers, shifted in the cold. The crowd of mourners, mumbling to each other, slowly got back into the waiting cortège of motor cars.

As midday approached Johnny took up his position behind a huge angel, its muscular arms extended in prayer. It began to snow as his hearse, a mere black van, and a couple of taxicabs trundled down the hill-side. His heart, as if to remind him that he was still alive, started to thump.

Victor Stone, Bill Fox and Henry Simkins emerged from the first cab; a priest and Lizzie and Matt from the second. Johnny was disappointed at the turnout. He had been hoping that Stella might come. Then again, they had only been on one date. Daisy, even if she were aware of his demise, would certainly not trouble herself

– unless she was in a mood to dance on his grave. As for Simkins, he was surely here out of curiosity rather than grief: not weeping but snooping.

The snow fell more heavily, an icy wind sending it in flurries round the headstones. His coffin – containing all that remained of the unknown man – was lowered into the hole. Johnny shivered: whether he liked it or not, this was a glimpse of his future. He felt a stab of guilt as Lizzie began to cry. However, it was mixed with gratification. She did care for him after all.

Matt, haggard yet handsome, put his arm round her and held her close. Johnny hoped he was not blaming himself for the death. Probably not: he had told Johnny to stop poking around. In his eyes he had probably dug his own grave.

The priest, hardly masking his boredom and eagerness to get back into the warmth, intoned a prayer as the five mourners each threw a handful of earth on to the cheap pine box. Johnny could not complain: Stone had promised to meet all his expenses thus far.

They had hardly turned away before a couple of gravediggers took up their shovels and started to fill in the hole. The snow soon covered their bending backs. To Johnny, staying put as the blizzard descended, they looked like a pair of statues coming to life.

Ten minutes later the job was finished. The two men lit fresh cigarettes with the dog-ends dangling from the corners of their mouths and ambled off to their hut. Johnny was so stiff he could hardly move. It was wonderful to feel the hot blood seeping back into his limbs.

Despite the killer's best efforts he was alive. He would not rest till the man responsible was sent to the gallows.

To Johnny, the mound of fresh earth, topped with two wreaths – he would give Matt and Lizzie the money for theirs – represented a new beginning.

The truth was not going to remain buried for long.

PART THREE
Snow Hill

TWENTY-ONE

Saturday, 19th December, 3 p.m.

Johnny took the Central Line from Holland Park to St Paul's. He'd had to force himself to get on as the doors opened, passengers and cigarette smoke flowing out on to the platform. Every single compartment of the train was packed with Christmas shoppers.

It was not a shopping expedition that Johnny was about to embark on – although he did plan to buy presents for Lizzie, Matt and Stella along the way. He was on the hunt for a psychopath.

Yuletide was, after all, the traditional time for ghost stories, and here he was: a ghost seeking vengeance on his killer.

Christmas had always been a double-edged occasion for Johnny. It had come as no great surprise to him that there was no such person as Father Christmas: he would have settled for a father for the rest of the year.

His excitement as a child had gradually been blunted by a growing awareness that his mother found the festive season an ordeal. It was then she missed her husband most.

Though she had stopped going to church when she was widowed, his mother had done her best to make the twenty-fifth a special day for her son. There would always be a small tree bought from the stall in Essex Road, presents wrapped in brown paper beneath it, a turkey with all the trimmings, crackers, sweets and carols, followed by comedies on the wireless. Even so, it would always come as a relief as the world woke up with a hangover on Boxing Day and resumed its daily routine. This was especially true now that Johnny usually spent the day alone. Once Matt and Lizzie had become engaged they'd started to spend Christmas with one or other set of in-laws.

A giant decorated Christmas tree stood incongruously and proudly in the courtyard of Bart's. It must have been especially awful to be in hospital at this time of year. Death and disease made no allowances for the holiday: many patients would not see in 1937.

His footsteps echoed in the deserted stairwells. There was no sign of the Grey Lady said to haunt the place. He didn't expect to run into the pathologist either; no doubt he would be heading towards the nineteenth hole about now. The inherent unfairness of life struck Johnny once again: the man who would slice open the bodies of those fighting for life in the wards around the quadrangle on Monday was at this moment blithely driving across the greens of Buckhurst Hill Golf Club. It was all balls.

Johnny pushed open the rubber doors of the mortuary. As he'd anticipated, Percy was alone.

"Can I help you?"

He was gratified to discover that Hughes did not recognise him.

"I hope so, Percy. Remember me?" Johnny took off his hat, hid his false nose, and winked. The boy stared.

"What you done that for? You look a right twerp."

"I'm working undercover. James H. Danton is the name."

The anagram of John Steadman had not taken long to work out. His time on the crossword pages had come in useful after all.

"What d'yer want this time?"

"Haven't you heard?" asked Johnny, his pride wounded. "I'm supposed to be dead. I was buried on Friday."

"Don't read the papers," said Percy with a sniff.

"You keep your ears open though, don't you? Aren't you curious why I'm dead?"

"Wrote something someone didn't like? Stuck your silly nose where it weren't wanted?"

"You're getting warmer. Like to guess whodunit? Like to tell me who torched the Urania Bookshop after killing Harry Gogg's bum-chum and then left me to be burned to a crisp?"

"No, no, no!" Percy turned pale. "I've said all I'm going to say about Harry. I don't want to end up like him."

"Well, tough luck. How d'you think you'll end up if I go to the cops and tell them everything I know about the death of a young cop called George Aitken – and how I came to know it?"

Percy moaned. Before he could say anything more, heavy footsteps could be heard coming down the corridor.

"Quick! Lie down on here." The lackey indicated an empty trolley. "For fuck's sake, move yer arse!"

There was no time to inspect the trolley for body fluids. Johnny lay down, crushing his new hat to his chest. Percy draped a sheet over him and wheeled him as far from the door as possible.

"Keep still and don't make a sound – or we'll both be for the high jump," whispered Percy.

The doors opened and closed with a sharp slap.

"Hello, Hughes. How's business?" It was Matt.

"PC Turner," stammered Percy. He was going to give the game away. "What can I do for you?"

"A friend of mine was killed last week. You may have heard about it. He was a reporter called John Steadman. I believe you knew him."

"I wouldn't say that I knew him," said Hughes. "Our paths crossed from time to time."

"And he didn't slip a shilling or two into your greasy palm now and again?" Matt sounded irritated.

It suddenly dawned on Johnny that Matt was trying to find his killer. He recalled their last conversation, when he had tried to tell Matt about the body that Vinson and Harry had delivered. He had seemed so unconcerned, as if he didn't want to hear about it. Perhaps that was all a cover; he had been trying to protect him all the time.

Johnny's heart swelled with gratitude. He resisted the temptation to reveal himself. If he did, he would only place his friend in jeopardy.

"Oh, he told yer about that, did he?" Percy's voice hardened. "Yeah, okay, once in a while I'd tip him off about a wrong 'un."

"Very commendable, I'm sure," said Matt. "That means we're on the same side. You can see that can't you?"

Matt's voice got louder. Was he coming towards the trolley? Suddenly it began moving. Johnny resisted the urge to cry out. One of its wheels squeaked. A door opened and, before he could do anything about it, Johnny found himself being slid into one of the refrigerators. The door slammed shut. He was in total darkness. Not again!

The irony of a dead man being put on ice was not lost on him. However, the fact that he could not hear or see anything re-awoke the claustrophobia that always lurked within him. He had been slid straight off the trolley at waist height, which meant that, as each fridge had three drawers like a filing cabinet, he was the filling in a corpse sandwich. Percy, angered by the fact that his anonymity had apparently not been preserved – and the further threat to implicate him – was trying to teach him a lesson.

Johnny shivered. Matt would not – could not be

allowed to – save him this time. If he did, all the subterfuge would have been for nothing. He would have to wait until the interview ended. Surely it would only be a few more minutes?

Keeping his eyes closed tight, Johnny tried to curl into a ball to preserve his body heat but there was insufficient room. He had no choice but to lie there as the warmth seeped out of him. He was glad that he was wearing an overcoat. And thank God there was no smell – except that of a heavy frost. He would just have to lie still and think of nice things: a cup of tea, a front-page exclusive, Lizzie, Stella . . .

He might have been all right, might have kept the suffocating silence and inky blackness at bay, had not the cadaver above him slowly started to drip on to his face.

What was it? Formaldehyde? Blood? Shit?

Johnny panicked.

TWENTY-TWO

The door opened. Percy slid him out of the fridge. Johnny immediately sat up, the sheet falling off him, and wiped his mouth vigorously. Blast! His fingers were smeared with make-up.

"It's only water," said Hughes, trying not to laugh. "Opening the door always causes a bit of a thaw."

"But what was thawing? That's the question. You bastard." It had always felt chilly in the mortuary but now it had the warmth of an open fire. "What did you tell PC Turner?"

"He wanted to know what I'd told *you*. I just said that Harry Gogg and PC Vinson brought in a body early Sunday morning and that it was sent on to the medical school."

Perhaps Matt would believe him now.

"That's good," said Johnny. "You did the right thing."

"He also asked me when I'd last seen yer. That's

when I wheeled yer over to the freezer. I was afraid he'd see I was telling porkies. I was trying to do what was best."

"You did," Johnny said, handing him a half-crown that was immediately pocketed.

Percy swallowed hard. His long, pale face watched him.

"Please don't mention my name to anyone else. We'd an agreement, Mr Steadman. I know I owe yer and all that, but still, yer oughter keep to it." He looked hurt and fearful.

"You don't need to worry about PC Turner. He's my best mate. You can trust him – he won't get you into trouble."

"Yer said I could trust you!"

What was he so afraid of? He must know more than he was letting on. Suddenly Johnny's heart sank. Call it intuition, a hunch or a bloody brainwave but he already knew that something had gone wrong.

"Are you sure you've told me everything that you told PC Turner? You didn't, for example, tell him that the body they brought in was that of a cop?"

Percy hesitated then nodded. "Sorry, I forgot."

"I told you not to tell anyone else. What did he say?"

"Nuffink. He turned and left without a word. Didn't even say thanks. 'Ave I done summat wrong?"

"Yes – which means we're quits now. I won't mention your name again – and you won't mention Aitken's body again."

"Deal. I never wanted to talk about it in the first place."

There was no point in blaming Hughes: Johnny had been telling Matt the same thing for ages. However, Matt would now be bound to tackle Vinson about that night – and, assuming Vinson was innocent, this could alert the killer.

There was not a second to lose. He produced the powder compact that Mrs Stone had insisted he carry and, using the mirror – which needed resilvering – above the double sink, repaired the damage incurred while in the freezer. Percy looked on in disbelief but wisely kept his mouth shut.

"I am going to get Harry's killer – and the man who killed the cop – even if it's the last thing I do. If you know who it is, Percy, this is your last chance to tell me. I'll pay double."

The attendant shook his head vigorously.

"I like my todger where it is, thanks very much."

"Have you always known?"

"I don't know, honest. I've told you as much as I can. As God is my witness, I hope you find the bugger."

Johnny was deep in thought as he made his way out of the hospital and hurried past Smithfield. Why did people walk so slowly? It was freezing.

Outside Partington & Sons, a tripe-dressing business, he saw a familiar face coming towards him. It would only arouse suspicion if he turned on his heels and went back the same way. There was nothing for it but to carry on.

Sweat began to trickle from his armpits as Stella's mother, her stringy hair hidden by an old blue hat, waddled towards him.

She looked him right in the face – and passed by without a flicker of recognition.

TWENTY-THREE

Saturday, 19th December, 5.15 p.m.

Although the encounter with Stella's mother had boosted his confidence, Johnny decided not to risk putting his disguise to the test with any other old acquaintances and took a roundabout way back to Honey Lane. His mind teemed with possibilities. Walking might help him to work things out.

He went over what Percy had said – and what he had not. As he cut through Cox's Court it occurred to him that Percy might have been telling the truth. What if he genuinely didn't know who the killer was? What if the killer wasn't a cop after all? Vinson may have helped take the body to Bart's, but he was unlikely to have been the man who dumped the knife in Passing Alley. Policemen did not kiss other men.

It came to him in a flash: Simkins. He had to be involved somehow. It would explain so much: how he had been first with news of the fire, how he had found Jo's fake suicide note so quickly, and how he had known that his rival was in the bookshop . . .

No, it was ridiculous. A crime reporter turning to crime? The job provided an ideal front for a killer: he would have every reason to follow closely the investigations of his own evil handiwork. But a sane man would hardly resort to arson and murder just for the sake of good copy. Then again, whoever was responsible for the mutilation of Harry Gogg could hardly be said to be compos mentis.

Was Simkins capable of going to such lengths? If he were responsible, he must know that it was only a matter of time before he'd be caught. Johnny thought back over their lunch together, discussing the case. It seemed to him now that Simkins had been playing with him, knowing all along that he was the person they were talking about.

Murder holds it's own fascination, doesn't it? Some might say the death of a male prostitute is of little consequence. In some ways, I have to say, I agree. However, who *killed him and* why *is tremendously important, don't you think?*

Simkins would have had no trouble mimicking George Aitken. And he was always hanging about cop-shops; it would have been easy enough to persuade someone to let him use a telephone.

What was his connection to Aitken, though? Perhaps there was none. Perhaps the cop's death was not connected to those of Harry and Jo.

A gang of urchins were loitering by the drinking fountain in Love Lane; Johnny quickened his pace, ignoring their outstretched hands and cries of, "Any spare change, guv?"

Why would Simkins kill? It always came back to motive. Johnny had little to go on, though he cast his mind back over every last scrap of gossip he'd ever come across on the subject of his rival's private life. Deep in thought, he barely registered his surroundings as Aldermanbury crossed Gresham Street, yet by the time he reached Milk Street all he'd managed to come up with was the possibility that Simkins had acted out of spite against his father. The scandal of his son and heir's arrest, trial and execution would certainly destroy Aubrey Simkins' political career. Was it possible Henry hated the old man that much? Johnny imagined trying to argue the case with Stone and immediately dismissed it as too far-fetched.

Honey Lane was now on his left. Simkins had been outside the brothel that day when he was thrown out. At the time, Johnny hadn't thought to ask him what he was doing there. He wondered whether Cecilia Zick might know. But assuming she did, how could he enlist her help? Blackmail? An appeal to her baser nature?

There was only one way to find out.

Saturday was evidently a busy day for the bum-boys. A pair of gentlemen were coming down the steps, their hats tipped forward, as Johnny reached the spot where he had been thrown to the ground. The gorilla on the door, about to shut out the cold, swung it open again.

"Afternoon, sir. Who should I tell Miss Zick is here?"

"Mr Danton." Everybody else probably used a false name too.

He was shown into the opulent parlour where a couple of other punters on either side of a roaring fire hid behind copies of *The Times*. Johnny doffed his hat and coat.

"Let me take those for you." Cecilia Zick appeared at his elbow in a miasma of perfume. The lap-dog, thank God, was nowhere to be seen. "I don't think we've met."

"No. It's my first time."

"May I enquire how you heard about us?"

"Personal recommendation from a gentleman who lives in Chelsea."

"There's a lot of gentlemen what live in Chelsea."

"Indeed. And quite a few of them sing your praises."

"You're too kind." She waited for the name.

"Henry Simkins." She tried to hide the flash of recognition, but Johnny glimpsed it beneath her batting eyelids. They were painted magenta.

"I can't say he springs readily to mind. Did he recommend anyone in particular?"

"In fact he did." Johnny lowered his voice. "Stanley."

"Ah," said Zick with a half-smile. "He's currently occupied but should be free shortly. Would you care for a drink?"

Johnny had never needed one more. "Scotch with a splash of soda, please."

"Coming right up. Do take a seat."

Johnny perched on the edge of the chesterfield. Eyes peeped over the top of the newspapers. One of them winked. Johnny looked away.

"There we are." Zick held out a silver salver. "How long will you be with us?"

"I can only spare half an hour."

"That's long enough, as your missus would say." Zick tittered. The two guineas quickly disappeared about her person. It was obviously more expensive at the weekend. "You just sit back and relax. He'll be here as soon as he's cleaned up."

The thought of Stan washing another man's semen off his body ruined the taste of the whisky.

A muscular lad dressed in a soldier's uniform entered the room. One of the men immediately flung down *The Times* and followed him out with a low growl, trying to grab his backside. The other man lowered his paper and studied Johnny.

"Don't be nervous. You're safe here." He smiled. He was about ten years older than Johnny and, judging from his clothes, much better off. His dark good looks – full red lips topped with a virile moustache – must have attracted any number of women and yet here he was, waiting his turn to abuse a young man. His wedding ring glistened in the firelight.

"I say, would you care to have dinner some time?"

Fortunately, before Johnny could answer, Stan came into the room and gave Johnny the once-over. The messenger boy made a mocking bow. "Pleased to make your acquaintance. This way."

Johnny expected to be led up to the attic but, having reached the first floor, he was shown into a much larger, warmer room. Its walls were hung with Chinese wallpaper decorated with a bamboo motif and the floor covered in soft, intricately patterned Persian rugs. There were two large mirrors and – Johnny could not help smiling – another on the ceiling above the king-size bed.

"You're in luck," said Stan. "All the other rooms are taken."

Perhaps this explained the higher price. The boy stripped off in seconds and hopped on to the bed. Johnny sat beside him. The sheets were still warm. It was all he could do to stop himself jumping up. There was a faint smell of male sweat – and other body fluids – in the room. He must not make the same mistake as last time. He would arouse suspicion if he immediately started asking questions. He had to appear keen: he did not want Zick interrupting again.

"Don't be shy." Stan started undoing Johnny's collar and slipped off his tie. His hand slid inside Johnny's shirt and tweaked his right nipple through his vest. Before he knew it the boy's lips were on his and his tongue, as strong and limber as an eel, was forcing itself into his mouth. The instinct to recoil was almost too much to resist. Johnny told himself: *Think about Stella. Pretend you're with Stella.* Christ, he better get a good story out of this.

Stan, he grudgingly had to admit, was a good kisser. Trying not to think about the assault in Passing Alley, Johnny was struck by the novelty of the act: it both was and was not like kissing a woman.

He opened his eyes and found himself gazing into Stan's. There were flecks of gold among the brown. The boy's hand dropped to Johnny's groin.

"Hello, hello. What do we have here?"

Johnny reddened. He could not help it. The kissing had turned him on. Was he queer after all?

He stood up, holding his hands in front of the bulge in his trousers.

"What's wrong?" Stan was evidently miffed.

"Nothing." He cleared his throat. "It's . . . it's just that I've never done anything like this before." He could still taste the boy on his lips. "You were recommended to me by a friend," said Johnny. "Henry Simkins. D'you know him?"

Stan's erection started to droop.

"I see a lot of men." A hint of pride crept into his voice. "You can't expect me to remember all of them. Is he a regular?"

"I've no idea. He's tall, willowy with long, wavy brown hair. Posh, throws his money about."

"Now, that I would remember."

"He's a journalist. I believe he's investigating the death of a cop from Snow Hill."

Before Stan, eyes wide with alarm, could answer, the door burst open.

"Mr fucking Steadman!" the irate madam stood in the doorway, Alf looming behind her. She was quivering with rage. "Think yourself cleverer than me, do you? Well, it takes more than a bit of slap to fool Cecilia Zick."

Stan grabbed his clothes and fled, the doorman taking the opportunity to smack his bare bottom as he did so.

Johnny put his head down and tried to follow but the fat woman grabbed his hair and pulled him towards her. He cried out as something sharp pricked his neck.

Within seconds his vision blurred, he lost the use of his limbs and, although he fought against it, darkness overwhelmed him.

An agonising pain brought him round. It was as if he were being split in two. He tried to move but his wrists and ankles were handcuffed to the brass bedstead. He was back in the attic. A blinding white light made him bury his face in the pillow. A camera shutter clicked.

Johnny was living Matt's nightmare. No wonder he had refused to explain it.

"He's coming round," said Zick.

"All the better," said a voice that Johnny knew he'd heard somewhere before. "The more resistance, the greater the pleasure."

His assailant jerked his hips again and Johnny cried out as the man's cock was driven where no cock had gone before. It was impossible not to resist. The sense of overwhelming fullness and the prodding of his stomach were unbearable. He wanted to vomit. The blood acted as a lubricant.

The click-click-click of the shutter told him that the unseen cameraman was recording every moment of his violation.

The rapist increased his pace, panting as he called

out every insult under the sun. Sweat, stinking of onions, dripped on to Johnny's back. He had not known such pain existed. How could men do this for pleasure?

There was one last vicious lunge, and Johnny felt the man's hot seed squirting into his bowels. Death was preferable to this.

He pulled out roughly, making Johnny yelp. Then a hand reached down between his outspread legs and grabbed his cock.

"Ha! It never fails. Rock-hard." He slapped one of Johnny's upturned buttocks and the springs creaked as he got off the bed. More flash-bulbs popped.

Johnny turned to look up. In the white glare of the camera's flash he saw Rotherforth's face sneering down at him.

"Think of me when your neck snaps," he spat.

He did not see the fist coming. The blow knocked out a tooth but put Johnny out of his misery.

Rotherforth did up his trousers and turned to the man who had been watching intently by the door. "You know what to do. The car's in Russia Row. Well, don't just stand there!" He raised his fist again. The young man flinched.

"Yes, sir. But can't I just have ten minutes first?"

"Very well, but only after you've helped Jim take his equipment back to the van." He picked up his jacket, brushed a speck of dust off the sleeve and began to button it up. "You never know, the bloody hack might have come round by the time you get back."

The inspector, back in uniform, stared down at Johnny's outstretched, soiled, bruised body.

"I'll say this for him: he was a stubborn little fucker." He sighed, suddenly exhausted. "Zick – a word, if you please."

He strode out of the room with the madam scurrying after him. The photographer and Rotherforth's accomplice silently picked up the various cases and bits of camera equipment then trooped downstairs.

Johnny remained out cold on the bed, naked and defenceless.

The little fucker! Talk about a bad penny. I thought I'd sorted him at the bookshop – that second corpse must have been some bum-chum of Jo's, hiding out in the flat. God knows how Steadman got out of there. And the sheer nerve – holding a fake funeral! He must have been so pleased with himself. I can just see the clever sod: revelling in his deceit, cock-a-hoop because he thought he'd got the better of me.

Well, he's not laughing now. He'll be in need of a real funeral before the night is out – except he won't get one.

There's a kind of poetic justice in him sharing Aitken's abuse. I don't think I've ever enjoyed making someone suffer so much. They don't realise that tensing up, fighting back, just makes it worse for them – and better for me.

He can't have been working alone though. Someone

must have helped him. Someone aside from PC Matt Turner. We'll have to see what Fox has got to say for himself. Why didn't the old queen tell me what was going on? Does he have a death wish?

And as for young Turner – if he thinks he's going to see me swing he's made a big mistake.

Now that Steadman's sorted it's going to be his turn to face the music.

TWENTY-FOUR

Johnny could hear whistling. It was the same haunting tune he'd heard back in Passing Alley: "Mad about the Boy". The kiss was the key to this whole story. He should have been more open-minded. Harry was not the only man whose love dare not speak its shame.

As he slowly regained consciousness he realised that someone was stroking his backside.

"Hello, handsome. Remember me?" The caressing continued. "I sometimes think there is nothing more beautiful in the whole world than a man's bottom. Two simple curves, thrusting out into space, defying gravity, arrogant yet at the same time so vulnerable. Only a god could design something so perfect."

Johnny, still mortified to be in such a compromising position, turned his swollen face. It was PC Vinson.

"You! You cunt."

"Now, that's not very nice." He spanked Johnny's backside lightly. "We're on the same side you know."

"I'm not queer," said Johnny. The rape had decided him once and for all.

"That's not the 'same side' I had in mind. I meant we're both against Rotherforth. Who do you think sent you the tip-offs? Who let you find the knife in the alley?"

"Why did you kiss me?"

"Felt like it, that's all." Vinson smiled. "What's the big deal?"

"I suppose you're going to fuck me as well," said Johnny, trying to sound braver than he felt.

"Thanks but no thanks. I'm Martha rather than Arthur. Believe it or not, you soon get used to the pain." Vinson laughed at his look of disbelief.

"If you say so. Why are you here?"

"To press your face into the pillow until you're dead." Vinson giggled. "Rotherforth was beside himself when he learned that you were still alive. I must say, I was rather surprised as well. He was absolutely livid . . . almost throttled Zick."

Johnny was traumatised but he was not going to beg. "Zick better hope I never set eyes on her again. What can I do to make you change your mind? I won't give you away, I promise. It's Rotherforth I've been after, not you. I can hardly believe what he's just done."

"You don't know the half of it. Now you're here, I've so much to tell you."

Johnny was shivering violently, his teeth chattering.

"Don't panic," Vinson said gently. "I was only having you on. I'm sorry it turned out like this. Any friend of Matt's is a friend of mine. I want you to nail Rotherforth. He's the bane of my life – and that of many others. He's a very sick man who needs stopping for good. From what Matt had said about you, I thought you were the man for the job."

"Well, look at me now."

"Your fake death hit Matt very hard. It certainly worked better than your false nose." He pointed to it on the floor. "Matt's very fond of you. I must confess I'm jealous."

"Shut up about Matt and get me out of these fucking things."

Vinson began to unlock the handcuffs. Even when they had been removed Johnny could not shift his arms. If he had been able to he would have knocked the bastard out.

The man who had been ordered to kill him helped arrange his limbs into a more comfortable position. Such was his state of mind, Johnny did not even mind being naked. His arse felt as though it were gaping open – and it burned. His head throbbed from Zick's drug and his jaw ached from Rotherforth's blow. It hurt when he talked but that did not stop him.

"How many more men has Rotherforth done this to?"

"Search me," said Vinson. "You're at least the fourth. Before that there was Matt, George Aitken, and me."

"Why didn't you go to the rubber-heelers?"

"I had no proof and the word of a constable against

that of an inspector would carry little weight. No one would believe me – I'd have just ended up the butt of endless jokes. It would have been impossible to stay in the force."

"You should have gone to Old Jewry. The top brass are terrified of scandal," said Johnny.

Though he could see Vinson casting glances at his cock, he was beyond caring. All that mattered was revenge.

"Why did Rotherforth need to rape unconscious men when there's plenty of willing boys available?"

"He doesn't tell me anything – except that he's not a poofter. He absolutely loathes homosexuals. The bastard carries a pearl-topped hat-pin with him so he can stick it into them if he can't be bothered to arrest them." He shook his head in disgust. "Only time I've known him to show any kind of tenderness is when he talks about a friend of his named Archie. The pair of them grew up together, signed up together, went to war together. Only Archie didn't come back. Rotherforth told me once he was trapped alone with Archie's corpse in a shell crater for two whole days on the Western Front. Archie died in his arms, apparently. I think they were more than bosom buddies, if you know what I mean, but I doubt they did anything about it." He shuddered. "I can't imagine the horror of seeing the man you love die before your eyes. Such an experience is bound to change a man – and not for the better . . ."

For a moment there was silence. Vinson sighed heavily. "Rotherforth refuses to accept that he might be queer.

Perhaps that's why he prefers his partners to be unconscious: if they don't know anything, he doesn't need to deny anything. A willing partner would force him to recognise himself."

"Why did he kill Harry Gogg? He didn't have sex with him, did he?"

"Christ, no! Rotherforth despised him. He'd only lay hands on him to hit him. Informants are supposed to be registered, but Harry wasn't – there was nothing official to connect him to Snow Hill. Rotherforth is a law unto himself like that. When he found out someone had tipped you off, he was convinced it was Harry. Then he saw him talking to you and he was afraid Harry would spill the beans about him. All Harry and I did was take Aitken's body to Bart's."

"How did Aitken die?"

"I'm not sure, but it happened in Snow Hill. Afterwards, Rotherforth tipped his corpse out of an upstairs window into Cock Lane, and we wheeled him round the corner on a barrow. I'd never seen Rotherforth look so frightened."

Johnny gradually began to rally. The murder of a cop in a cop-shop – by a cop – was a sensational story. With Vinson's testimony it ought to be possible to expose the bent copper.

"Does Rotherforth know you're here now?"

"Of course. I'm supposed to suffocate you and take your body to the mortuary at Bart's. I saved your life by asking if I could have some fun with you."

"Thank you." Johnny was going to shake his hand

but in such a ridiculous position – nude, bleeding, tear-stained and sickened – there was no appropriate gesture he could make. His tongue found the hole left by the absent molar. "I suppose I owe you a great deal."

"Yes, you do," said Vinson. "I'm doing it for Matt more than you, though."

Johnny sat up.

"Does he know I'm alive?"

"Not likely," said Vinson. "Rotherforth would kill me if Matt were to find out. He's better off not knowing. Besides, he's the one in danger now. Rotherforth won't rest until he thinks everyone's been silenced – one way or another."

"In that case, what about yourself?"

"I'm too useful. He can't operate by himself, and I'm the only one he remotely trusts." He got to his feet and held out a hand to pull Johnny up. "Come on, let's get you out of here while Zick's still occupied."

Vinson handed him a heavily darned collarless shirt and a pair of trousers. They were not his own clothes – perhaps they belonged to one of the boys – but they would have to do till he could find a cab back to Holland Park. He was still shaky so Vinson helped him dress.

"I presume you won't tell anyone of my escape," said Johnny.

"Are you kidding? I like being alive."

Johnny stared into Vinson's eyes. Could he trust him? The man had saved his life. On the other hand . . .

"You misled me about Aitken. Said that he was still alive."

"I had to. I was hoping to keep myself out of the picture. I wanted to tell you when we met outside the Viaduct Tavern, but I didn't know what Rotherforth was going to do then. He still scares the hell out of me. Did you know he was in the pub?"

"No, I didn't – but that doesn't matter now." The presence of the inspector that night would, however, explain why Matt had left so abruptly. "You knew that Aitken was dead. You knew Rotherforth had raped you – and Matt. Wasn't that enough to make you do something?"

"I did do something: I contacted you."

Footsteps came trudging up the wooden stairs. The two men looked at each other and dived under the bed. The footsteps passed the door. Another whore and his client.

"We better use the back passage," said Vinson.

"Is that some kind of joke?" Johnny did not feel like laughing.

"No, of course not. Sorry." Vinson peeped out of the door to make sure the coast was clear. Johnny followed the policeman along a corridor and down the servants' staircase into the basement. His legs felt as if they were going to give way at any moment. Only anger and adrenalin kept him going.

The black Wolseley was unlocked.

"I can't take you home," said Vinson. "Rotherforth will check the odometer."

"That's all right," said Johnny. "I should be able to

get a cab in Holborn." He stared through the narrow windscreen. Russia Row, apart from a pair of rats scuttling along the gutter, was deserted. He could still feel Rotherforth plunging away. He had never felt so unclean. "Got any fags?"

Vinson produced a packet of Greys. He lit Johnny's first, then his own.

"Thanks." He let the magic smoke trickle slowly out of his nostrils. "It's a dead give-away, that."

"What is?"

"When you struck the match, you held it away from yourself like a woman. Men strike towards themselves."

"How d'you know?"

"I'm a person who notices such things."

Vinson turned the key in the ignition.

"Hold your horses," said Johnny. "I've got a few more questions. Why did Rotherforth – I'm presuming it was him – send Matt the photographs?"

"When he saw him talking to you in the Viaduct, he feared the worst. He thought blackmail would be the best way to shut Matt up. Then you showed up at the Urania, flashing the photo and asking about Aitken and Gogg. Rotherforth and his associates were behind the bookshop as well as the brothel. You've no idea how many pies they've got their grubby little fingers in and how profitable they've been. When you went back to the shop, he panicked. Jo was already starting to ask questions about what happened to Harry, so he couldn't be relied on. Rotherforth thought destroying the shop and everything in it – including you – would safeguard the operation. However, here you are, back from the dead."

"So who was the other person who died in the shop?"

"I've been wondering about that," said Vinson. "It must have been Charles Timney. Poor kid. I was wondering where he'd got to. You've just met his father."

"I have?"

"He's Rotherforth's pet photographer. Jim shares his hatred of homosexuals and takes great delight in catching them in compromising positions. Those mirrors in the bedroom downstairs are all two-way; Jim stations himself in the adjoining room and records the action at leisure. The victims will pay anything for the negatives – and they've no choice but to cough up again when Rotherforth produces a second set. It works every time – well, almost. One sad sack went home to Whitechapel and hanged himself instead."

"So much for *The Preservation of Peace and Public Tranquillity*." The mantra encapsulated the primary duty of a policeman. "Why was Charles in the bookshop?"

"He'd been thrown out by his father. I expect Jo, having lost Harry, needed some company and let the lad stay with him on the quiet."

"What made his father throw him out?"

"Can't you guess? He showed too much interest in the dirty photographs. He was Jim's assistant – until he realised that he was like me and Harry. Jim went berserk, disowned him on the spot, threatened to kill him if he ever saw him again – which is why Charlie hid from

Rotherforth each time he visited the shop. Jo put it about that Charlie had joined the army."

"Could you get me a photograph of him?"

"Why?"

"Why d'you think? It's a tragic story. He's another of Rotherforth's victims. It's a real shame. If Charlie hadn't been exposed to all that filth, met the likes of you and Harry, he would have stayed normal."

Vinson laughed.

"Come off it! Pictures don't pervert your personality. He was born that way, just as I was. Most men like women, some men like men. As Harry used to say, 'If God had meant men to fuck each other, he'd have given them holes in their arses.'"

"Charming." Johnny shifted uncomfortably. "Poor Charlie. He was caught between the devil – Rotherforth – and the flames of a real hell-fire. I tried to save him, you know, but the floor gave way. I'm going to ensure he gets a proper headstone. Why does his father work for Rotherforth?"

"He's got no choice. Rotherforth has enough dirt on Jim to get him sent down for years."

"What kind of dirt?"

"Never you mind. Jim knows the true value of silence."

"Well, it's my business to break that silence."

He turned to look at Vinson, who was still in his constable's uniform.

"Why did you really send me the tip-off? You could have sent an anonymous letter to Aitken's fiancée telling her to demand an investigation."

"There was no body. The powers-that-be would have said there was nothing to investigate."

"But policemen don't just vanish into thin air! Surely they have a duty of care to the people who work for them."

"Rotherforth informed the top brass that Aitken had run off back to Scotland. A family emergency."

"He has no family."

"Precisely. Rotherforth knew that – and he knew that news of a cop suddenly walking out of the job would reflect badly on the force. He counted on the determination of the top brass to keep the disappearance quiet."

"Are you prepared to testify against him now?"

"Absolutely not. Besides, what proof have you got that Rotherforth is guilty of anything? Everything I've told you is hearsay. There's no concrete evidence that he was in any way involved in Aitken's death, the murders of Harry and Jo or the bookshop arson. Zick and Timney would deny everything."

He was right. Johnny's heart sank. He still was not thinking clearly.

"He's just raped me – and there are photographs to prove it. Could you get hold of them?"

"Are you sure you want the world to know?"

"Of course not: but they would be proof of Rotherforth's pornographic interests. If he knew I had them, if he knew his fate lay in my hands, he might turn himself in."

"Not a chance. He'd just try to kill you again. Besides, you've got to promise me that you'll keep away from him.

If he knows you're still alive, he'll kill me – slowly. At the moment Matt is his main concern. The only way we can stop Rotherforth for good is if we catch him trying to bribe Matt into silence or, if that fails, trying to kill him. Rotherforth really wouldn't want to do that though. He adores him."

"Not as much as you do."

"Hark at you!" Vinson laughed. "I've seen the way you look at him. You love him."

"Yes, I do. More than any other man – and I'm not ashamed to admit it. But I don't like him the way you do."

"And what way is that?"

"You know, sexually."

"You may be right – although I wouldn't be too sure about it. Anyway, I've just saved your life. Promise me you'll lie low until I say so. Tomorrow's Sunday and Rotherforth won't be on duty. He's unlikely to do anything until Monday."

"Okay. I promise – but the sooner he's arrested the better. I'd still like you to get hold of the photographs and their negatives though. I don't want perverts getting off on what happened tonight."

"I'll do my best. Where can I contact you?" Johnny gave him the number of the Stone residence. Vinson started the engine.

"Aren't you worried about what Rotherforth will say when he's arrested?" Johnny was still unsure of his saviour's motives. "The scandal could destroy your career as well."

"Why should it? Rotherforth can't say anything about me without incriminating himself. I'm a victim too." Vinson stared off into the night as if recalling the moment when his life switched tracks. "So where should I drop you?"

"Holborn Circus will be fine. That's hardly out of your way."

"You'd better lie down on the back seat – just in case."

They turned into Milk Street and headed towards Cheapside. Neither of them saw the big man who had just entered Honey Lane and, at the sound of the car, stepped back into the shadows.

But Matt had recognised the Wolseley – and its driver.

Johnny, running on empty, said good evening to the butler and tried to sneak across the cold marble floor. The Stones, however, had just returned from a dinner party in Kensington. As soon as she saw Johnny, Honoria rushed to his side and, ignoring her husband's volley of questions, helped her "wounded soldier" to the bathroom.

There were angry welts on his wrists and ankles where the cuffs had cut into him as he had writhed on the bed. A devout nudist, she tut-tutted at his reluctance to undress but the blood on the inside of his trousers made her hold her tongue. She added disinfectant to the water. Its lingering sting made him wince as he lowered himself gingerly into the claw-footed tub.

"I'm sorry," said Mrs Stone.

"It's not your fault," said Johnny. "Cuts and grazes must be cleaned."

"I wasn't talking about them." The water was turning pink.

"Oh," said Johnny, averting his eyes as she gently raised his chin to wipe away the blood. He really did not want to discuss his assault – especially with a woman, even if it was usually women who got raped. He was ashamed. "Please don't tell anyone."

He meant, of course, her husband. The last thing he needed was for this to get back to the office. He could hear the comments now: *A real man would never let himself be used like a woman*; *He must have secretly wanted it*; *I'd kill any man who touched me like that.*

All he had tried to do was uncover the truth about how a cop had died. Three other young men had subsequently been killed, and Johnny himself – like Matt before him – had been treated like a mere piece of meat.

Even so, he refused to be a victim. It was up to him to avenge all their deaths.

In the meantime, though, all he wanted to do was sleep.

TWENTY-FIVE

Sunday, 20th December, 9.20 a.m.

The next morning, when Rotherforth's semen came spluttering out, Johnny vowed that the inspector would not see the next Christmas. Rotherforth had in effect killed him three times: in the freezer, in the fire and in the bed. The last time, though, he had done more than end his life: he had robbed him of his manhood.

Johnny was intelligent enough to know that he must not allow it to ruin his life. He *would* get over it, eventually – and Matt would too.

He had survived. He was just sore all over – inside and out – and missing another tooth.

Nevertheless, it was difficult not to feel like a virgin ravished on her wedding night.

Johnny, unlike many members of his generation, had not had to get married to lose his virginity. He was twenty-one when a secretary on the local newspaper, perhaps seeing the glint of ambition in his green eyes, invited him to the pictures. They had been flirting for weeks – but then Johnny flirted with all the secretaries. He could not remember the film that they had seen but he remembered Ann's parents returning earlier than expected – fortunately after the event. Her father had taken one look at their flushed faces and tousled hair and thrown him out of the house. Johnny did not care – he was a real man at last!

Now, however, he wondered whether it might have been better to wait and do it for the first time with someone he loved.

Ann had not loved him and he had not loved Ann. He'd been relieved to discover that she was not a virgin: in fact, he could not have had a more expert guide to the intricate and delicate parts of a woman. She had taken hold of him, told him what to do and he had done it – all too quickly.

Something in her masterfulness, her no-nonsense pleasure-seeking had made a part of him recoil. Their feelings were of the body, not the mind, and, while they were wonderfully intense, they left his thumping heart untouched. Johnny was a romantic. Perhaps it came of having seen too many films.

Matt, he was pretty sure, had been a virgin when he married Lizzie. As usual, Matt had gone about things in the right way; Johnny the wrong. Perhaps he would have fallen in love with Ann, had they continued to see each other. However, she had made it abundantly clear that her father would not countenance such a thing. Johnny had stopped flirting with her and gone on to bed other good-time girls, but the steady supply of uncomplicated sex had proved to be unsatisfying. Lizzie was the only woman he loved.

Alas, as R. Wilfer Esq said in *Our Mutual Friend*: "What might have been is not what is."

Johnny could detect no change, no matter how subtle, in the manner of his boss when he described the progress he'd made with the investigation the night before. It was clear that Mrs Stone had kept her word.

"There's still no evidence though," said Stone, getting up from his desk to poke the fire. Silence settled in the room as he stared into the flames and thought.

It was now four o'clock and already a servant was closing the shutters in the massive house across the road. The gilt of an ornate French clock on the mantelpiece gleamed in the light from the gasolier.

Finally, Stone cleared his throat. "You think this Rotherforth is going to try silencing your friend Turner as well?"

"That's what Vinson said. Rotherforth doesn't know how much I told Matt." Johnny tried not to grimace as he shifted on the sofa. "Vinson promised to call as soon as he got his instructions. I gave him the telephone number here. It will probably be tomorrow."

"Excellent. If he doesn't telephone, we'll have to consider other ways of catching Rotherforth. We could have him tailed – by professionals. It might be a good idea to bring a couple of your colleagues into the investigation as well. Bill Fox has not made much headway." Stone, unaware of Bill's secret proclivities, held up his hand to silence Johnny's objections. "Vinson's testimony and that of the photographer, even if we could trace him, only amounts to hearsay. There's only his word that Rotherforth shoved Aitken – who may still have been alive – out of the window. For all we know, Aitken could have jumped."

Stone hung up the poker and returned to his desk. He was frowning.

"We can't rely too much on Vinson's word. For all we know, he could have been the one who killed Gogg, and who's to say whether he was acting under Rotherforth's orders when he did it? Same goes for Moss. You didn't actually see who strangled him and set the fire in the bookshop; you only heard the murder." He shook his head. "No, Rotherforth needs to be caught in the act. And the more witnesses there are, the better. It will be difficult, mind – if not downright impossible. The devil must be very clever to have remained undetected for so long. Don't worry," he added, noticing how crestfallen Johnny seemed, "the fact that a cop is running a pornography racket and a brothel is a great story, even if we can't pin the four murders on him."

Johnny gave a splutter of indignation, but Stone waved him down.

"I know, I know. You've had a very tough week – one that most people would not have survived. But trust me: it will be worth it in the end."

"I won't be happy till the bastard's dead," said Johnny.

The Christmas tree ornaments sparkled in the firelight. Lizzie watched Matt snoozing in the armchair. He was still not himself. The nightmares had been bad enough, but since Johnny's death he'd been not only grieving the loss of his friend but also blaming himself for it.

It did not seem to occur to him that she was upset too. His nightmares were getting worse all the time and his refusal to discuss their possible cause was driving a wedge between them. They had almost had a row as they decorated the aromatic fir, its needles already beginning to drop.

"There's nothing for you to worry about," he said when she tried, yet again, to help him. "You just look after yourself and my baby."

My baby – not *our* baby. It was all right for men: one spasm of pleasure and a woman was destined for months of discomfort. No doubt the first glimpse of her child would make all the back pain and morning sickness worthwhile, but she didn't know how she would cope with a newborn if Matt was still in this terrible state.

The photograph, never far from her mind, rose to the surface of her thoughts for the thousandth time. It was carefully hidden under her withered bridal bouquet, which was stored, wrapped in tissue paper, in a shoebox on their wardrobe shelf. Since she could not bring herself to ask Matt about it – the fact there was something she could not ask her husband niggled her; there should be no secrets between them – she would have to find out the answers for herself.

Inspector Rotherforth had advised her to burn the "offending item" – which was probably an off-colour joke that had backfired – and remain silent. It was, he assured her, bound to be a fake – perhaps concocted by so-called friends at the gym. Much wiser not to mention it to Matt. His patronising tone suggested that she should not worry her pretty little head about such nonsense.

But Lizzie was worried. And she wasn't about to stop trying to find out the truth.

Rotherforth was sitting at the dining table with his devoted wife and three children. They were playing Ludo. On the wireless, toothy George Formby was busy cleaning windows.

Edith, the inspector's eldest daughter, who would be fourteen next month, was winning. The youngest, Elsie, was bored of the game. Thinking she might bring it to an early end, she waited until no one was looking and then surreptitiously shifted a counter.

She should have known better. Her heart leapt when she caught her father's coal-black eyes boring into her.

He did not utter a word. He just flipped the board into the air, sending the die and counters everywhere.

The game was over.

Lilian Voss sang the words to "All Things Bright and Beautiful", but her heart was not in it. Her world had turn to ashes. Everything was black and grey.

John Steadman had been a good man, she could tell – he'd had a face that invited trust – but now he was dead. She could think of no one else to turn to.

Since George's disappearance she had prayed constantly for his return yet found no relief.

No matter what anyone said, he was not the sort of man who would jilt a girl.

Something bad must have happened. Something told her she would never see him again.

Tears trickled down her colourless cheeks.

Henry Simkins, pleasantly exhausted after the day's shoot, wallowed in a bath that was big enough for two. Poor old Steadman, six feet under. He actually missed the dear boy.

Johnny had always reminded him of his closest schoolmate. He could see Freddie Cumming now, his lovely green eyes – the midnight green of a magpie's tail feathers – blazing in panic.

One afternoon there had been an impromptu tuck-box inspection after lessons had finished for the day. Freddie had stood, frozen in fear, his hands resting on the unopened lid. It turned out he was trying to hide a tatty old teddy bear which, if seen by his confederates, would have earned him hours of merciless ribbing.

Simkins remembered the look of gratitude he'd received when he lifted the lid of his own box, which had already been inspected, and let Freddie slide the stuffed toy into it. The approaching prefect – Gibbs, or was it Darbyshire? – had seen nothing.

This small act of kindness had earned him Freddie's undying friendship. Thereafter they were inseparable – often visiting each other during the vacations – until one Christmas Freddie's father went bankrupt.

Freddie had never returned to school and all Simkins' letters had come back marked *Unknown at this address*.

Where was Freddie now? he wondered, taking another swig of claret.

His thoughts returned to Johnny Steadman. He had watched his rival go into the bookshop but the only person he saw leaving the premises was Rotherforth. When he'd questioned the inspector afterwards, Rotherforth had sworn that he'd seen someone slip out via a rear entrance and he'd assumed it must have been Steadman.

Unable to prove his suspicions, Simkins was afraid to ask more questions. The inspector was too good a source to alienate. The promise of photographs that would compromise his father's beloved Tory party was enough to force even him to have the patience of a saint. However, that did not mean he would stop sniffing around.

Could Steadman's death have been connected to the photographs? Had he found out about them? Had Rotherforth killed him to stop them falling into his hands? If that were the case, why kill Joseph Moss as well?

Rotherforth, sounding uncharacteristically flustered, had banned him from Zick's bordello: *If you ever show your face there again, I can guarantee you'll see never your precious pictures.*

What Simkins needed now was a stooge, someone who would do his dirty work for him and take the rap if discovered – but who? It would come to him.

He held his nose and sank under the expensively perfumed water, his long hair spreading out like the tendrils of an exotic plant.

Bill Fox had followed his usual Sunday routine: a walk along the canal to Kensal Green Cemetery to place flowers on his wife's grave – the gasometers sinking as a million roasts cooked slowly in the oven – then back home to a cheese and piccalilli sandwich and the afternoon spent reading all the newspapers.

Rotherforth had told him – no, ordered him – to stop nosing around. The bookshop fire had been investigated thoroughly. Johnny's death was a tragic accident, nothing more.

He had no choice but to believe him. He was going to miss the extra cash when he retired. Besides, he had no wish to spend what time he had left in prison.

The bottle of Scotch was almost empty. The open book of naked youths slipped off his lap.

Tom Vinson had his own copy of the photograph that lay hidden under a bridal bouquet in Devonia Road. He did not need to look at it: every detail was etched into his brain.

Matt had a beautiful body. He was the embodiment of perfection. Just the memory of those miraculous minutes when they were alone together – moments he had longed for and never dreamed would come true – still made him hard.

He didn't care that Matt thought people like him were sick, a disgrace to humanity. Matt was his ideal man; he really did worship the ground he walked on.

In this respect he was by no means alone. Although he flushed with anger at the memory of his idol's defilement, he knew that if it hadn't been for Rotherforth, his abiding fantasy of making love to Matt would never have become a reality.

Still he hated Rotherforth more than any man alive. The humiliation he had felt when his abuser, sensing his enjoyment, had immediately withdrawn, never to touch him again, still stung.

His efforts to do the right thing had ended disastrously. Images of the dead flashed through his mind: Aitken, looking over his shoulder in the showers, soap suds snaking down his spine into the cleft of his buttocks; Harry, his arm round Jo's shoulders, happiness radiating off them; Charlie, rejected by the father he loved, putting a brave face on his pain. All of them killed by Rotherforth.

And now Matt was in mortal danger. Rotherforth's attempt at blackmail had already failed, and though he might think he could buy anyone, where Matt was concerned bribery would never work.

Matt had only one hope. And he wasn't about to let him down.

Whatever it took, he was going to protect him.

TWENTY-SIX

Monday, 21st December, 2.25 p.m.

Lizzie's feet were aching. It was strange: they seemed less resilient after a day of rest. Gamage's, with just three days to go before Christmas, was heaving. The aisles were so crowded she had retreated behind the counter. Besides, she had no time to spray passers-by with scent. She was too busy helping clueless husbands, excited children and bored ladies who lunched.

A whiff of sandalwood made her look up: the gentleman was in the wrong department if he was looking to buy cologne.

"Good afternoon, Mrs Turner."

"Good afternoon, sir. Have we met?"

"Very briefly. At the funeral on Friday – Henry Simkins." The reporter held out his hand. Lizzie shook it.

"Of course. Forgive me."

"Did Johnny ever talk about his work?"

"Sometimes. Why?"

She studied him. Yes, he had been at the cemetery.

A customer tapped a coin on the glass-topped counter. "Excuse me . . ."

Simkins sniffed the various perfumes on display while Lizzie attended to the old woman who wanted something nice for her niece.

"Sorry about that." Lizzie smiled thinly. "I really haven't got the time to stand and reminisce." She remembered how Johnny had raged against his amoral rival.

"I can see that," said Simkins, oozing what she presumed he thought was charm. "However, I'm sure you'd like to see his killer brought to justice."

Lizzie frowned. "What are you talking about? His killer died in the fire."

"It seems not." Simkins nodded gravely. "Another man was seen leaving the bookshop shortly before the fire began."

"How do you know? Have you told the authorities? My husband is a policeman and he hasn't said anything about another suspect."

"The police are aware of the situation. Has your husband told you what kind of shop it was?" Simkins raised his immaculate eyebrows. He could see that his guess had been correct: she was in the dark.

"It was a bookshop."

"Indeed. However, it sold books of a specific kind. Books with pictures of naked men in them. And as for what was sold under the counter . . ."

A blush spread across her cheeks. It made her even more attractive.

"Johnny wasn't interested in that kind of thing." He was really beginning to annoy her now.

"I'm not suggesting he was." Simkins looked straight into Lizzie's eyes. "Which begs the question: what was he doing there?"

"I've no idea. Investigating a story, as likely as not."

"Snap!" Simkins sounded like a teacher who had just made a particularly dim pupil see the light. "My thoughts entirely. Wouldn't you like that story – the story Johnny gave his life for – to be published?"

"And for you to take all the credit?"

"Of course not. That would be impossible now that Johnny is part of the story."

Lizzie excused herself once more while she saw to another customer. Why had this snake come hissing round her?

"Why me?"

"I'm sorry?" Simkins pretended to be puzzled.

"Why are you telling me all this?" asked Lizzie. "It isn't going to bring Johnny back and, truth be told, the idea that his killer might still be at large is unsettling."

"I thought you might ask your husband why the police seem to be doing nothing to find this other man. At the very least they should interview him. Your husband might have heard something while he's been out and about. After all, he and Johnny were bosom buddies, weren't they? I'm sure he must be making investigations of his own . . ."

So that was it: he had got nowhere through official channels and was consequently trying a different approach.

"Yes, they were – ever since they were toddlers." She fought back tears. She was relieved that she finally knew what the reporter wanted – but the thought that someone had so far got away with murder was shocking. "Very well, I'll ask my husband this evening." She would be interested to hear what Matt said, but she had no intention of passing on any information to this muck-raker.

"I'd be most obliged." Simkins produced his business card with an unnecessary flourish. Lizzie slipped it into a pocket of her uniform. "One more thing: last Monday I saw Johnny coming out of an establishment in Honey Lane. I believe it was number six. An establishment for gentlemen who have special tastes – tastes shared by the bookshop's clientele. I believe both establishments are – or rather, were – owned by the same people." He smiled at her confusion. "I'll bid you good-day." He touched the brim of his hat and sashayed out of the store.

Lizzie watched him in astonishment. In one minute he had turned her world upside down.

Johnny's killer was still at liberty. Why had Matt not told her? Surely he knew? This would explain why he had become so withdrawn. Perhaps he was trying to solve the case himself, against the orders of his superiors and without their knowledge.

But why had the odious Simkins not approached Matt himself? Reporters were supposed to ask awkward questions.

And then it hit her: the photograph must have come from the bookshop or at the very least have some connection with it.

Well, she could not go there now – but she could visit the place in Honey Lane. Those sort of men would hardly pose a threat to her.

The call finally came at a quarter to four.

"It's me," said Vinson when Johnny, summoned by the butler, ran to the kiosk under the stairs and, having made sure the door was closed, picked up the receiver.

"Who else would it be? You're the only person who knows James Danton is here." Johnny was not good at waiting. He had started writing the story of the four murders but found it impossible to concentrate. Not knowing, not being able to do anything, was exhausting.

"Don't get shirty with me, sunshine."

"I'm not your sunshine," said Johnny.

"What a difference a day makes," said Vinson drily. "So much for gratitude."

Johnny sighed. He would never be allowed to forget the events of Saturday evening. Though he had tried to put them out of his head, he was reminded of them each time he sat down.

"Just get to the point."

"Meet me outside the Globe tonight at quarter to twelve."

"On the corner of Hosier Lane, yes?"

"Correct."

"And . . .?"

"That's it. I'll give you the details when I see you."

"Oh, come on!" Johnny snorted with impatience. "You can tell me more than that. What has Rotherforth arranged? What has Matt done? How is he? Hello . . .? Hello . . .?"

The line was dead.

Matt finished putting on his uniform and, glancing at the photo of Lizzie stuck on the back of the door, closed his locker.

"God knows what she saw in you!" Watkiss, passing by, slapped him on the back.

One by one his colleagues left, taking their banter with them, until the room itself seemed to issue a sigh of relief. The air was humid from the showers in the adjoining bathroom and smelled slightly of sweat.

He sat down on the bench, glad to take the weight off his feet, bracing himself for the conversation – and probable confrontation – that he had been putting off for days.

Matt was nearing the point of exhaustion. His original nightmare of agonised paralysis and blinding light had been joined by another in which he could only stand and watch as Johnny was consumed by the flames.

He blamed himself for Johnny's death. When there was no one else he could turn to, he had gone to Johnny for help. The fact that Johnny had been pleased to be asked – had been glad of the chance to pay him back for all the times Matt had helped him – was no consolation. Johnny could never see that, in their own ways, they were as strong as each other. He wished he could swap some of his brawn for a few of Johnny's little grey cells. The sergeant's exams were only a month away.

And how had he repaid his friend's help? By threatening to frame him for murder. All because that second photograph had arrived, with a threat that the next one would go to Lizzie.

Matt knew the pictures were connected to his nightmares. He had to accept that, one way or another, he had been molested. It was in everybody's interest – especially his own – that the truth about them never come out. He loved his job and he was not going to let a couple of perverts – there had to be more than one, because someone had to have taken the photo – ruin his chances of promotion. All his life he had wanted to be a cop; it wasn't just a question of following in his father's footsteps – it was who he was, it was everything he cared about. Apart from Lizzie.

Lizzie. Sweet Lizzie. He had almost let the cat out of the bag yesterday. The temptation to come clean had been almost overwhelming. But there was the baby to think of now. The idea of being a father made his heart swell. For some reason he was convinced that it would be a girl. Whatever happened, his duty now was to look after his pregnant wife; he couldn't risk jeopardising her well-being – they had already lost one baby. And they'd come close to losing this one; when he had to break the news of Johnny's death to Lizzie, he'd been convinced that history was about to repeat itself.

Johnny's murder had hit them both hard. But in Matt's case it was not just the loss he had to deal with but a sense of having betrayed his friend. He had refused to listen to Johnny's theory about a dead cop because dead cops did not make phone calls. It wasn't until Harry Gogg's deranged lover had murdered Johnny that Matt finally took the trouble to question the morgue attendant. Only then did he discover that his friend had been right all along: George Aitken was already dead when he took the phone call from someone claiming to be George. That call could only have been made by the person responsible for Aitken's death: which meant that the killer – who had reached him on an internal line – had to be on the inside.

Footsteps interrupted his train of thought. Here he came, whistling that bloody tune again. It was time to wipe the smirk off his face.

Vinson entered the changing room and went to over to his locker. Matt, standing round the corner, pressed himself against the cracked, white tiles and watched as he took off his uniform and put on his own clothes. A birthmark on his lower back made Matt flush with rage but he did not move.

Instead of just checking that his hair was okay, Vinson stood in front of the mirror and combed the jet black strands over and over again. He should have suspected him long ago. Such behaviour was not normal in a man.

Matt stepped into view. Vinson jumped.

"Oh, hello. I thought was alone."

"Obviously," said Matt. "Got a date?"

"In a manner of speaking." Vinson met his eyes in the mirror. "Why d'you ask?"

Matt ignored the question. "Would it be in Honey Lane by any chance?"

Vinson turned to face him.

"Certainly not. Why would I be going there?"

"I heard you were a friend of Zick."

Vinson laughed, a little too loudly. "Whoever told you that?"

"Never you mind."

Vinson went over to a bench and sat down. "What's up, Matt? Why the interrogation? I thought we were friends."

"So did I." Matt could tell that Vinson had expected him to join him but he stayed where he was. The discrepancy in height only made Vinson more nervous. He stood up again.

"I've always been on your side."

"Then what were you doing in a male brothel on Saturday night?"

"That's an odd question," said Vinson. "What makes you think I was there? Were you there – and if so, what's your excuse?"

"I was trying to find the killers of Harry Gogg and George Aitken. You?"

"Saving someone's life."

"Whose?" Matt's contemptuous tone made it quite plain that he did not believe his colleague.

"It's none of your business. Besides, you wouldn't believe me if I told you. We all have to rely on the discretion of others occasionally, don't we?"

"Is that a threat?" Matt stepped towards him.

"Not at all." Vinson swallowed. "Matt, believe me. I would never do anything to hurt you."

"Then tell me what you were doing in Honey Lane!"

"I can't. Not yet. Maybe tomorrow but not now. Look, I have to go."

Matt sat down, alone once more. There was no doubt: he had seen Vinson's birthmark, which resembled an ink blot, before: on the kneeling man who was greedily fellating him in the second picture. Yet he had not even been able to broach the subject.

Zick had recognised him from somewhere – *Perhaps I've seen you in a photograph . . .* – but refused to elaborate until he had wrapped his fingers round her neck. Her henchman had been useless: one blow to his fat belly had seen him collapse like a burst balloon.

The thought of Vinson's wet lips around his cock made Matt feel sick. Vinson was involved in blackmail and at least one sexual assault. He was unfit to be a cop. The problem was how to expose this without using the pictures as evidence. He did not want the world to know that he had been taken advantage of. Furthermore, Vinson had to be in league with someone else. Alas, Zick had proved much tougher than expected. The madam had clammed up and refused to name anyone apart from his erstwhile friend. Stupid bravery or sheer terror? Matt could not decide. Whatever the reason, he had been unable to extract any more information before the repulsive creature blacked out.

What should he do next? Inspector Rotherforth would know.

The afternoon dragged on as she wrapped the overpriced little boxes that would be ripped open in four days' time. As soon as the hands of the clock stood to attention at 6 p.m. she scurried to the staff quarters, slipped on her coat and stamped her card. Once outside she zigzagged through the foot-traffic to the kerb and hailed a yellow taxi-cab. This was no time to watch the pennies. She explained her intentions to the flat-capped driver and sat back to enjoy the ride. Matt regarded taxis as an unnecessary extravagance but, before they had got married, she had taken them all the time.

She retrieved the photograph from its hiding place in Devonia Road – fortunately Matt was on duty till midnight – and placed the envelope in her handbag. The waiting cab then set off for Honey Lane. Butterflies started fluttering in her stomach. What was she going to do when she got there? Something would come to her. A bunch of fairies did not frighten her.

The cab picked up speed once it had negotiated the Angel which, as usual, was clogged with trams, buses, vans and carts – and their vociferous, gesticulating drivers. It rattled down St John Street, went round the Central Markets of Smithfield, past Bart's and paused at the end of Giltspur Street. Her husband was probably patrolling his beat but he might equally well be just yards away round the corner. The thought of what he had been through brought tears to her eyes. She admonished herself for being silly – he was a big, brave man – and rested her hands on the new life growing inside her.

When they arrived at Honey Lane, the young driver, who had been eyeing her in the rear-view mirror, actually got out to hold open the door for her. She rewarded him with a big tip.

"Sure you got the right place, madam?" She looked up at the imposing house with its glossy black front door. The fanlight above it was decorated with a large figure six.

"Yes, thank you."

"I can wait for you, if you like. I'll turn the meter off."

"That won't be necessary, thank you."

"Suit yourself." He touched the peak of his cap, hopped back into his cab, executed a perfect U-turn and headed back towards Cheapside. A cloud of grey fumes hung in the icy air. It was beginning to snow. The silence was unnerving.

She climbed the steps and raised the lion's-head knocker but, before she had even let go, the door opened and a mountain of a man looked down at her.

"Sorry, no women allowed." He slammed the door in her face. Lizzie immediately used the knocker and did not stop until the brute glowered over her once again.

"I'd like to see the manager, please."

"And what would you be doing with Miss Zick?"

"I thought women weren't allowed."

"Miss Zick runs the place."

"Well, tell her I'd like to talk to her about John Steadman."

The name produced a look of confusion.

"Come in." He stood aside to reveal a wide entrance hall with wooden panelling. A large jardinière took pride of place on a Queen Anne side-table. "I'll see if she's available." He lumbered off down a corridor that led to the rear of the building.

Lizzie listened. She had never been in a brothel before. She had imagined a place of loud music and lewd behaviour, laughter and raucous conversation. This house of ill-repute was as quiet as the grave. A well-dressed gentleman clattered down the stairs carrying a top-hat. He did not seem the slightest bit abashed to see her.

"Most convincing, I must say." He let himself out.

The doorman returned followed by a corpulent woman in a dress that was at least two sizes too small for her. She was wearing too much make-up but her French perfume, to Lizzie's trained nose, seemed expensive. They did not sell it in Gamage's, that was for sure. A little dog trotted behind the madam, its claws clicking on the polished floor.

"Cecilia Zick. How may I be of service?" The question was not accompanied by a smile.

"I'm here about a friend of mine," said Lizzie. "John Steadman. I don't know if you're aware, but he was killed last week."

"I had heard something to that effect. And you are . . .?"

"Mrs Elizabeth Turner. My husband is a policeman at Snow Hill."

"How nice for you." The ageing flapper put a hand to her neck. The powder did not quite conceal what appeared to be bruises. "Coppers are some of my best customers." She laughed at Lizzie's look of horror. "Just my idea of a joke. What exactly d'you want to know?"

"Johnny was a reporter investigating the murder of Harry Gogg. It's said that both of them were killed by the boy who set fire to the shop in question. However, I've been told by another reporter – who is working on an exposé of your sordid set-up – that someone else may be responsible for Johnny's death."

"What? That's poppycock. Who told you that? I can assure you there'll be no newspaper stories about me – that's what I pay insurance for. What's the name of the toe-rag?" Lizzie knew better than to reveal her source. Johnny would have been proud of her.

"Why don't you tell me what Johnny was doing here?"

"He was bothering one of my boys, that's what. He was disrupting business, making a right nuisance of himself. I got Alf here to throw him out."

Lizzie retrieved the photograph from her handbag and reluctantly showed it to the woman.

"Have you seen it before?"

"Can't say as I have." Zick picked up the lap-dog that was yapping at her feet.

"Could it have been taken here?"

"Certainly not. We don't provide souvenirs."

A stocky man, forearms covered in red and blue tattoos, emerged from the parlour on the right.

"I haven't got all night, Cecilia. Got to be back in barracks by ten."

"A thousand apologies, Sergeant. Roberto shouldn't be much longer. I'll bring you another Scotch." The soldier went back into the waiting room. Zick turned to Lizzie. "As you can see I've clients to attend to. I'm sorry I couldn't be of more help. Show Mrs Turner out, Alf."

"One moment please. When did you last see Johnny?"

"Oh, I don't know. I see so many people. The days all blur into one. Saturday, wasn't it? No, silly me. It was last Monday. Just one week ago."

"Hold yer 'orses," blurted Alf. "The little squirt was 'ere on Saturday. Your memory's playing tricks, Cissy. It were only two days ago."

"But he was buried on Friday!" Lizzie stared at the mismatched pair of criminals. "You're lying to me. If the City of London police are in your pocket, the Metropolitan police will still listen to me. They'll no doubt be only too happy to expose their rivals' corruption."

"Idiot!" said Zick, glaring at Alf. However, she swung her fist not at him but at Lizzie, catching her right on the chin.

She packed a hell of a punch for a woman.

When Lizzie came round she was in a threadbare armchair in an old-fashioned kitchen. A single tap dripped into a stone sink. Grey laundry aired on a frame suspended from the peeling ceiling. Her jaw ached. Cecilia Zick was seated at the table watching her. The chihuahua was asleep in front of a feeble fire.

"You wait till Inspector Rotherforth hears about this," said Lizzie, checking to see if any of her teeth were loose. Apparently not. Zick gave a hollow laugh.

"That will be much sooner than you think." Lizzie rubbed her face.

"What d'you mean?"

"Rotherforth is my guardian angel. In return for a share in my considerable profits he ensures that my business is not interrupted. It's taken years for me to find the ideal premises and build up a list of trustworthy clients. It makes sense to have the police on my side."

"I don't believe you."

"Well, you'll be able to ask him yourself later. He and his associates owned the bookshop too."

If Johnny had found all this out, thought Lizzie, it was hardly surprising he had been murdered. And, fool that she was, she had gone to Rotherforth for help. The photograph of Matt must be incriminating evidence. No wonder the inspector had told her to destroy it. If only she could get a message to Matt. Rotherforth had to be stopped.

"I'd love to stay and chat, but there are a lot of hungry men upstairs. In the meantime it's the dungeon for you, my love. Don't worry, there aren't any rats."

Lizzie knew it was now or never. *Go for the eyes,* her father had told her. *It doesn't matter how big or strong someone is, their eyes are as vulnerable as yours.*

She launched herself at the woman, her carmine nails ready to scratch and gouge.

Zick, however, was ready for her. She grabbed Lizzie's wrists before her nails could find their target and wrestled her to the floor. The dog woke up and, in a ridiculous attempt to protect its mistress, leaped on top of Lizzie, yapping for all it was worth. When she instinctively brought her knees up, one of them, by fluke rather than design, found her captor's groin. The woman let out a huge groan, rolled over and shrieked. Her wig had fallen off.

Of course – that was it! – she could see it now.

This woman was a man.

She should not have laughed. However, the sight of the roly-poly man in a dress rolling around clutching his wig was too much for her.

Zick, unfortunately, could not see the funny side. He flung the syrup to the floor and finally got to his feet.

"Let's see if you're still laughing in a minute." He dragged her out of the kitchen and down the back stairs. "Alf! *Alf!*" The gorilla came up to meet them. "Put her in the dungeon."

The hulking doorman slung her over his shoulder and carried her, kicking and screaming, down another two flights of stairs into the cellar. He unlocked a door, switched on the light – a bare bulb of low wattage – and dropped her into what appeared to be a real-life torture chamber. Lizzie gasped in disbelief.

Three of the walls, which were painted black, boasted a vast array of whips, chains and other restraints. She could not even begin to guess what some of them were designed to do. A large, full-length mirror took up most of the fourth wall. There was a cage in the shape of a man, rather like a cross between an iron maiden and a suit of armour, at one end of the room and, at the other, an X-shaped board tilted at an angle of seventy degrees.

Alf dragged her across the lino to the board and, having slapped her face when she tried to resist, cuffed her hands and feet to it.

Zick, breathing heavily, in female guise once again, came in and stood on the spotted rubber mat in the middle of the floor. The lap-dog was nowhere to be seen or heard.

"What's the matter? Lost your sense of humour?" He was still livid. "I've got better things to do than deal with interfering bitches like you."

"Wait till my husband finds out about this," said Lizzie. "You'll be sorry then."

Zick laughed. "What makes you think you're going to see him again?" He turned on his high heels and left.

The faithful henchman gagged her tightly with a filthy rag then trailed after his boss. He locked the door behind them.

The transvestite's cruel words hung in the air. Lizzie felt a stab of fear – for herself and Matt. What had she done?

A sense of dread spread through her veins.

Sooner or later Simkins is bound to realise that I haven't got any photographs of frolicking Tory grandees – yet . . . I can't keep increasing the price to fob him off. "They're worth every penny, Simkins. Wait till you see what they're doing . . ." If he gets too pushy, I'll have to get Timney to fake some. Shouldn't be difficult.

Mind you, I can't see Simkins being a major problem. He's too ambitious. With the right handling, he might well be a good substitute for Fox.

Zick will keep his trap shut, too. Living off immoral earnings is a slap on the wrist compared to what he'd get for conspiracy to murder. He's in too deep now to risk blabbing.

What I don't get is why Moss sent Turner's wife the photograph. Was he after revenge for Gogg's death? Maybe it was him rather than Gogg that sent the tip-off to Steadman. Well, it's lucky for him I didn't know about that when I throttled him – I'd have made him suffer a lot more if I'd realised he was going to cost me the bookshop and the brothel.

Still, we'll soon be back in business, poncing in pastures new. There's only a couple of loose ends left to tie up tonight and then this mess will all be sorted.

If Turner's got any sense, he'll fall in line like a good lad. He won't want that pretty wife of his coming to any harm. And he'll be signing both their death warrants if he doesn't do as he's told.

In the meantime, I'll have to put off dealing with Hughes. He's become a liability, that one – since he found out Aitken was a cop, he's been scared shitless. He'd rather be exposed as a corpse-fucker than take the drop for murder. Well, thanks to Turner, he's got a few hours' reprieve. I'll let him stick around long enough to dispose of the bodies – then I'll dispose of him.

TWENTY-SEVEN

Monday, 21st December, 11.45 p.m.

Johnny stood outside the Globe and shivered in the borrowed overcoat. He had lost his own in Honey Lane and was waiting for the right moment to ask if he could claim for a new one on expenses. The clearing sky had sent the temperature plummeting. The public house had long since shut its doors. Most of its patrons would now be tucked up warm in bed.

The prospect of kicking his heels till closing time had been unbearable, so he had left the luxurious warmth of Stone's home – without his irksome false nose – at 9 p.m. Before leaving he had taken the precaution of writing down the details of the rendezvous. If he was not back by breakfast-time, the butler would pass the note to his master. Of course, it was a futile gesture: it would surely be too late by then.

The snow, as he had correctly surmised, was causing

transport chaos. As he'd made the journey, Johnny's excitement had been mixed with something else: not fear exactly but a sense of dread. Something was not quite right. Too many things could go wrong. Was he walking into a trap?

Vinson could have killed Gogg. Stone's words haunted him. Vinson had been outside the cold-store that night. The taller man Johnny had seen with him must have been Rotherforth. From what he'd observed, Johnny had assumed that Vinson was following Rotherforth's orders in trying to get rid of the knife. Except . . . he had not got rid of it: he had ensured that it was found by a journalist. Why? Vinson said that he was trying to expose Rotherforth.

But what if neither of the two cops had killed Harry Gogg. What if they were both following orders, protecting someone else?

Johnny wondered how long it had taken Vinson to realise he was being followed. Had he planned to lead him down Passing Alley, or had he simply reacted to unforeseen circumstances?

The trouble with this story all along was the lack of concrete evidence. There was the bloody butcher's knife and that was it. The rest was nothing more than hearsay. He only had Vinson's word for it that Rotherforth the rapist was also a killer.

Given Vinson's jealousy over his friendship with Matt, perhaps the tip-off was actually a set-up designed to get him killed. With him out of the way, the love-sick Vinson would have Matt all to himself – assuming Lizzie were ignored.

No, it was too outlandish. He was being paranoid. Had Vinson wanted him dead, he could have knifed him in the alley or suffocated him at the brothel. But then, either way he would have ended up with blood on his hands. If, however, Vinson made it look as though he'd saved Johnny's life, Matt would be extremely grateful to him.

The tip-off had been a clever move: whether or not it succeeded in unmasking Rotherforth, whether or not his supposed rival for Matt's affections lived, the anonymous Vinson could not lose. All the cop had to do was light the blue touchpaper, stand back and watch.

Johnny was bitterly regretting the two pints of IPA he'd downed before the pub closed. It was no good. He had to go. He nipped round the corner into Hosier Lane and relieved himself in a dark doorway.

He looked over his shoulder at Bart's. Its brightly lit windows recalled an advent calendar. For months after his mother's death Johnny had not been able to go near the hospital. Its very name was enough to bring back the endless, sleepless nights of pain. The smell of people rotting from the inside. The shame of waiting for loved ones to die – and the grief and guilt when they did.

"I could arrest you for that."

Johnny jumped. He buttoned himself up hastily. He had not heard Vinson coming. A ligature could have been round his neck before he knew it. The snow muffled sound – which was probably in their favour.

"Don't you ever hang up on me again."

In truth Johnny was no stranger to having the phone

slammed down on him, but that did not mean he was going to let Vinson get away with it.

"Or what?" The copper towered over him. "Do you want my help or not?"

"You don't frighten me," said Johnny. "Don't forget your job is on the line as well. Boys in blue aren't meant to be bum-boys. Tell me, why did you become a cop?"

Vinson studied him for a moment, as if checking that he was being serious.

"I suppose I craved a sense of belonging. All my life I've felt like an outsider, different from everyone else. Wearing a uniform, looking the same, made me feel safe. Besides, I wanted to do something worthwhile and exciting, to help people, not waste my life in a factory or an office. It wasn't just about spending a lot of time in the company of men." He gave a sigh. "And it was all going so well until Rotherforth got his claws into me."

"I'm still not clear why you sent me the tip-off."

"I told you: you're a friend of Matt's. I knew you were bound to turn to him for help. It worked like a dream to begin with: he got all the credit for finding Harry Gogg. How do you think he found you in Green Hill's Rents? Harry thought he'd win favour by telling Rotherforth about your meeting." Vinson shook his head. "Fatal mistake. Rotherforth was furious: he was certain that Harry had already squealed – then, with his hat-pin, really made him squeal. Harry swore on his life that he hadn't told you anything, that he hadn't sent you the tip-off, but Rotherforth didn't believe him. He persuaded him to go ahead with the meeting and told him exactly what he was supposed to say – some cock-and-bull story."

"But he was dead when I got there."

"I don't think Rotherforth ever intended for him to actually meet with you. It's more likely he'd decided the cold-store would be the ideal location to kill Harry and maybe get rid of you in the process. Leaving Harry's corpse displayed like that was intended to be a warning to everybody else to keep their mouths shut."

"But if you knew all this –"

"I didn't know it then; I put it all together, bit by bit, afterwards. At the time, I thought I could put a stop to Rotherforth's games by making sure Sergeant Dwyer passed on the report of a possible break-in at the store when Matt called from the police-box on his beat." He sighed. "I never meant for Harry, let alone Jo and Charlie, to die. I really liked George Aitken, too. Now Rotherforth is finally going to pay for all the things he's done."

"Hang on a sec – you do realise that you could have sent Matt to his death? What if he'd turned up as Rotherforth was butchering Harry, or trying to kill me? There's no way you could have guaranteed he'd arrive after my meeting – or the killing."

"It was a risk worth taking. If Matt had arrived sooner and seen Rotherforth entering the cold-store, he might have been able to save Harry as well as you."

"Okay." It was a valid point. "When did you realise I was following you?"

"In the alley. It was a strange moment. I was going

to see that Matt found the knife, but then I recognised your scent."

"I don't wear scent!"

"I know you don't, but everyone has a scent unique to them. Yours is a mixture of soap, sweat and something else. It reminded me of freshly baked bread. It's nice. I decided to leave the knife with you." He met Johnny's gaze. "You still don't trust me, do you?"

Johnny remained silent.

Vinson gave a sorrowful shake of his head. He produced a white envelope from his greatcoat and gave it to him. "Here you are."

Johnny moved into the moonlight. It was a photograph of a football team. Vinson pointed to the boy holding the ball. He was tall, narrow-shouldered but by no means weedy. His curly hair softened his chiselled features. A big grin lit up his face.

"Charlie was the leading goal-scorer that season," said Vinson. "He represented St Mary's in Stoke Newington. The local rag ran a picture when they beat a team from Tottenham in a really rough derby. There wasn't much turning of the other cheek."

"Thank you." Johnny could still hear the boy's scream as he fell to his fiery death. "Have you told his father?"

"The bastard didn't shed a single tear. He's apparently very grateful to you for arranging the burial. You saved him a lot of money."

"And that's all he said?"

"Yes, apart from *good riddance*."

Johnny's blood ran cold.

"And Rotherforth?"

"He just shrugged and said something like *only another few thousand to go.*"

Johnny could not think of a suitable response.

Vinson shivered. "Come on. Matt's already there."

"And where is 'there'?" asked Johnny as they tramped past the Watch House – once a defence against resurrection men – in Giltspur Street. The snow, blue in the moonlight, was a foot-deep in places.

"Here," said Vinson, stopping at the mouth of an alley which ran alongside the Bluecoat School where the poet Charles Lamb had once been a pupil. "Rotherforth sent a message to Matt telling him to be at the foot of St Sepulchre's bell-tower at midnight."

Johnny stared down the passage into the darkness. It was a good place for an ambush. He hesitated.

"Don't worry," said Vinson. "I'm not going to kiss you."

The church did not have much in the way of a graveyard. Its original one, south of Cowcross Street, had long since been built over. A barnlike structure, with no division between nave and chancel, it was nevertheless known to generations of children. The great bell in its tower was rung each time prisoners began their final journey from Newgate to Tyburn. The night before, a handbell, still on display in the church, was rung outside the condemned man's cell. These were the "bells of Old Bailey" in the nursery rhyme.

The priest, who entered the gaol via a tunnel which

ran from the crypt, would recite the following verse as he rang the handbell:

All you that in the condemned hole do lie,
Prepare you for tomorrow you shall die,
Watch all and pray; the hour is drawing near
That you before the Almighty must appear.
Examine well yourselves, in time repent,
That you may not to eternal flames be sent,
And when St Sepulchre's bell in the morning tolls
The Lord have mercy on your souls.

The few square yards at the foot of the tower had been given the grand name of Snow Hill Court; a short passage connected it to Snow Hill itself. Two other alleys also led into it: one from Giltspur Street – down which Johnny and Vinson were making their way – and a longer, narrower snicket which wound past the rear of the Rolling Barrel. Anyone who turned down the latter soon found their progress blocked by a black door without a lock or handle. This door was a fire escape for those inside the police station.

It slowly began to open.

Matt, who had been standing anxiously in the shadows for five minutes, heard a noise from the alley leading to Giltspur Street. He tapped his night-stick against his leg. Nothing happened. Had he imagined it? Perhaps it was a cat – although most living things seemed to have vanished from the face of the earth. He strained his ears

– and thought he detected a sound coming from the other alley.

Why had Rotherforth suggested they meet here rather than in the comfort of the station? He had promised to explain about Aitken's death and Vinson's role in it. He had also impressed upon him the need for absolute discretion. Matt supposed the inspector had his reasons. He was in no position – and had no authority – to question them.

Johnny, forced to wait behind Vinson, was as impatient as ever, keen to see their mutual friend. He peered round the cop and into the courtyard which was sliced diagonally in half by the tower's shadow. The contrast between the darkness and the moonlit snow was dazzling.

Unable to stop shivering – nervous anticipation only made it worse – he stepped even closer to Vinson and tried to absorb some of his body-heat.

Suddenly he heard Matt's voice whisper, "Sir!"

Rotherforth emerged into the yard and stood there for a moment in silence. What was he going to do?

Vinson and Johnny, not daring to move, watched intently.

Above them the great bell began to toll midnight. All over the city, church bells cut through the icy, crystalline air.

The shortest day of the year – which in so many ways had been the longest – was ending.

* * *

Rotherforth cleared his throat. "I'm not the man you think I am, Turner. However, I can assure you Aitken wasn't murdered. His death was an accident. When Steadman found out about it I sent you those pretty pictures to make you stop him digging around. Alas, the plan backfired."

Matt, unable to comprehend his superior's confession, simply stared at him.

"But where did the photographs come from? How did I come to be in them?"

"We'll get to that in a minute – maybe. First you have a decision to make. Some people are prepared to pay a lot of money for such photographs – especially when they feature in them."

"You're talking about blackmail."

"I prefer to call it punishing perverts. Whatever it is, it's extremely lucrative. Couldn't you and your wife, with a baby on the way, do with some extra cash? You'll be paying a mortgage soon."

"What would I have to do?"

"Nothing. Absolutely nothing. Just keep your mouth shut."

"No."

"Can you really afford to turn down hundreds of pounds? We're branching out into moving pictures. One of my associates works at Gainsborough Studios. In the meantime, imagine the hoo-ha if your debut were to appear on the station notice-board."

"I'm a copper: I can't just ignore blackmail and murder."

"And I can't let you just walk away." The two men stared at each other. "You'll be sitting the sergeant's exam next month. A good report from me will be essential."

"What makes you think you'll still be in the job?

"This –" Rotherforth pulled out a gun. It glinted in the moonlight.

"If you're planning to kill me too, you might as well tell me how you managed to photograph me in such a compromising position."

"Does it really matter?" The inspector's voice took on an air of resignation. "Okay, I suppose I do owe you an explanation. Someone who had no choice took them for me. You were – what's the word? – selected because you're a fine figure of a man. I doped your cocoa one night when you were staying in the station."

"And Aitken?"

"He wasn't as strong as you. I overdid his dose. It was an accident. A stupid bloody accident. Vinson and Gogg, acting under my orders, took the body to Bart's."

Matt groaned, took a step forward but stopped dead when Rotherforth raised the gun.

"That's right. You just stay there and listen," said the inspector. "I don't expect you to understand. I never wanted it to come to this – believe me, I like you – but if you hadn't rescued Steadman from the cold-store that would have been the end of the matter. Gogg should have known better than to blab. He deserved everything he got. As did Steadman – a persistent bugger, if ever there was one."

"I didn't tell him anything," said Matt, fighting back the rage, trying to keep his voice low and even. The temptation to shout abuse – if not cry for help – was almost irresistible.

"Don't tell lies, Turner. I saw you talking to him in the Viaduct."

"So what? I didn't know about Aitken until Johnny came to me! Later on, I told him that Aitken had called me – which he obviously didn't as he was already dead."

"I was surprised you didn't recognise my voice." Rotherforth smiled wolfishly.

"Well," said Matt, "there are a lot of Scots in London."

"Indeed. Though there's one less now." Rotherforth paused.

It was a bit late to pretend he was sorry – but, thought Matt, the bastard was going to try anyway.

"I really didn't mean for Aitken to die, you know. It was an accident, I swear. I did my best to revive him. He was a lovely lad." A catch crept into his voice. "I just couldn't wake him up afterwards."

For a moment Matt thought Rotherforth was going to break down. He took another step. He so wanted to kill him.

"Don't move!" hissed the inspector. "Another inch and I'll blow your head off."

Matt swallowed. "You said *afterwards*. After what?"

"Christ, you can be a dumb ox," said Rotherforth bitterly. "In a way, that's what first attracted me to you. I couldn't wait to have you."

The scales finally fell from Matt's eyes. "You knocked me out so that you could sodomise me?"

"What's the problem?" said Rotherforth. "You survived, didn't you? You'd never have known if you'd kept your mouth shut. I didn't mean any harm." If he could not persuade Turner then he would humiliate him. "All I did was enjoy your beefy arse. All the hours at the gym have certainly paid off. You should thank me. You were the best, Turner. Much better than Vinson. Mind you, he didn't go round blabbing. He took it like a man."

"Like a man? What do you know about being a man?" Matt said with a sneer. "Real men don't have sex with other men."

Rotherforth cocked his old service revolver. The click seemed incredibly loud.

"You're doing it again, Turner. Saying things you shouldn't. I should never have given you a second chance. I should've killed you straight away."

"Why, though? You're married. I don't understand why you did it."

"Why not? I did it because I could. Because it felt right."

"You cunt." Matt's teeth – and fists – were clenched. "You won't get away with this. I told PC Watkiss that I was meeting you. If anything happens to me, he's got a letter for Superintendent Inskip."

A sad smile spread across Rotherforth's face.

"Bad choice, Turner. You might as well have written in invisible ink."

Matt had recovered from the initial shock. His racing mind was full of questions. "You're bluffing – you're not going to fool me again. That said, you can't have done it all by yourself. Who helped you?"

"PC Vinson, of course. He's besotted with you. He was so grateful when I let him have his way with you. But then, you can see that just by looking at the pictures. I believe you've seen the one where he has his mouth full. There are dozens more like that. He'll be most distressed when he sees your corpse."

"So you're going to kill me after all?" Matt, ignoring the gun, stared straight at the murderer. All he had was his night-stick. His luck had finally run out.

"'Fraid so," said Rotherforth, and pulled the trigger.

TWENTY-EIGHT

The bullet hit Vinson in the chest, the force of it, at such close range, spinning him round. He crumpled like an empty paper bag.

It took Matt a couple of seconds to realise that he was unscathed. He knelt down beside Vinson and raised him into a sitting position. The blood turned the snow black.

The gunshot had been deafening in the close confines of the courtyard. Johnny's ears were still ringing. It was so much louder than in the movies. He had been sure Matt was a goner. Vinson had come out of nowhere, moving with such speed that Johnny had not even had time to react – and neither had Rotherforth. He was still standing in the same spot, gun in hand.

With a roar, Matt rushed the inspector. More out of annoyance than surprise, Rotherforth swatted him on the side of his head with the hot gun. Stunned, Matt collapsed beside Vinson on the ground.

Vinson's eyes opened. "I'm sorry," he said. Then he coughed and blood gushed out of his mouth.

"Don't be silly," muttered Matt. "You saved my life. Hang on. Someone's bound to have heard the shot. Help will be here any minute."

"It's too late," said Vinson, grimacing. "Fuck, it hurts. I've nothing left to lose now . . . I love you, Matt. Always have, always will."

He did not say another word.

"Very touching," said Rotherforth. Wisps of smoke still curled from the gun. "On your feet, Turner. A gentleman doesn't shoot a man when he's down."

Matt, still dizzy, got up. His greatcoat was soaked with snow and Vinson's blood.

"Go on then, if you're going to do it," he said, flinging down his night-stick. "What are you waiting for? One more dead body isn't going to make any difference. They can only hang you once."

"You're the last one," said Rotherforth grimly. "There's no one else. If it's any consolation, I meant it when I said you were the best."

"It isn't," said Matt and spat at him.

The spittle landed bang in Rotherforth's left eye. He did not even bother to wipe it away: he merely raised the Webley and aimed it at Matt's head.

Johnny felt as if his feet were rooted to the ground. Surely they'd have heard the shot from inside Snow Hill. Where was the sound of running footsteps and police whistles?

But there was just a click as Rotherforth thumbed the hammer back on the gun.

It was down to Johnny. He had to do something *now*.

"Put the gun down, Rotherforth," he shouted. "You're surrounded. The whole world knows about your sexual depravity and the murders of George Aitken, Harry Gogg, Joseph Moss, Charles Timney and John Steadman. You're a disgrace to that uniform. Your crimes will disgust all right-minded people."

Rotherforth, startled, turned and fired three shots into the darkness. Acrid smoke hung in the air.

Matt dropped into a crouch and picked up his night-stick.

Desperate to keep the gun from swinging back towards Matt, Johnny jeered, "Is that the best you can do?"

Another shot whizzed past him. Johnny had ducked his head back round the corner just in time.

"Give yourself up before anyone else is killed," he shouted. "Aren't you sick of death?"

Raised voices could be heard in the distance. All three men turned to look in the direction of Snow Hill police station. They had woken up at last – and they were running this way.

"Ah, fuck it," said Rotherforth.

And he pulled the trigger again.

TWENTY-NINE

Blood and brain tissue spattered the wall of the church and stained the snow-covered ground. The sound of the shot ricocheted round the courtyard. For one astonishing moment he remained on his feet, then he toppled like a felled oak.

The two on-lookers did not move. They had only seen people shot on the silver screen: real life was different. The inside of someone's head was a fascinatingly ugly sight.

Matt, who had involuntarily shut his eyes when the gun went off, could not believe them now. Rotherforth had eaten his last bullet. The bullet he'd thought would end his life. He stared at the rapidly cooling corpse.

The excited voices got louder as they came up the hill.

"Matt! Come on!" Johnny stepped into the moonlight. Matt clutched his heart and stared at the black-haired double of his friend. Try as he might, he could not speak.

"Snap out of it. I'm not a ghost!"

Matt remained stock-still as Johnny embraced him joyfully.

"See, it really is me!" Johnny said, tugging at his arm. "Come on, we have to get to Zick's before word gets out Rotherforth is dead and the rest of the gang do a runner."

Matt, in a daze, followed Johnny down the alley to Giltspur Street. They broke into a run as policemen's whistles began to shriek.

The bodies had been found.

The snow made it hard going but Johnny did not care as they skidded and slid alongside the massive walls of the Old Bailey. He was so glad to be reunited with Matt.

He had felt like whooping when Rotherforth had topped himself – the bastard had had it coming for a long time – but now he was beginning to realise that the inspector had escaped justice once again. His death had been too quick and too painless.

Johnny had been counting on Rotherforth being brought to trial. He'd wanted to see him in the dock, forced to explain why he had turned from enforcing the law to breaking it. Now they would probably never know.

Though they didn't know it, they were following the same route that Lizzie's cab had taken hours earlier. There were few footprints on the pavements of Newgate

Street. The snow, which had long since leaked into Johnny's shoes, made his socks chafe.

To begin with the two men said little; each was too wrapped up in his own thoughts. Eventually Matt broke the silence:

"Well, at least we know what – or rather who – caused my nightmares," he said, attempting a jocular tone in an effort to hide his embarrassment. "It makes sense now. I'd kind of suspected as much, but was hoping against hope there'd be another explanation."

"There's none so blind as those who will not see," said Johnny. Did that sound like an accusation? It was not meant to be. "He did the same thing to me, more or less. God, it hurt."

"He did? When?"

Johnny was touched by Matt's concern.

"I went back to Zick's on Saturday to have another go at questioning Stan the messenger boy, but she saw through my disguise."

"*She?*"

"The madam. She's Rotherforth's business partner."

"You mean 'he'. Surely you knew Zick was a man?" Matt stopped in amazement. "Didn't you notice the size of those hands? He used to work down the docks. Sometimes, Johnny, you're so naïve."

"I had my mind on other things," Johnny said huffily. At least the darkness hid his red face. Everybody must have assumed he had known all along and was just being polite. He did not like cross-dressing and found pantomime a bore.

"Well, I'm sorry that Rotherforth got to you as well," said Matt. "Now you know how I felt. One thing's for certain: I'll never drink cocoa again."

They laughed, too loudly, the noise echoing off the sleeping buildings in Cheapside. It was like old times: the two of them against the world, safe in each other's company.

"You're not going to write about it, are you?" Matt looked down at the virgin snow.

"There's no need," said Johnny. "I've got enough evidence that Rotherforth was a killer and a pornographer on the side without going into everything that happened. Some truths are best left untold. What about Superintendent Inskip, though?"

"Without proof, there's nothing we can do. I don't like the idea of anyone being untouchable. I'll try and keep tabs on him. The odds are he'll slip up sooner or later."

"So what's the plan?" asked Johnny as they turned into Honey Lane.

"It's simple," said Matt. "I'm going to beat the crap out of Zick – and then arrest him for living off immoral earnings."

Johnny suddenly halted.

"What is it?"

"Simkins," said Johnny. "He was outside when I got turfed down the stairs on my first visit. He never did say what he was doing here."

"Same as you, probably," said Matt. "He came to your funeral. He's not a bad fellow – for a hack. He claims to have alerted the fire brigade when the bookshop went up."

"Perhaps he was following me," said Johnny. "Or just following the same clues. I was at the cemetery."

"You were?" Matt shook his head. "You're a piece of work, causing all that grief."

"I'm sorry. I will, of course, reimburse you for the wreath. The fire was too good an opportunity to miss. I heard Rotherforth kill Joseph Moss, but there was someone else there as well – the son of the man who took the photographs. He was the one whose body they found and buried in my name."

"Shame it wasn't the photographer himself."

"He's called James Timney."

"Well, we'll see what he has to say for himself." Matt took off his helmet and scratched the side of his head. "I presume Rotherforth killed Harry Gogg as well."

"Indeed. You wouldn't have really framed me, would you?"

"Of course not," said Matt. "I was going out of my mind at the thought of Lizzie being dragged into it all. I thought if I could just get you to back off, I'd be able to sniff around and do a bit of investigating on the quiet myself. Knowing how persistent you can be when you're on the trail, I had to come up with something pretty drastic to make sure you took me seriously. I was just trying to protect you really."

"I know," said Johnny. "But you'd saved my life at the cold-store and I was determined to unmask your blackmailer."

"Well, we're quits now. As for Simkins, I wouldn't worry about him. You know something that he doesn't: you're alive!"

"So I am," said Johnny. "I suppose he would look rather stupid if he blames Zick or Rotherforth for my demise."

"Zick will be able to tell you what Simkins knows. Rotherforth's death may loosen his tongue – and if it doesn't, we'll loosen it for him. Okay, here we are – are you ready?"

The house was in total darkness. Not a chink of light showed through its shutters and blinds. It was the dead of night: most law-abiding citizens – and many who were not – would be fast asleep at this hour.

Matt hammered on the door but no one came. Johnny stepped forward and tried the knocker himself.

"What?" asked Matt.

"The sound," said Johnny. "It's different."

He knelt down to peep through the letter-box.

"It's blocked up!"

Matt put a hand on his shoulder. "Did you hear that cry for help?"

"No," said Johnny.

Matt rolled his eyes.

"Well, I did," he said, and rammed his massive shoulder against the door. It hardly moved. "I could do with a little help here."

It took a while but eventually the pair of them, breathing heavily, managed to break into the brothel.

"Zick clearly didn't like unexpected visitors," said Matt, wiping his brow.

"We're too late," said Johnny. He stamped on the bare boards. There was no trace of the Turkey rug that had covered them.

The chesterfield, wing-back armchairs and aspidistras had vanished from the parlour. The brocaded drapes had been taken down. The bedrooms on the first, second and third floors – where so many illicit liaisons had been enjoyed and recorded – were without their enseaméd beds.

Johnny stared through the two-way mirrors in amazement. A window in the floor of a walk-in cupboard looked down on the bed where he and Stan had kissed. He hoped there were no pictures to prove it.

The boys, the bouncer and the little mutt had all vanished, along with their boss.

"The turd has flown," said Johnny. "What do we do now?"

A crash in the cellar startled both of them. They rushed down the stairs. All the doors were open except one. It was locked.

"Stand back," said Matt. It took just two kicks with his regulation boots for the lock to give way. He switched on the light. For a moment he stood frozen in horror.

Johnny pushed past him. Lizzie was spread-eagled on a cross that was now lying on the floor. When she saw him she gave a muffled scream.

"It's all right. I'm not a ghost." He knelt down, removed her gag and undid the straps that held her wrists and ankles.

Matt swept her up in his arms and buried his face in

her neck. Even though she had been through a painful ordeal – as her bruised face testified – it was her husband who was in tears.

"Put me down, Matt. I've wet myself. Apart from that, I'm all right, honest. You know I like to stand on my own two feet."

But her legs were still too wobbly to support her, so Matt took most of her weight as she hobbled towards the door.

"What the hell are you doing here? Are you mad – and in your condition? You could have been killed!" Matt's distress manifested itself in fury.

"I was trying to help!"

"How did you even know about this place?"

She produced a business card from her pocket. "He came to see me today."

"Henry Simkins!" Matt turned to Johnny, anger distorting his features.

"Don't look at me. I had nothing to do with this."

"He gave it to me this afternoon," said Lizzie. "He said that Johnny's killer was still at large and that he may have been killed because he was investigating this place. I thought a woman would be safe in a queer brothel."

"Well, you were wrong," said Matt, relief suddenly replacing his rage. "Why didn't you tell me what you planned to do?"

"You were at work. And I knew you'd stop me from interfering. Can't we just go home?"

"Not yet," said Matt. "What happened here? Why did everyone clear out?"

"I don't know – I was locked up down here so I couldn't tell what was going on. Suddenly there was a lot of running about and banging of doors and heavy things being moved. Then everything went quiet. It didn't take them long to clear out," said Lizzie. "They must be used to doing a bunk. They forgot all about me."

"I hate to think what would have happened if we hadn't found you when we did."

"I heard your footsteps and, in a panic, the only thing I could think of doing was tipping the damn contraption over."

"It was a stroke of genius," said Johnny. "How's the baby?"

"Fine, I think."

"We'll let the doctors decide that," said Matt firmly. "We're going to Bart's before we go home."

"I need to go to the office to write this up," said Johnny. "It'll take me the rest of the night. You don't need to speak to Simkins immediately, do you, Matt?"

"No. Relax. You can have your moment of glory. Remember what we talked about though."

"Don't worry, I'll ensure both our reputations are enhanced. Why don't you go and find a cab? It won't be easy on a night like this. I'll stay with Lizzie."

As soon as she heard Matt tramping up the stairs Lizzie opened her handbag and gave Johnny an envelope.

"I was trying to find an explanation for this." He recognised what was inside immediately. "I assume you've already seen something like it."

"Unfortunately I have," said Johnny. "Matt was drugged by Rotherforth. He had no idea what was happening to him. The pictures were being used to blackmail him – but you must never let on you know. It's all over now. Rotherforth has just shot himself."

"Oh! I went to him for help. He told me to burn it."

Johnny studied the envelope. "Is this what it came in?"

"Yes. You recognise the handwriting?"

"I'm afraid so. Remember Daisy, the chorus girl who claimed to be an actress?'

"We only met the once."

"She found the photograph at my place – Matt had given it to me so that I could try to find out what was going on. Daisy jumped to the wrong conclusion and stormed out with it. She told me later that she had burned it. It looks as though sending it to you was her way of getting back at me – and Matt."

"I did notice she was most put out when he wasn't bowled over by her cheap charms."

"Unlike me, you mean?"

"You aim too low, Johnny, always have."

"Then how come I'm in love with you?"

"You're not. Not really. Once, perhaps – but not now. You needed me, especially when your mother was ill, but you have to let go of the past. You're a good-looking, kind young man. It's time you stopped behaving like a randy schoolboy and found yourself someone who actually meant something to you. You'll always have a special place in my heart though."

Matt came clomping down the stairs. "Thank God for this uniform. You can drop us off at the hospital on your way to Fleet Street, Johnny."

THIRTY

Tuesday, 22nd December, 7.35 a.m.

Johnny was roused from his slumber by a well-aimed kick. He had been out cold beneath his desk.

"I thought you were dead! What on earth have you done to your hair? Trying to copy my good looks?" Louis Dimeo stood over him grinning, his scrubbed skin glowing with health. The football fanatic was fitter than many of the sportsmen he wrote about.

Johnny groaned and stiffly clambered back into his chair.

"The report of my death was an exaggeration – as Mark Twain once said." Adding, as an afterthought: "He was an American writer."

Dimeo wagged his finger.

"Don't patronise me. 'The Creator made Italy from designs by Michael Angelo . . .'"

Johnny was impressed. "Where's that from?"

"No idea. Anyway, why the subterfuge?"

"I was working undercover. A bent cop tried to kill me – three times. It's the scoop of the year."

The young Italian must have been surprised. He handed him the mug of tea he was holding.

"Here you are. I'll get myself another one."

"Thanks." He took a sip and winced.

Dimeo must have put at least four sugars in it.

The article was finished by 4.30 a.m. Johnny knew that he should go home, catnap, wash and change, but the effort had left him completely drained. Every ounce of energy had gone into the writing: it was as if the three thousand words had just flowed. The problem had not been what to include but what to exclude. As Twain told Rudyard Kipling: *Get your facts first, and then you can distort them as much as you please.*

He had portrayed the popular and widely respected Rotherforth as a corrupt pervert who had drugged a young constable under his command with the intention of raping him, only to accidentally kill him in the process. To cover up what he had done, he'd murdered Harry Gogg, a police informer who had spoken to the *Daily News*, and then tried to kill a *News* reporter by locking him in a Smithfield cold-store. Matt's role in the story was restricted to his role in rescuing Johnny.

The article had gone on to describe the inspector's torching of the pornographic bookshop, and the murders of Joseph Moss and Charles Timney. Rotherforth's association with Cecil Zick and his brothel was also outlined, without mentioning the names of any of the boys. It ended with an account of the heroic death of PC Tom Vinson, who had first tipped off the *News*, and the moment when Rotherforth, faced with exposure and disgrace, had shot himself.

Johnny omitted to mention the fact that Gogg and Moss were lovers, knowing it would cause most readers to have less sympathy for them. Nor did he mention Vinson's homosexuality.

He decided to leave Percy Hughes' name out of the piece because the mortuary attendant had been acting under duress – and his gratitude should ensure his future co-operation.

And, because the peace of mind of the living – Matt, Lizzie and himself – was more important than the further denigration of the dead, he made no mention of the photographs.

The lift-boy sniffed when he saw Johnny's unshaven face and smelled his stale clothes.

"Did you miss me?" asked Johnny.

"If I say yes, will you give me a Christmas box?"

The lad's cockiness reminded him of his younger self.

"Nice try. How about, if you don't say yes, I'll box your ears?"

Victor Stone was already sitting behind his enormous desk when Johnny was admitted to the inner sanctum.

While Johnny sat fidgeting on one of the sofas, his editor read the article not once but twice.

"Well, this should set the cat among the pigeons!

The police will no doubt want to speak to you, but the fact that Rotherforth and Vinson cannot contradict you means they can't refute the accusations – although they're bound to try. And if Cecil Zick has any sense he'll keep his mouth shut."

"He's probably in Paris by now," said Johnny.

"I dare say you're right. Well done, Steadman. It's too long – but the subs can take care of that. We'll lead with it on tonight's front page and continue it on page two. A sad tale's best for winter." He paused for a moment, seemingly ambushed by a painful memory. He cleared his throat. "It's about time you became a fully-fledged crime reporter. I'll speak to Patsel, see what we can do. In the meantime, I'm going to raise your pay by ten shillings a week."

"Thank you, sir. And thank you for your hospitality. Please give my regards to Mrs Stone."

Much as he'd been well looked after by the Stones, Johnny couldn't wait to go home. He was accustomed to waking up to windows paisley-patterned with frost. Steam-heating made you soft.

"You're welcome. Honoria, for some inexplicable reason, took quite a shine to you. Now, I suggest you make your first priority a visit to the barber's – there must be something they can do about the colour of your hair. You look like a tiger-cub. I assume you'll want to look your best in the photo that will accompany your exclusive. You're going to be famous – for a day or so."

* * *

Bill was banging away on the typewriter, cigarette dangling from his lip, when Johnny returned with his cheeks glowing and his bleached hair almost back to its natural orange.

"Coppernob! What a surprise. I never thought I'd live to see the second coming. You're the talk of the town. I've read the piece – it's one of your finest. We must celebrate your miraculous survival."

"Indeed. It is most marvellous." As usual, Patsel had crept up on them. He moved with uncanny stealth for a lumpen man. "You have done a great service, Steadman, in ridding the world of such a degenerate. Rotherforth's suicide has a certain last-ditch nobility, but he would have done us all a favour had he shot himself sooner."

"He also shot a lot of Germans in the war," said Johnny.

"Mr Stone tells me that he's promoted you to the position of crime reporter." Patsel's tone suggested he disagreed with his superior's decision. "I shall have to find a replacement for you at the Old Bailey."

"I hear Louis Dimeo is very keen to broaden his horizons," said Johnny.

"Really?" Patsel's eyebrows shot above the rims of his glasses. "Are you joking with me?"

"No, sir," said Johnny.

Dimeo, seated a few desks away, behind Patsel, shook a fist at him.

"I will consider the matter," said Patsel. Then with a curt bow he turned away and moved on through his micro-Reich.

Bill looked at the clock. "I'll just finish this item about

a serious assault in Cornhill last night and then we can go for an early lunch."

Johnny waited until they were sitting at their favourite table in the Tipperary – a quiet spot in the corner from where they could monitor the comings and goings of other drinkers without being overheard – two full pints and meat-and-potato pies in front of them, cigarettes lit, before going on the offensive:

"You lied to me."

"When?"

"When you said your contacts at Snow Hill had assured you that everyone was accounted for. You said someone was sacked, not transferred or injured. Rotherforth told you to say that, didn't he?"

"What makes you think I took orders from him?"

"I saw you coming out of the Urania Bookshop."

"Ah." Bill took a long swig of beer. "So my little secret is finally out."

"Which one? Your collaboration with Rotherforth, or your taste for young men?"

"One led to the other, actually. It started the usual way: he would give me the odd tip-off and I would occasionally write something favourable for him. He paid good money. How d'you think I could afford to help you with your mother's medical bills?"

Johnny put down his pint. The notion that pornography had paid for her treatment was an unpleasant one. Then again, at least some good had come out of the whole dirty business.

"Look, Johnny, I had no idea what the murdering bastard was up to. He seemed like one of the good guys – war hero, family man, all-round decent cop. He lied to me. When I learned about his involvement in the bookshop it was too late – and seeing its wares stirred something inside me." He leaned forward to whisper: "What harm is there in looking at books? So what if I like looking at naked men as well as women? You'd be surprised how many people do."

"Nothing surprises me any more," said Johnny. "I owe you a lot, Bill, and you can rely on my discretion. But if you'd told me the truth about Rotherforth, three lives could have been saved. It's not something I'd like on my conscience."

"Who are you to lecture me about conscience! You've no right to come on all holier-than-thou. Gogg, Moss and Timney – who, by the way, was a good lad – would all be alive today if you hadn't been so concerned about boosting your career."

"It wasn't just about that," said Johnny, shifting uncomfortably. "I was trying to help a friend."

"You mean PC Turner? He can look after himself."

Johnny hung his head. "You're right. I always knew that. Perhaps I was using him as a pretext."

"Don't be too hard on yourself, lad. You were doing what I taught you to do: following the truth wherever it led."

"One thing I have learned," said Johnny. "Queers – no disrespect intended – are just like the rest of us. Only having seen them in the dock, I was looking at them from a false perspective. When it comes down to it, there are just good men and bad men – and most of us are a mixture of both. Good and bad, I mean." He gazed into his glass. "You don't fancy me, do you?"

Bill's laughter dissolved in a fit of coughing. "My dear boy! I adore you – but not in that way. Never have, never will."

Johnny was relieved yet at the same time vaguely insulted. The expression on his face made Bill laugh – and cough – all the more.

"Just three more months, Coppernob, and you'll be shot of me. They'll put me out to grass like a purblind pit pony. I shall go into enforced exile like Trotsky – although in my case it'll be Margate not Mexico." He raised his glass and winked. "Bottoms up!"

There it was in black and white – KILLER COP SHOOTS HIMSELF – and in smaller letters underneath: John Steadman *Crime Reporter*.

He gathered up three copies, said goodnight to Bill, flicked Louis' earlobe as he passed, and made his way to the lift. The cries of congratulation, some mixed with envy, were only cut off by the closing doors.

Lilian Voss was just emerging from the gate by St Bartholomew-the-Little when he arrived. He'd had to dash to get there in time for the end of her shift. She looked taken aback when she saw him, said something to her two colleagues who carried on towards Little Britain, and crossed the road to join him on the recreation ground where, thirteen days earlier, he had first spoken to Harry Gogg.

He handed her a copy of the *Daily News*.

"I wanted to give you this personally. I'm afraid George is dead. He died in Snow Hill. His inspector drugged his cocoa – his intention was to molest George while he was under the influence of the drug, but he miscalculated the dose. George would have known nothing about it: he never woke up. The inspector shot himself last night. The exact circumstances leading up to their deaths are unlikely to be revealed."

"I knew he wouldn't have jilted me." There were no tears, just a dignified stoicism. Perhaps her job had inured her to untimely death and the viciousness of human nature. She held out her hand. "Thank you."

Johnny took her hand in both of his. "I'm so sorry. By all accounts, George was a fine man. I know it's too soon for you to think of such things, but I don't believe he would want you to live your life in mourning; he'd want you to be happy, to find another man to love. When that time comes, I'm sure you won't be short of suitors."

"You're very kind. You may be right, but I've always believed that we each have just one soul mate. I'm lucky that I found mine. Nothing and nobody can take away my love for George. I'll always love him."

Johnny handed her a large brown envelope. It contained a copy of the photograph from the *Smithfield Sentinel* that had been used to illustrate his exclusive.

Inspector Rotherforth, Tom Vinson, George Aitken and Matt stood proudly among their colleagues on the steps of the Old Bailey.

Lilian traced George's outline with her index finger. She was shaking but she still did not cry. "Thank you. You're a true gentleman. Goodbye."

As soon as she'd got the words out she turned and ran across the road.

Johnny had one more errand to run before he could go home to get some much needed sleep, but first he needed a drink. On the other side of the recreation ground, he could hear sounds of jollity as shift-workers made their way into the Cock. The place was packed with office workers, porters and postmen determined to make the most of the festive season.

Stella, helping out behind the bar, did a magnificent double-take when she clocked him.

"Full of surprises, aren't we?" Looking genuinely pleased to see him, she placed a Scotch on the bar.

When she refused to take any payment, he gave her a copy of the newspaper. "I don't think your father will have any more trouble. This will explain why I had to, er, lie low for a few days."

"Thanks. I've already heard about your exploits. What are you doing on Christmas Day?"

"I hadn't really thought about it." He was lying: he'd been expecting to spend it by himself as usual.

"Why not come for dinner? About one o'clock? We'll be closed, but there will be about ten of us. Pa will want to shake your hand when he realises that you're the man who cleaned out Snow Hill."

"He'll want to shake me by the neck when he realises my plans for you."

Her blush gave him a warm feeling inside. It was a long time since he had felt that way.

The receptionist at the *Daily Chronicle* looked him up and down with disdain as she tried Simkins' extension.

"I'm sorry, sir. There's no reply."

"That's because I'm here," said a posh voice. "Come to gloat, Steadman?" He held a copy of the *Daily News* in his hand. "Congratulations, anyway. You had me fooled. I'm on my way to Trump's. Fancy coming along?"

Johnny had several things he wanted to say, but the foyer of a newspaper was not the place to say them – after all, he might want a job there one day – so he reluctantly agreed to endure Simkins' company a while longer.

It took less than a minute for his rival to hail a cab. His height and assurance seemed to bend the world to his will.

"Cheers!" Simkins swirled the brandy in his glass. "Here's to a brilliant exclusive and a well-deserved promotion. We're equals now."

"Hardly," said Johnny. "You're far more experienced in so many ways. It was your gift for accents that tipped me off someone might have impersonated Aitken on the telephone to create the impression he was still alive. So thank you, thank you, thank you."

Simkins frowned. "But that wasn't the only tip-off you had."

"No, it was Tom Vinson who started me on the trail."

"Ah, yes. Satan's little helper."

"Satan – yes, that was Rotherforth, all right. How much did you know about him?"

Simkins looked uncomfortable. "I knew about the bookshop and his connection to Zick, but had no idea he was one for the boys."

"I suppose you got all that out of your system at school."

"Something like that. You?"

"It wasn't that kind of school."

"No. I suppose not. I saw you go into the bookshop that night. I was the one who called the fire brigade."

"Then you must have been following me."

"I was actually waiting for Rotherforth. He'd promised me some photographs."

Johnny's blood ran cold. Simkins noted his reaction.

"Photographs of what?" asked Johnny.

"Members of Parliament playing with other – how shall I put it . . .? – members."

"And did you get these photographs?"

"He swore he'd get them to me after Christmas – provided I kept quiet about seeing him leave the bookshop just before it went up in flames."

"Did you believe him?"

"What else could I do? It was far too late to rescue anyone. Besides, Rotherforth told me he'd seen someone leaving via the back door and he was certain it was you."

"There was no back door."

"I wasn't to know that. When you were listed as one of the dead, I assumed it must have been the arsonist Rotherforth saw slipping out. Had I realised that he was responsible, I would have gone straight to Scotland Yard. At the time, I thought the porn-racket was his only guilty secret. I hoped my silence would persuade him to cough up the photographs – anything to outrage my dear pater and his party."

"Did he tell you what to write the day after?"

"No one tells me what to write – but he did tell me where to find the suicide note. I thought it was a nice little exclusive. How was I to know it was a fake? Anyway, as well as letting Rotherforth off the hook, it lent credence to your cunning little plan. You should thank me."

"Thank you? Not only did you leave me to burn, you had no qualms about sending a pregnant woman to Zick's place. Would you like me to thank you for that too? She – and the baby – could have died."

"You mean Mrs Turner? I had no idea she had a bun in the oven, and I didn't send her anywhere. I simply asked her to quiz her husband. The cops were stonewalling as usual. I knew Gogg worked at Zick's and I was trying to put the pieces together. I would have exposed Rotherforth eventually."

"Only after you'd got your manicured hands on those photographs."

"I haven't given up yet."

"As a matter of fact, PC Turner is doing his best to

trace James Timney, Rotherforth's pet shutterbug. But I'd steer well clear of Matt if I were you."

"Thanks for the advice. I look forward to further developments. Ha ha!" He nodded at Johnny's empty glass. "Another?"

"No thanks." Johnny stood up. "I'll be seeing you."

"You can count on it. Yuletide felicitations."

The next day, Wednesday, 23rd December, Johnny was interviewed at Snow Hill.

Though his inquisitors were coolly polite rather than hostile, they grilled him on every last detail of his article and admonished him for leaving the scene of a murder.

He neither expected nor received thanks for ridding the station of a man who had brought their force into gross disrepute.

Lizzie was released from hospital after a night spent under observation.

She and the baby were said to be unlikely to suffer any long-term ill effects.

Matt had already returned to patrolling the streets of the City.

Beat patrol in the small hours of the night left him with plenty of time to think about recent events.

He vowed that one day, no matter what pile of dung the scoundrel had crawled under, he would find Cecil Zick and see him brought to justice. He took every opportunity to grill any rent-boy he encountered about the vanished brothel-keeper. His natural good looks, and air of understanding – if only they knew how much he understood! – soon overcame their initial suspicion and reluctance. He persuaded them that not all cops were queer-bashers.

Johnny arranged for a monumental mason to replace the temporary marker on his erstwhile grave with a headstone bearing the name Charles Timney. Having ascertained his date of birth from the Public Records Office, he ensured Timney's life-span was recorded too. It was the least he could do. The coroner had been informed, but Timney's next-of-kin seemed to have fallen off the edge of the world. The family home in Stoke Newington was empty. Former neighbours implied the Timneys had done a midnight flit.

Having laid some chrysanthemums on his mother's grave, Johnny stood at the foot of Charles' last resting place. Apart from that moment when he'd heard the boy's footsteps on the floor above him, followed by the sound of coughing as the bookshop went up in flames, they'd had no contact. Yet he couldn't shake off the feeling that he was partly to blame for Charles' death. More troubling still had been the discovery that the boy's own father had rejected him just for being himself.

Fathers and sons . . . There was Matt, determined to outshine his. Simkins, consumed with hatred for his. It was almost enough to make him glad that he had not known his own father. Almost – but not quite.

* * *

Inspector Rotherforth's funeral was a small, private affair for immediate family only.

His body was buried in the far corner of a Holloway churchyard, reserved for suicides and tramps, where the nettles grew unchecked.

On Wednesday, 30th December, the funeral of PC Tom Vinson was held at St Sepulchre's. He was afforded full police honours, and in his eulogy the priest praised Tom's bravery and selflessness. Every pew was filled.

After the service, Johnny and Matt joined the cortège for the slow journey to the City of London cemetery in Manor Park. There they watched Tom's coffin being lowered into the ground.

Johnny bit his lip so hard it bled. Only Tom's mother and sister were crying.

As they left the graveyard, Johnny handed Matt an envelope. "No prizes for guessing what it is. Returned as promised."

Daisy's vindictive stunt had failed. He had no intention of ever seeing her again.

"Thank you," said Matt. "At least this is one secret that did not come out."

Johnny remained silent for a few moments, then he asked: "D'you think Tom loved you the way Lizzie does?"

"What sort of question is that?"

"A reasonable one."

"I don't want to talk about it."

"He saved your life."

"He did a few other things as well."

"I know, but we both owe him a great deal."

"Drop it, Johnny."

"Okay, okay. All I'm saying is, I'm glad you're still with us. I don't know what I'd do without you."

Matt looked round to see if anyone was watching, then put his arm round Johnny's neck, pulled him close, and, as if they were back in the playground, ruffled his ginger hair.

AFTERWORD

The germ of this story was told to me by the son of a cop stationed at Snow Hill in the 1930s. An inspector took to doping the cocoa of constables in his care so that he could have sex with them. One evening he misjudged the dose with the result that a young man tragically died. The inspector went home and hanged himself. For a while, around Smithfield, *Snow Hill* became a slang term for *limp-wristed*.

Perhaps unsurprisingly, despite extensive research, I have been unable to find any evidence to corroborate the story.

Whatever the truth may be, the rest of this novel is certainly impure make-believe.

BIBLIOGRAPHY

Four books in particular proved invaluable in my research:

This Small Cloud: A Personal Memoir by Harry Daley (Weidenfeld & Nicolson, 1986)

Smithfield: Past and Present by Alec Forshaw and Theo Bergström (Robert Hale, 1990)

The London Encyclopedia edited by Ben Weinreb and Christopher Hibbert (Macmillan, 1993)

Islington's Cinemas & Film Studios by Chris Draper (Islington Libraries)

ACKNOWLEDGMENTS

I would like to give heartfelt thanks to my agent Jonny Geller and my editors Julia Wisdom and Anne O'Brien – *Snow Hill* would have been a very different book without them. Roger Appleby kindly showed me round the museum at Wood Street Police Station, London, EC2. Finally, a special thank you to Brian Case who set the snowball rolling.